Crimson Dreams

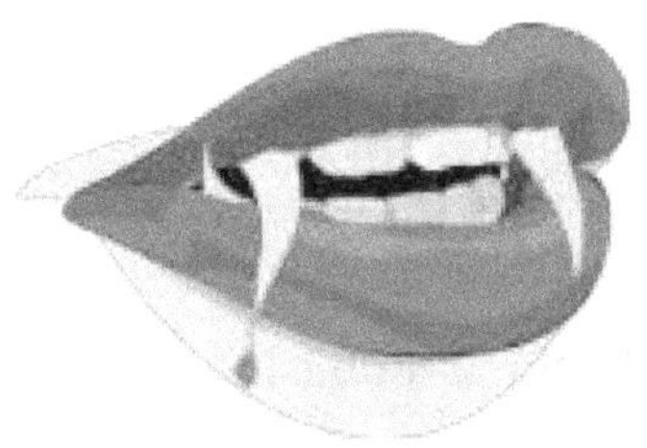

By Margaret L. Carter

Writers Exchange E-Publishing

http://www.writers-exchange.com

Dedication

To Dawn, with thanks for the encouragement and the VAMPIRE'S CRYPT artwork.

Prologue

The first time she saw her dream-beast, she thought her date had just missed killing it.

Heather Kincaid sat wedged against the front passenger door of Ted Gaines' car, wincing every time he whipped around another curve on the dark mountain road. He glared straight ahead through the windshield as they roared toward her family's summer cabin at ten miles over the speed limit.

Even though she'd just turned eighteen, her parents had expressed doubts about Heather's going out alone with Ted, who had a reputation for being "wild". But he was, after all, a cross-country star at the local high school and son of the local storekeeper whom they knew from years of summer visits. Heather had been thrilled when he'd asked her out, shy bookworm that she was.

She didn't feel so thrilled now, after they'd parked at the scenic turnoff and she'd had to bat his hands away one time too many.

Eyes flashed in the headlights, and something darted across the road. Deer-

-

Ted swerved, with a squeal of tires.

Heather caught sight of a second figure charging in the wake of the deer. Man? Beast? The shape conveyed nothing normal to her brain. But the car was about to ram it--

"Ted, stop!" She wrenched the wheel away from him, and they veered away from the creature.

Ted slammed on the brakes. The car screeched to a stop with a bone-jarring jolt, and the engine stalled.

In the headlights' beam, Heather saw a hulking thing with glowing red eyes glance at them, then lurch toward the bushes on the roadside.

Ted seized her wrist and yanked her hand off the steering wheel. "Are you crazy? What the hell do you think you're doing?"

"Didn't you see him? I think you hit him."

"What are you talking about? All I saw was a stupid deer."

"There was a man, too! Or maybe some other animal--something." She felt lightheaded; her pulse pounded in her temples.

"You're seeing things." He started the ignition.

"Wait a minute, we have to find out if he's hurt."

"Is this some kind of excuse to get away from me?"

"No, Ted, I really saw another..." Person? She didn't know; the whole experience had been a blur. But she couldn't just ride away. She opened her door.

"I'm warning you, if you get out, you can just walk home."

"Fine! There's a full moon." Clutching her purse, she stepped onto the shoulder and slammed the door. The car peeled out and vanished around the next curve.

Real smart, Heather, she scolded herself. *The cabin's at least three or four miles from here. I'll bet I won't get to go on another date till I'm thirty.* Never mind that now;

she had to find out whether the car had really hit someone. She peered along the embankment at the edge of the woods.

A rustle in the underbrush drew her attention. She picked her way down the slope. As her eyes grew accustomed to the moonlight, she made out a shape crouched under a bush.

For a second, the creature looked inhuman. A lupine muzzle contorted in a snarl. Then the apparition melted into the face of a man with crimson, glowing eyes.

Ted was right, I am seeing things! Trembling, she edged closer. *Trick of the light, that's all.* "Hey," she called in a shaky voice. "Are you hurt?"

"Go away!"

The voice certainly sounded human. She glimpsed dragging movement, as if he unsuccessfully tried to stand.

"No, you *are* hurt. I'd better get some help."

"No!" The snarl in his voice paralyzed her. "It's only my leg, thanks to your quick action. The doe is right over there." She heard him drag in a rasping breath before he continued. "Its neck is broken. Bring it to me."

"What--"

"Do it!"

His voice compelled her. She didn't stop to question again until she leaned over the still-warm body a few yards away. *What does he want with the deer? And why am I doing this?* she wondered as she grasped the animal's forelegs and dragged it closer to the injured man.

As soon as she came within the man's reach, he grabbed the animal and shoved her away. "Stay back--not safe--" He rolled over and buried his face in the doe's belly.

What's he doing? Is he some kind of maniac? In spite of his warning, she tiptoed nearer and knelt down, trying to see what he was doing. After several minutes, he raised his head. She saw a dark stain around his mouth.

"I told you to stay back."

Heather scrambled to her feet, ready to flee. Too late--she didn't see the man move, yet he was at her side, his fingers around her wrist. With his other hand he wiped the--blood?--from his mouth.

"I mean you no harm. I owe you thanks for your help. Without it, I might have lain there for hours, in pain or unconscious." He stood firmly, as if he weren't injured at all.

What's going on? I thought he had a broken leg. But her fear ebbed away and she said, "Oh--no problem. I'd better get home now."

"You'll forget all this. You imagined what you saw a moment ago." His rich baritone vibrated beneath her diaphragm.

Now she saw his face as fully human, saw a pale young man with thick, dark hair and bushy eyebrows. Like Ted, he was much taller than she, but he carried himself proudly, without the slouch that characterized Ted's posture. The man's eyes held hers captive, while his thumb stroked the pulse point on her wrist, sending shivers up her arm.

How did I ever think Ted was sexy? She swayed toward him, yearning for the caress to go on and on. "What do you mean, imagined?"

"You were confused. Go home and forget."

"I'm not crazy! I know what I saw!"

The man's free hand brushed her temple, the curve of her jaw, the hollow of her throat. His fingers felt refreshingly cool in the humid air. "What you saw wasn't real. You don't want it to be real, child. Why complicate your life?"

She fought against the whirlpool sucking her thoughts into oblivion. *It's real, and I don't want to forget!*

The sound of a car's engine shattered her trance. She jerked her hand free, eliciting a snarl from the man.

Yelling for help, Heather scurried up the embankment. A station wagon stopped for her frantic waving. Its occupants, an elderly couple, vacationers like her own family, didn't question her half-true story about a tiff with her boyfriend.

To her relief, she managed to slip into the cabin without her parents' realizing that strangers, not Ted, had dropped her off. She mumbled a quick goodnight and headed straight for the shower.

That night, she received the first "visit". She dreamed of waking up in her bedroom in the cabin, to find the creature from the woods standing over her. He looked like an ordinary man now, except that his eyes glinted red again. She realized at once that this encounter wasn't real, because he wore a ruffled shirt with lace collar and cuffs, topped by a swirling black cape with crimson lining. Anyway, a live, solid man couldn't have gained access to her room. She wasn't a heavy sleeper, so if he'd broken in through the front door or climbed in a window, the noise would have awakened her before he'd reached her bedside. Not to mention waking Mom or Dad. Therefore, he was a dream.

He seated himself on the edge of the mattress. She felt it sag. *Wow, what a realistic dream!*

"You are a very stubborn child," he said. His voice made the air vibrate around her.

"You're not really here," she murmured. Assured of that fact, she wasn't afraid. He was actually attractive, in a wild sort of way. Like Heathcliff. Heather and her best friend had tried to read *Wuthering Heights* that spring; the other girl had quickly given up, but Heather loved the book.

"I'm glad you're taking that sensible attitude now. I enjoy my life here and don't want to leave. Nor do I want to use excessive force. That always complicates matters." His cool fingers trailed over her face and neck.

Delightful shivers coursed through her. "What you thought you saw this evening was your imagination. Don't tell anyone."

"I didn't plan to," she said.

"Good. Then you can forget it. It wasn't real."

Here we go again. Her head seemed to be floating. "I don't care if it was real or not, I still don't want to forget." His hand stroked her hair, making her feel like purring. "Only exciting thing that's ever happened to me. I want to remember. Won't tell anybody."

He gave an exaggerated sigh. "I've never encountered anyone quite so difficult. Well, as long as you understand that this is only a dream, how much of it you remember doesn't matter." He leaned over to kiss her forehead, her cheek, her neck, then still lower. Alternate waves of heat and cold rippled over her. She was burning, melting. An electric spark zapped her. Then, darkness.

Chapter 1

Halfway out of the driver's seat, Heather stared at the dead animal sprawled on the gravel driveway in front of the cabin--a bobcat, looking like a discarded stuffed toy except for the dark blotch on the belly. With her heart racing, Heather retreated into the car, leaving the door open. She pressed her lips together and tried to slow her breathing. Dizziness rocked her.

The image leaped to life in her memory: Six years ago, a summer evening on a moonlit mountain road. A man crouched over the bleeding body of a deer. Glowing eyes.

Heather shook herself back into the present. *I imagined that; didn't I settle that long ago?*

She picked up her purse and leaned out of the open door. A flicker of movement in the side-view mirror caught her eye. A glint of red--

She squeezed her eyes shut. *No, it's not going to start again! I won't let it!*

When she nerved herself to glance around, she saw no sign of life. Removing the car keys from the ignition and digging another ring of keys out of her purse, she stood up and slammed the door behind her. She marched up to the dead bobcat. Blood still oozed over the matted fur, and no flies buzzed around it yet. A dog must have killed it, mere minutes before, probably scared off by the sound of the car. Nothing to get upset about.

Skirting the body, she walked up the two sagging steps to the front porch and inserted the key into the cranky lock. Boards groaned under her feet, as always. Dead leaves littered the porch, which needed a coat of paint. *Look at this mess! Mom will have a fit.*

No, would have had. Laura Kincaid would never see this place again. Uterine cancer had ensured that. Heather blinked away tears more of anger than sadness. *It wasn't time. I wasn't finished with her yet. With them.* Her father had outlasted her mother by less than four months. Heather recognized his "accident" as suicide, although, as a doctor, he'd been careful to make it appear otherwise. He'd left her with what their minister, a thirtyish woman with a counseling degree, called "unresolved issues".

Again Heather shrugged off the temptation to sink into gloom. The issue for this month was cleaning out this place and putting it on the market. Brooding on the porch wouldn't get that done.

A breeze followed her into the living room. She sneezed at the dust it raised from the scratched hardwood floor. A glance at the ceiling confirmed that the oval water mark on the plaster had expanded since her last visit. Mom had constantly complained about the defects in the place, ranging from the uneven floorboards and leaky roof to the hard water from the well and rust stains in the sinks and commode. Definitely no rich folks' summer cottage, just a four-room cabin--well, five rooms, if the screened-in back porch counted--with a fake Lincoln log façade. Dad had bought it early in their marriage, as soon as his medical practice began to prosper. Heather had often wondered why they'd kept the place and vacationed here every year, if Mom disliked it so much. *Who knows, maybe complaining was a form of relaxation for her.* She'd spent half of every month-long "vacation" cleaning. Everything had to be perfect.

Including me. With a cardiologist for a father and a professional volunteer-- PTA president and chairman of countless hospital charity committees--for a mother, Heather had always had standards to meet. Honor roll was expected; only straight A's merited special notice. Her friends were subjected to a security check worthy of the CIA.

Heather took off her gold-rimmed glasses and rubbed her damp forehead. *Cut that crap, right now! You're not a kid anymore; you don't have to swallow that stuff. Time to get to work.*

She trudged back and forth from the car, carrying in a couple of grocery bags and stacks of flattened cardboard boxes. She'd brought her mother's station wagon, since her own compact was too small to transport much junk. Heather averted her eyes as she passed the dead animal, thinking, *First thing, get rid of that.*

Out back, on the screened porch, she found the shovel in its usual corner. A few hundred paces into the woods, she dug a shallow pit in the soft loam on the edge of a weed-choked ravine. Then she scooped up the carcass, which was heavier than she'd expected, and lugged it out back to bury it.

Good, that's over, she reassured herself a few minutes later, scrubbing her hands at the kitchen sink. *Now I won't have any more hallucinations.* On second thought, she mustn't label that glimpse in the side-view mirror a hallucination, which implied a crack in her sanity. Call it an optical illusion, a trick of light and shadow, enhanced by memories.

The kitchen faucet dripped, and the mineral stains in the sink looked worse than she remembered. Fishing a notepad out of her purse on the counter, she jotted down "Plumber". Noticing a missing handle on a cabinet as well as a hole in the window screen, and recalling the leaky roof, she added a hyphen and the word, "Handyman".

Who's going to buy this dump? She felt a twinge of guilt at her disloyalty. After all, her parents had valued the cabin enough to keep it for over twenty years. And Heather had enjoyed the place herself, until that summer when she'd turned eighteen. *Be honest, I kept on enjoying it, a little too much. That was the problem.* She wasn't sentimental enough to want to hold onto the cabin. She didn't need a vacation home she hadn't visited since the summer after high school graduation.

She'd had an excellent reason to renounce the mountain vacations, despite her parents' obsession with fresh air and exercise for their bookworm daughter. Her mother's peculiar about-face, forbidding her to join them on future trips ("Your father and I want some time to ourselves for a change"), had come as a positive relief, though Heather wouldn't have admitted that relief at the time. She had needed to escape the powerful allure the dreams exerted over her. The dreams she'd experienced only at the cabin that strange year, delusions so real she could touch and taste them...

Heather shook her head and brushed a tangle of auburn hair out of her face. She must not think about her dream-beast. He'd been a phantom of her imagination, and she was too old to need a fantasy lover.

Right now, she needed the phone number of a local handyman. Pausing in the living room to jiggle the fireplace damper, she wiped sooty fingers on a tissue pulled from her jeans pocket and wrote down "chimney sweep"? The cabin had a phone, since her father, as a doctor, couldn't spend a month without one. In later years, he'd even had cable installed. But no local phone book. She would have to visit Ted's father's store first thing in the morning, where she could get names and numbers as well as more groceries.

Nothing to worry about there, either. In the years since she'd last seen Ted Gaines, he had probably married and even moved out of town. And if not, so what? She had dated him once, during her last summer at the cabin. As a date, it had turned out a dismal failure, but they'd parted as friends, more or less.

She unloaded her laptop, resisting the temptation to check her e-mail. Never mind that a message from her online gaming partner, "Nightblade", would be more fun than any of the chores looming over her.

Deciding to get a little work done before supper, she scoured the kitchen sink, making a mental note to ask Ted or a plumber about stronger cleansers to obliterate the hard-water stains. Then she swept and mopped the kitchen and bathroom floors, ran the upright vacuum over the braid rugs in the living room and bedroom, and decided she'd done enough cleaning for the first day. After scrubbing the grit off her face and hands, she gobbled a sandwich at the Formica-topped kitchen table. She had saved her bedroom for an after-supper treat.

The twin bed had been left freshly made up, as usual, with a stuffed Winnie the Pooh on the chenille spread. The desk and dresser were neat, though dusty. Heather skimmed her hand over a three-shelf bookcase crammed with volumes of varying sizes and ages. These would go home with her, not to charity. *The Lord of the Rings. She.* Madeleine L'Engle's *A Wrinkle in Time.* Five Ray Bradbury collections. Dozens of paperback Tarzan and John Carter of Mars adventures.

I'm surprised Mom didn't give them to Goodwill. She always swore reading stories about "unreal" stuff was a waste of time. She had thrown away Heather's cache of Wonder Woman comic books, bought out of her allowance, without a word of warning, a memory that still ignited a flare of resentment. *Forget that! I was twelve years old, for goodness' sake.* Heather folded a box and began piling books into it. A few minutes later she settled on the floor, her back braced against the bed, to read a library-discard edition of *The Borrowers.*

She finally looked up when natural light became so dim she couldn't focus on the print. A twinge of guilt assailed her for frittering away an hour or more. *Don't be silly, I've got a month, or all summer if I want to use it.* She switched on the bedside lamp and collected nightgown and toiletries from her suitcase.

Before taking a shower, she gave the bathroom a quick scrubbing. She'd found dead insects in the tub. *I'll never be a perfect housekeeper like Mom, but there are limits!* While cleaning the bathroom sink, she noticed a rip in the window screen. Another repair to add to the list. *Tomorrow, I'll think about it tomorrow. Yes, Miss Scarlett.* She giggled. She realized she must be more tired, or nervous, than she'd thought.

The hot shower made her drowsy. Returning to the bedroom wearing a translucent, powder-blue nightgown that flowed to her ankles, Heather became aware of the quiet. She heard only crickets, none of the intermittent traffic noises she could always hear from her Charlottesville apartment. If anybody decided to break in and attack her, nobody would hear her scream. *There you go again! Quit looking for trouble!*

She forced herself to concentrate on the image in the age-flecked mirror above the dresser as she picked up the hairbrush and yanked it through her hair. *I need a haircut, and my eyes look like they've got purple bruises under them.* Beautiful eyes, anyway--or so the man in her dreams had always said.

He isn't real, remember? I came back here partly to prove that, didn't I? She stuck her tongue out at her reflection.

Something stirred in the corner of her vision. She wheeled around. Nothing there, of course. It was just the curtain rustling in the breeze. Why did she feel as if eyes rested on the back of her neck, then? She brushed her hair with long, vigorous strokes, refusing to look behind her again. Gradually the rhythmic motion lulled her into a fatigued daze. Minutes later, another movement in the background broke her trance. She blinked. Again the glass reflected only the stillness of the bedroom, without the shimmer of mist she thought she had glimpsed. *I'm falling asleep on my feet. Nobody here but me, myself, and I.* Her eyes drifted shut, with the hairbrush suspended halfway to her head.

The brush slipped out of her grasp. A second later, she felt it drawn through her hair, in gentle, languorous strokes all the way down to her shoulders. Cool fingers alighted on the nape of her neck to lift the locks of hair and massage the tight muscles of her scalp. Alternate waves of warmth and chills chased each other down her spine. Sighing, she relaxed into the caress. *I like this dream.*

The brush stopped. The phantom hand that had held it grazed her cheek as it tucked a strand of hair behind her ear. The fingertips skimmed along the curve of her neck to her shoulder, then insinuated themselves into the bodice of the nightgown. Heat blossomed in her chest. She leaned against a hard, male body, while a ghostly touch teased one of her nipples--

Her eyes flew open. The tantalizing sensations ceased. But in the mirror, a man stood behind her, staring over her shoulder. He had a pale, lean face with dark hair swept back from a high forehead. Dark, thick brows almost met over his nose and bristled like a bobcat's ear-tufts over deep-set, silver-gray eyes. When he shifted his gaze as if to meet hers in the mirror, his eyes flashed with a crimson glow. Heather screamed and spun around.

Nothing. The room was empty.

Her mind whirling, she fell to her knees and groped for the brush she must have dropped. *Of course I did, because he wasn't real.* Even if he had existed in the past, he couldn't be here now. She had fallen asleep for a minute and dreamed him. Otherwise, how could he look exactly the same as he had that first time, six years earlier? He had appeared about twenty-five then, and he hadn't aged. *Since I imagined him anyway, why should he?*

It was only natural to conjure up the face that had shadowed her dreams in this very room every night after that encounter on the dark road. The visions had transformed her vacation refuge into something wild and strange. They had both thrilled and frightened her, luring her into a realm whose forbidden pleasures had made real life seem faded and drab. She didn't need to be told that those sensations were forbidden. While Mom never discussed sex, aside from the pragmatic necessity of preparing Heather for her first period, the implied boundaries were sharp enough.

Heather threw herself face down on the bed, nuzzling into the pillow and hugging the stuffed toy. She recalled how lethargic she had become, dozing for hours on the screened porch or wandering under the trees, eventually stopping to lie on her back on the ground and gaze at the leaves rippling in the filtered sunset. Only her increased appetite and her father's medical assurances had quelled her mother's suspicions about her health. Mom had ascribed Heather's behavior to "adolescent moods". Since the dreams and the lassitude vanished as soon as they'd returned home to Arlington, Heather hadn't worried about her condition, either.

The visions she experienced at the cabin weren't bizarre and fragmented like ordinary dreams, but coherent, concrete--like slices of an alternate reality. In college she'd encountered the term "lucid dreaming" and recognized part of her own experience. She had known every time that the events were products of her sleeping imagination, but she hadn't wanted to cut them short. She clasped her secret to her breast and enjoyed it.

Now, when she closed her eyes, memories flashed on her mental screen: Her dream-beast came to her as her favorite TV hero, Zorro, masked and cloaked, to sweep her away on a black stallion in the moonlight. Or she lay awake like Guinevere in her bower, waiting for Sir Lancelot, clad in his golden armor, to remove his helmet and kneel at her bedside to worship her with his kisses.

He appeared in the guise of an elven lord, with pointed ears, silver eyes, and green robes. As he sang "The Demon Lover" and "The Great Silkie" and other ballads, his voice reverberated in her veins as if she were a living harp that he strummed.

Sometimes they shed their human bodies and ran side by side, on four feet rather than two. The pungent scents of moist loam and fleeing prey made her nostrils flare with delight and hunger. With him, she soared above the treetops, feeling cool wind on bare skin. She viewed the night through his eyes. The landscape glimmered in silvery pastels, punctuated with the infrared auras of small animals. He swooped down upon a fleeing doe, and the animal's heartbeat surrounded Heather like the pounding of surf on rocks.

He talked with her, too. After the first night, he called her by name instead of "child". He listened without dismissing or scolding her. She trusted him with fantasies and ambitions she wouldn't mention to her parents. She'd told him how much she wanted a computer system before she'd summoned the nerve to ask her parents. (Her mother had grumbled, "Waste of money, you'll probably use it for a lot of silly games." Yet a few weeks later, they had agreed to buy her a PC and even let her subscribe to an online service.) Some nights ended with his gently kissing her goodnight. Others ended with a fiery, melting sensation and a piercing, painless chill at her breast. Either way, she never saw the man depart; he simply vanished.

Later, during a couple of psychology courses in college, she'd decided her unconscious mind had latched onto the man she'd met in the woods--who couldn't have looked the way she remembered--and shaped him into the companion she needed at that point in her life. A companion who offered, in the safety of fantasy, what she lacked in reality. She assured herself that if she were actually an incipient schizophrenic, she would have imagined the man everywhere, all year round, not just at the cabin. Still, she'd felt relieved to stop the summer visits. Her one attempt to tell her best friend back home about the dreams had evoked the response, "Heather, you're weird," accompanied by a nervous giggle.

I'm grown up now, with a life and a budding career. I won't let it start again.

With that resolution, she turned off the light and burrowed under the covers. The buzzing confusion in her head didn't stop her from falling asleep within minutes.

He stood beside her bed, gazing down at her as calmly as if they had last met just the night before. This time he wore no exotic costume, only an open-necked, short-sleeved shirt and very snug jeans.

"Heather, why did you stay away so long? I feared I would never see you again."

Still half-asleep, she reclined against the pillows and scowled at the apparition. "You aren't here. And I told you I wasn't coming back, remember?" Asking an imaginary man to remember a conversation didn't register as a contradiction in her sleep-clogged brain. She dimly noticed that her fear that the visions might resume had dissipated, as it always did when face to face with him. She accepted his dream-presence as easily as she had at eighteen.

"You did, and I begged you to reconsider. But as you'll recall, I used no force. I hoped you would return of your own accord--and you did." He sat on the edge of the bed; she felt his solid weight. He lifted her hand to brush his lips against it, a sensation like the tickle of a kitten's whiskers.

Damn, this feels real! She vividly recalled their final conversation, which had ended with an incandescent kiss that made her feel as if she would shatter like crystal, never to be whole again. And after that, in the velvet darkness before oblivion, a sweet taste burning on her tongue, and his farewell like a caress inside her mind.

She snatched her hand away. "I stopped coming here because I didn't need you anymore. I have a life now."

"Did you ever consider that I might need you?"

She pulled the sheets up to cover her bosom. "Yeah? For what?" Already she was falling into the trap, talking to him as if he existed in the same reality she did. "Why should I apologize to you? You're nothing but a Fig Newton."

"A what?" His bristling eyebrows arched.

"A figment of my imagination. So what could you possibly need me for?"

"The pleasure we shared, for one thing. As for what else you gave me--well, perhaps I can explain some other time." His fingers captured a strand of her hair and trailed along the curve of her chin.

A shiver coursed through her. She had trouble catching her breath. "Don't--you can't imagine what--"

He withdrew his hand. "Yes?"

"You made me think I was losing my mind!" Anger flared up, blotting out the insidious delight she'd almost succumbed to. "Damn you, you fractured my whole sense of reality. I didn't know what was wrong with me." She wiped her eyes with the back of her hand. "Just like I don't know what's wrong now, why I'm conjuring you up after all these years. I thought I'd finally turned normal."

"My dear girl, I never meant to cause you that kind of pain." He smoothed her hair, comfortingly rather than sensuously. "If 'normal' means you have to become a person I can't touch or speak to, I hope you'll decide against it. Can't you relax and accept me, as you always did before?"

"I don't know." Again she discovered herself speaking to him as if he were real. Those books on lucid dreams never mentioned anything like this! Well, why not treat him like a separate individual, as long as she kept in mind the difference between dreams and her daytime life? "It's not that simple. You...spilled over...into the rest of the world. You even spoiled me for real men." She blushed.

He responded with a low laugh that made her heart stutter.

Oh, Lord, I didn't mean to say that! But it was true; her loss of virginity in college had been anticlimactic, and she'd soon realized she hadn't loved the man after all. She hadn't dated seriously since.

"As a gentleman, I suppose I should ignore that remark. But I can't deny I'm flattered." He raised her hand to his lips again. His tongue flicked over her palm and lingered on the inside of the wrist.

Her insides churned with excitement. She imagined she could feel her pulse leap at his kiss. "Stop that! I'm not in the mood. I have too much on my mind." Dream or not, she refused to be an easy lay.

He obediently released her. "I apologize for my lack of consideration. Your parents' recent deaths must have been hard for you. Would you like to talk about that?"

How did he know? *Why not? He's a product of my own imagination, so he must know everything I know.* She sat up and wrapped her arms around her knees. "Mom died of uterine cancer in November. After that, my father just...went downhill. Gave up."

She recalled watching Dad sit at the kitchen table, night after night, with a bottle of Scotch and a juice glass full of ice. He would drain the glass, stare at nothing for several minutes, then refill it. He had drunk heavily as long as Heather could remember, though he'd never let the habit interfere with his cardiology practice. Between his workaholic hours and the alcohol he used for stress relief, she'd seen even less of him than most doctors' children might expect. He never became raucous, much less violent; he simply withdrew. Holidays always ended with his drinking himself to sleep on the couch after dinner. But only after his wife's death had he taken to drinking on week nights in addition to his usual weekend "relaxation".

One evening Heather had sat up with him, nursing a single Scotch and soda while he rambled on about his failure to save his wife.

"You're not an oncologist," Heather had said, with no real hope of penetrating his depression. "What could you have done that didn't get done? Didn't you say yourself that you hired the best specialists in the D.C. area?"

"I'm a doctor; I should have known." The liquor sloshed onto the table as he poured a fresh shot. "I should have made her get check-ups more often, should've noticed the warning signs." His normally crisp speech was slurred, the only mark of intoxication he ever displayed.

"You gave her the best care anybody could have. Stop blaming yourself."

He didn't seem aware of Heather's touch on his hand. He rambled in this vein for some time, then started maundering about Heather's uncle, Mom's brother.

"I let Ken die, too. The omnipotent M. Deity, can't do a thing when it really matters."

Uncle Ken, whom Heather remembered only as a sickly young man who liked to draw vividly lifelike sketches of animals for her, had been a hemophiliac who'd died of AIDS.

"But nobody could do anything for him. By the time the danger of transfusions became public, it was too late." Heather had read up on hemophilia as well as the early progress of the AIDS epidemic, as soon as she became old enough to understand.

"That's a load of--" Her father had bitten off the words, as if he still worried about exposing his grown daughter to vulgar language. "I should have known. The contamination of the blood supply was suspected long before the blood banks admitted to it. If I'd investigated properly--"

Finally Heather had stopped her futile attempts to argue him out of his depression. The conversation only deepened her own sadness. The best she could manage was to stay close when Dad wanted company. She talked out her own residual guilt with Sharon Lane, the minister of their church.

She told the man in her bedroom some of this. "Four months after Mom died, Dad killed himself. Oh, he made it look like an accident. I think he wanted to make sure there wouldn't be any trouble with the insurance company."

Her visitor made no comment on her bitter tone. He asked in his deep-velvet voice, "How do you know it was suicide?"

"He planned it so efficiently, right down to clearing up all his complicated cases so he wouldn't have to leave them to anybody else. That night, he had two drinks--just enough to make driver error plausible without raising his blood alcohol into the illegal range. Then he phoned the hospital to say he was driving over to check on a patient scheduled for surgery the next day. He even picked a rainy night--one when I was in Charlottesville instead of at home. He drove off an overpass at sixty miles an hour, judging from the skid marks." She swallowed the unshed tears trying to choke her. "They called it an accident, but I know better. He deserted me. I wasn't worth living for."

The man smoothed her hair. Heather felt as if his palm radiated warmth that spread like a cloak around her shoulders.

"No one could think that of you," he said.

"I was never perfect enough for them. They were always criticizing. If my report card had one B, they wanted to know why it wasn't straight A's." She gulped a deep breath. "I was an accident. They never planned to have a baby. With Mom's brother being a hemophiliac, she knew she might be a carrier."

"There are tests, surely?"

"Tests to find out whether the baby is a boy or girl after it's conceived. Mom didn't want the risk of producing a boy and facing the choice of whether or not to abort."

"She told you this?" His voice was very low.

Heather nodded. "When I started my periods. She had to explain the hazard, since I might carry the gene myself. I'm not taking the chance she took.

I got my tubes tied over spring break. If I ever get married, there won't be any risk of children."

He took her hand. "Why do you say 'if'? I imagine men must pursue you constantly."

She said with a wry smile, "Not so I've noticed. Like Mom said, a girl has to avoid acting too serious or too smart, and I never mastered the trick. Doesn't matter." She shrugged. "After you got through with me, none of the real men I dated measured up. And who'd want to marry a crazy woman, anyway?"

He tightened his clasp on her hand. "Heather Kincaid, you are not crazy."

"Yeah? Then how did I dream you up?" His cool, firm grasp sent an electric current up her arm that felt anything but dreamlike. Her fingers stirred, exploring the contours of his palm. She discovered a silky patch of fine hairs in the center. Intrigued, she stroked the spot with the ball of her thumb.

He shivered, squeezing her hand still harder. "Sweet Heather, don't do that, if you want me to retain any self-control at all." He swallowed, then drew a long breath. "So you've decided that you're to live as a spinster. What else will you do with your life?"

She told him about earning her bachelor's degree at William and Mary, followed by the graduate program at the University of Virginia. "I'm working on a master's in library science. I plan to specialize as a medical librarian. The job market's better than in schools or public libraries."

His eyes glittered as they held hers. "Is this your own desire?"

Good grief, as a therapist, he cuts even deeper than Sharon.

"Of course! Well, okay, maybe at first it was to please Dad, spend time with him. All through high school, I worked in his office or for one of his colleagues. But I got really excited about medicine. I knew I didn't have the drive to become a doctor, but books always interested me."

"The popular lore states that all doctors are rich," he said with an ironic smile. "Surely your father left you funds sufficient that you no longer need to work?"

She laughed at the question--just the naive assumption she ought to expect from a dream lover. "He left enough to support me till I finish my degree, without working other than as a graduate assistant. I'm not about to deplete the capital by trying to live on it long-term. And why are you asking about money, anyway? I get enough of that stuff in the real world; you're supposed to act like a fantasy."

"You said you weren't in the mood."

She felt a hot blush suffuse her face.

"If you're so dissatisfied with my performance, why did you return?"

"To sell the cabin," she said.

His expression turned somber. "Why, if you don't need money... Then you don't intend to come back?"

"This place is nothing but a maintenance headache. I have no reason to spend summers here alone, so why should I hang onto it?"

His grip grew painfully tight. When she emitted a suppressed gasp, he let go. "Am I not reason enough, Heather?"

She edged away from him, wedging her back against the headboard. "You're the main reason not to! I told you, I don't need you anymore!" Something in her chest constricted. She had to struggle for the next breath.

"And I said that I need you! My dear, if I'm a product of your imagination, I cannot exist without you, can I? If you stay away, you condemn me to nothingness."

"That's the most twisted argument I ever--" She wrapped her arms around herself, fighting an inner chill. "Whatever you are, you appeared the minute I got here. I saw you in the mirror, out in the driveway, and later in this room." Could he possess some sort of real existence, after all? Could her starved imagination have projected her longings so powerfully that he had acquired a visible, tangible form? *That's even more insane than a simple erotic fantasy.*

"Yes, you did. I felt you approaching, after so many years of separation. I couldn't resist watching you, being near you. Mirrors betray my kind. I can cloud human vision, but a sheet of glass can't be beguiled." He placed his hands on her shoulders. "I came here to give you pleasure, not to frighten you. Forget all these doubts. They aren't important."

The silver gleam of his eyes, with the spark of red at the centers, captured her gaze. She felt as if she were floating, pleasantly lightheaded, as if from a glass of champagne. Her fears melted away. *That's right, it isn't important where he came from. Might as well relax and enjoy him.* She snuggled into his arms. His ragged breathing ruffled her hair.

"Ah, Heather, it's been so terribly long!"

His hard body trembled in her embrace. Laying her head on his shoulder, she heard the hammer of his heartbeat. His lips nibbled her ear, traced the arch of her jaw, and claimed her mouth. His kiss burned. She savored a tangy, metallic flavor as his tongue darted in quest of hers. She heard a second drumbeat throbbing along with his heart and realized it was her own pulse. The double rhythm filled the air with thrumming echoes. A crimson mist veiled her sight. Her head spun. Pleasure as blinding and deafening as a lightning bolt exploded at her core, an ecstasy whose power she had forgotten, so piercingly intense that she wondered how the girl she'd once been could have summoned the resolution to renounce it--and how, now that she'd found it again, she could ever maintain her resolve to leave it behind.

Chapter 2

She sat on a low, three-legged, wooden stool in front of a pantry-size fireplace where a kettle simmered, suspended over the fire. Though she identified with the dream figure, Heather couldn't recognize the girl as herself. The girl had auburn hair like Heather's, but she was smaller in both height and girth. She wore her hair in a long braid that fell down the back of an ankle-length blue dress topped by an apron.

Another kind of lucid dream, Heather thought from somewhere outside the scene. This time she had no doubt about the unreality of the experience, but unlike most dreams, it played out as coherently as a videotape.

"Judith, what is this foolery about not wanting to marry young Michael? You've been betrothed most of your lives." Heather recognized the querulous woman with the worry creasing her face as her--no, Judith's--mother.

The stern man who loomed over the seated girl said, "Hush, Sarah. We both know this matter is far more serious than breaking a troth. Lass, you were seen with--someone. Can you explain yourself?"

Judith shook her head, her cheeks aflame with anger. "I know not what you mean, Father. If the village gossips choose to besmirch my name--"

The man slapped her across the mouth. Tears sprang to the girl's eyes. She pressed her hand to her lips.

The woman caught her husband's arm. "Thomas, what are you thinking of?"

He shrugged her off. "This is no time for mistaken kindness." He gave Judith a brusque shake. "The vicar has summoned the magistrate. They're talking of witchcraft. If you can't give a proper account of yourself, they'll bring you to trial. Do you want to be hanged for a sorceress?"

Through Judith's perceptions, Heather sensed fear as well as anger in the father's tirade.

The mother stepped to Judith's side and wrapped an arm around her. "Thomas, you know she's a God-fearing girl. Our own child couldn't possibly-_"

"Silence, woman! Whatever she's done endangers all of us--you, me, and the little ones." He squeezed the girl's chin and made her look up at him. "Well? Folk say you've consorted with the Devil and entertained a fiend in your bed."

She jerked away from his grasp. "It's a lie! He's not a fiend!"

"He? Then you admit your whoring! Damned slut!" He hit her so hard that she toppled to the floor before her mother could catch her.

Heather reeled under the pain, and darkness enveloped her. When her eyes cleared, she stood on the cabin porch. Her own parents blocked the door, glaring at her.

"How dare you let a man into your bedroom?" said her mother. "Do you want the whole world to think you're a tramp? And what if you end up pregnant? Do you want to have a baby that's going to die?"

Tears blurred her eyes. "No, I can't get pregnant--I had the operation. And we never--"

"Don't try to snow me," her father said. "I know how men are with girls like you. I'll bet that's all you've been doing since you got here--daydreaming and waiting for him to show up."

"That's right," said her mother, arms folded across her chest. "I know how lazy you are. I mean, look what a mess this place is!" She swung the door open. From inside the cabin, a miniature whirlwind of dead leaves swept across the porch to engulf Heather like a tornado.

Again she sank into darkness.

Heather woke at dawn, euphoric with the sheer relief of glimpsing sunbeams through the crack in the curtains and recognizing her nightmares as just that-- nightmares. She stretched her arms wide, luxuriating in the delicious languor that enveloped her. *Why do I feel this way?*

Memories of her dream visitor flooded her like the gush of a cold shower. Her eyes snapped wide open. *It's happened again! On the first night, too!* That settled the matter; she could get rid of the delusion only by staying away permanently.

Sitting up, she opened the curtains beside the bed and squinted at the pale daylight seeping through the trees until her vision adjusted. Her throat rasped with dryness. *Do I really want to escape from it--from him?* She moaned aloud, remembering the thrill her dream-lover had roused.

She crawled out of bed and stumbled upright. She felt as enervated as if she really had spent half the night in passion instead of sleep. Her cheeks warmed at the thought. *Enough! Time for a real shower.* She needed the cool water to clear her head. A tall glass of juice, a solid breakfast, and a few hours of manual labor would help even more. Not to mention a trip to the general store. Just the thing to exorcise night-haunters.

While dressing, though, she couldn't resist checking the room for any signs that another live person had entered. She found none, of course. *I'm losing it for sure, if I'm starting to think my phantom is a real man. Think straight--how would he have gotten in, night after night?* She resolutely tuned her mind to real life.

After years of famine, he could scarcely believe his good fortune. He had to extrude mental antennae every few minutes to reassure himself. *She's finally back!* And she hadn't lost her vulnerability to his allure.

Those few luscious minutes before he'd soothed her to sleep proved that. He smiled at the thought. Why did she matter so much to him? *Is this a trap I'm setting for myself? Am I fixated on her?* Well, what of it? "Trap" was too strong a word; he could handle one barely-grown girl. The critical question was whether to lull her into the continued belief that he was imaginary, or confront her in waking life.

He'd work out strategy later. Right now, he wanted only to sleep off the sensual languor she'd instilled in him. Dawn was close enough to let him sink into the restorative daylight dormancy of his kind. He lay down and relaxed his grasp on consciousness...

Pain--terror--not mine--Judith's! The stab of anguish spurred him instantly alert, nerves bristling at the threat.

Get a grip! No danger, just a dream. Not much of a comfort, since his kind seldom dreamed so vividly. And he hadn't succumbed to memories of Judith in over a century. Could Heather's embrace have revived those buried anxieties? *Nonsense. She isn't Judith. The cases are nothing alike, nothing.*

After breakfast, Heather plunged into the work waiting to distract her. Sorting household items into throwaway and giveaway piles loomed as too large a task for the first day. Instead, she dusted and scrubbed. When she surfaced for a drink of water, she found she had distracted herself so thoroughly it was already lunchtime. After a peanut butter sandwich, she decided she couldn't put off her drive to the village any longer.

She locked the cabin and drove toward town. It wasn't much of a town, just a hardware store, a gas station, movie theater, a few year-round residents' homes, and the Gaineses' general store, "The Skyline Shoppe", with the post office occupying a cubicle in the back. The village hugged the shore of Bear Paw Lake. A little farther around the lake, a boat rental facility and the lodge, with restaurant and cocktail lounge as well as a few rooms for those who preferred not to rent cabins, catered to tourists.

After a short drive, she clutched her purse and stepped out of the car in the store's parking lot. Gravel crunched under her tennis shoes. She blinked at the building. It bore the same fake-rustic look, with weathered brown siding, tourist trinkets displayed in the poorly-lit window, an ornamental arrangement of dried corncobs on the door, and a life-size statue of an Algonquin chief on the wide porch. Heather tapped the Indian's chest as she walked by. His paint was flaking.

The inside of the shop looked familiar, too. Postcards, cookbooks, and wildlife guides on rotating stands by the door. Several shelves of souvenir items, followed by a selection of camping needs. Groceries on the other side of the room. The place hadn't changed at all since her last visit. *Well, I have! I'm not a confused eighteen-year-old anymore.* She filled one of the undersized carts with cereal, canned goods, fruit, deli meats, paper products--all the staples she might need for a month's stay. Nearing the counter, she reminded herself to include flashlight batteries and matches. A small stack of firewood remained behind the cabin, and the nights could get cool enough to make a fire pleasant.

Instead of Mr. or Mrs. Gaines, Ted himself, in a T-shirt bearing a silk-screened image of the Blue Ridge Mountains, stood behind the checkout counter. He wore his hair shorter than he had in high school, and his slim frame had filled out, but she recognized him instantly. He stared at her for a few seconds, then broke into a grin. "Heather Kincaid--is that really you?"

Glad that no other customers were in the store at the moment, she answered with a jerky nod. "In the flesh. Hi, Ted."

He showed no sign of embarrassment, as if he'd forgotten that their last encounter had consisted of a tussle in the front seat of his car after a movie. On that single date, Heather had discovered that the two of them had nothing in common. Her earlier crush, she realized, had blossomed mainly because he was the first boy ever to pay romantic attention to her. After the ill-fated date, he'd not only left Heather alone; he had avoided her when they accidentally crossed paths, as if afraid of her--afraid of her anger at his cowardice, maybe. She hadn't minded a bit, since it had, in fact, taken her a long time to forgive him for deserting her.

Ted's fear or humiliation had long since faded away. He reached across the counter to shake her hand. "Welcome back." He switched off the smile. "Hey, I was sorry to hear about your mother."

"Dad, too," she said. Might as well set the record straight to avoid awkwardness later. "He died this spring."

"That's rough." He lowered his eyes. "My mother passed away two years ago. Heart."

"Oh--I didn't know." After they'd finished exchanging condolences, she asked about Ted's father.

"Semi-retired. I pretty much run the day-to-day operation, and he checks up on me and mans the register when we're busy. We've got some part-time help, too, but it's mostly me." No surprise there; it had been a foregone conclusion that Ted would inherit the business.

"And how's Pam?" Ted's twin sister Pamela had cruised in loftier social circles than Heather; they'd known each other only as speaking acquaintances.

Ted's smile faded again. "Okay, I guess. She teaches junior high math in Richmond. She's sort of engaged to some guy down there, one of the other teachers, but you'd never know it from the way she's been acting since she got here."

"She's here?"

"On vacation. I've been wondering whether she's sick or something. She's driving Dad nuts." He shrugged. "Sorry, you don't want to hear this. Anything else I can help you with?"

As Heather unloaded her purchases on the counter, she said, "I'm trying to get the cabin in shape to sell it. It needs a lot of work--starting with a bad leak in the kitchen faucet. Could you recommend a repairman? And maybe a realtor?"

"Sorry to hear you're not sticking around." He sounded sincere. He jotted down a few names and phone numbers, then rang up her groceries on a computerized cash register, the only obvious change in the store's equipment. As he packed the bags, a golden retriever emerged from the back room and sat at Heather's feet, politely thumping its tail. Heather let the dog sniff her hand, then scratched behind the silken ears. The dog lifted a paw to be shaken.

"Is this Ginger? The one that was a puppy last time I was here?"

Ted's grin reappeared. Heather began to recall why he had once attracted her. "Yeah, sure. She has pups of her own at the moment. They're five months old--we've found homes for all but two, a male and a female." He emitted a shrill whistle and called, "Here, dogs!"

A pair of half-grown retrievers with golden-brown fur wiggled their way out of the stockroom. While one lingered at Ted's heels, the other sniffed the cuffs of Heather's jeans. When she petted the dog, it gave her hand a generous lick.

"That's the female. We call her Brown Sugar. Sugar likes you--right, girl?" He returned to packing the groceries. "Say, wouldn't you like to have her? Just what you need."

"Whoa, wait a sec!" Heather retreated from her tail-wagging admirer. "I don't even know if my apartment in Charlottesville allows pets. Never gave it any thought." Her family hadn't had a pet since the death of their old cat when Heather was twelve. Her mother had refused to consider another animal, because it was "too painful" to watch them get sick and die. She'd stuck to plants instead, another area where Heather had proved herself incompetent. Four or five of Mom's potted ferns had already died on her.

"Think about it. The offer stays open." When she scooped up two of her grocery bags, he said, "Hang on, I'll take the rest."

She caught a whiff of sweat and aftershave as he hefted one of the remaining sacks.

At that moment a young woman entered the store from the stockroom behind the counter. Heather recognized Ted's sister at once. Pam still looked like a cheerleader, with honey-blonde hair trimmed in a perky, shoulder length style.

"About time you got up and wandered over here," Ted said to her over his shoulder. "I need you to watch the register. You remember Heather Kincaid, don't you?"

Pam gave Heather a cool glance and muttered, "Sure. Hi."

"Hi," Heather said, embarrassed by the open antagonism between brother and sister.

Pam slumped on the counter and said, "What do you care when I wake up? I came home to get some rest, not work in this crummy store. I've got a splitting headache."

"Maybe you'd feel better in the mornings," Ted said, "if you didn't hang around the Shenandoah Lounge until closing time every night." With a disgusted shake of his head, he shouldered his way out the door with an armful of Heather's groceries. Heather and the half-grown female pup followed him.

Heather was happy to wait at the car while Ted carried and loaded the rest of her purchases.

"Sorry about Pam," he said as he closed the trunk on the last bag. "She's been acting weird since her second night here. Staying out late every night, spaced out all day--I think it's a guy." He sighed. "Or maybe she's sick or, for all I know, on something."

That didn't sound like Heather's memory of Pam. "I hope she feels better soon." That seemed a safe enough comment. She didn't want to be rude, but she didn't want to hear his family troubles, either.

She drove off, guiltily glad to escape.

Back at the cabin, she lugged her bags into the kitchen and then stepped onto the screened back porch to gaze over the green treetops of the valley at the sunset tinting the sky above the ridge opposite. *Maybe I could get to like it here again.* She shook her head at the errant thought and retreated to the kitchen to shelve the groceries. Sure, the mountains were beautiful in spring, summer, and early fall, but she could only imagine what it was like to live here in midwinter. Could people appreciate a Christmas card landscape when trapped in their houses for days at a time? How could families like the Gaineses stand to live here year-round? *They know how to handle it, I guess. Four-wheel drive, and all that.*

She spent the rest of the afternoon rereading *A Princess of Mars*. At supper, she realized she had done nothing about contacting either a handyman or a realtor. *Oh, well, tomorrow is yet another day, Scarlett.*

That evening, she anticipated her first game session in weeks. She logged on and checked her e-mail. Nothing urgent, only a long series of posts from the mailing lists she subscribed to. She messaged her role-playing partner, whom she knew only as Nightblade, dashing adventurer. *He's probably a middle-aged insurance salesman or something like that, but who cares? It's only a game.* To him, she was "Krystal". All he knew of her mundane life was that she had recently lost her parents, information she had shared to explain the recent slowdown in her online activities.

The words {Good Evening, Krystal} appeared on the screen.

{Good evening, Nightblade. Ready to play?}

{Yea, fair damsel. The quest awaits.}

The premise of the game rested on the theft of the Sunstone, a jewel that maintained the health and prosperity of the kingdom of Teranthia. The quest, which entailed a convoluted tree of subplots, could be pursued by a single player or a team of several. When Nightblade and Krystal had last "met", they had been about to approach the cave of a giant ogre, where the tracks of the villain's party had led them. Heather, as Krystal, played the role of a sorceress whose only weapons, aside from her spells, were her bow and enchanted dagger. Nightblade played a warrior who also happened to be a were-dragon.

Their avatars appeared on the screen, frozen against the backdrop of the rocky mountainside and yawning cave-mouth. Krystal, taller and more buxom than Heather, with an impractical cascade of golden hair, wore lightweight leather armor, enchanted for protection, over body-hugging doeskin trousers. Heather sometimes wondered whether Nightblade's true appearance and his computer persona differed as far as hers did. She had played Sunstone Quest with Nightblade since her freshman year in college; she'd met him online, and he'd persuaded her to take up the game. Although she knew nothing about his off-line life, his character appeared as a knight in black plate mail, with a mane of dark hair and a rakish mustache.

The restored game segment switched into motion. After a brief conference, they agreed that Nightblade would sneak up to the cave and issue a surprise challenge to the ogre, goading him into emerging. From her hiding place, Krystal would then attack the monster with her spells, once it stood exposed. Since ogres' traditional stupidity balanced their strength, the tactic should work.

The plan proceeded smoothly until the giant humanoid charged out of the cave, straight for Nightblade. He used his superior agility to dodge, aiming a sword-slash at the creature's midsection. At the same moment, Krystal fired flame darts from her fingers at the ogre. They sizzled into nothing, like red-hot embers dropped into water.

It has some kind of shielding against spells, she thought.

She typed in the instruction {Krystal examines the ogre}.

The computer responded with details about the monster she saw on the screen: {You see an eight-foot-tall ogre wearing roughly cured animal hides, carrying a club, and wearing a ring on his left hand.}

The ring probably held the magical protection. If her spells wouldn't penetrate the enchantment, she had no recourse but the bow. While she pondered, the ogre raised its club to strike at Nightblade. The warrior, barely evading the crushing blow, swung at the monster and inflicted a belly wound. Krystal fired several arrows in succession into its torso. It staggered and howled in pain, but an ogre was too tough to bring down so easily. Its club landed a glancing blow on Nightblade's left arm. Now he couldn't use his shield, though his sword arm remained functional.

{Nightblade, perhaps you should transform} Heather typed.

The game allowed him to assume dragon-shape only a limited number of times per "day", so he reserved the power for desperate circumstances. Apparently he had already decided that this skirmish qualified, for his outline blurred into gray smoke. Perhaps the program had gifted the ogre with an invulnerability to spells specifically to force Nightblade into wasting a change on this minor conflict. Later he might find his options limited at a more critical juncture. But he had little choice. If the ogre killed them here, conserving power wouldn't benefit them.

Nightblade's human form melted into that of a black dragon with glossy wings. With a roar rendered in bloodcurdling clarity by the sound card, the dragon charged the ogre. One swipe of Nightblade's talons knocked the monster to the ground. Taking no chances that the ogre might rise for a counterattack, the dragon used his fangs to rip out its throat.

{Will you change back now?} Krystal asked.

{No, this shape may still be needed.}

Too large to maneuver inside the cave, the dragon stood guard outside while Krystal crept in through the gash in the rock. The computer informed her that the area stank of rotten meat. Conjuring up a light spell, Krystal drew her dagger and slinked forward. The remains of gutted animal and human corpses littered the cave floor. No new opponents attacked. The only sign of nonhuman life was a nest of bats overhead, which proved to be atmospheric rather than dangerous.

She recognized the livery on the dead fighters nearest the entrance; they were hirelings of the villainous wizard Adregon, stealer of the magic jewel. She searched the men and pocketed the few coins they carried. In a belt pouch, she also found a map, obviously planted to guide the quest to Adregon's next destination. She emerged from the cave and wrenched the magic ring off the dead ogre's hand.

{What have you found?} Nightblade typed.

She showed him the map.

{We have a great distance to cover} he typed. {You must ride upon my back.}

She hadn't previously flown on the dragon, but she gingerly climbed aboard. Once he soared into the air, the panoramic graphics delighted her. She suspected the program wouldn't allow this indulgence too often. No doubt

Nightblade would require an extra day, at least, to recuperate from the exertion.

As the sky changed color with approaching sunset, Nightblade glided to a landing in a sheltered glen. Krystal made a quick inspection, assuring herself that the area was safe for camping, while the dragon resumed human form. He strode up to her, and the screen's caption announced {Nightblade kisses Krystal}. The two computer personae carried out the action.

{What was that for?} she asked, startled out of character.

{A celebration of our victory and escape, fair lady.}

{Not that big a victory} she retorted. {It's getting late, real-time late. We'd better sign off.}

{With regret I accede to your wishes.}

They arranged for their next session and exited the program.

After cutting the power, Heather stared at the blank screen for several minutes. Her pleasure at the cybernetic kiss dismayed her. It occurred to her that she'd embraced two equally illusory substitutes for real-life relationships--an electronic construct and a recurring hallucination. *What's wrong with me? Why don't I date regularly, or at least pretend I'm interested in flesh-and-blood men? Am I that much of a coward? Or that hard to satisfy?* Even if she never married, she could still date. And with luck she might eventually find a man who'd want her despite her self-imposed sterility. Some men weren't interested in fatherhood, and in any case, adoption could fill the void. *Don't kid yourself; all men, deep down, want to reproduce their own genes.*

Just as she started to get out of the chair, the landline phone rang.

When she answered, the caller said in a harsh whisper, "Good, I wasn't sure this number still worked."

"Hello, who is this?"

"It's you, isn't it? You're the one he's after now."

Heather realized that the hoarse voice was deliberately disguised. *Who do I know that would harass me with anonymous calls?* She felt that the caller was a woman, but she couldn't tell for sure. "If you don't start making sense, I'm hanging up."

"He came to you last night, didn't he?"

Heather's annoyance yielded to alarm. "How on earth did you know--"

"Then it is you. I knew it!" The voice rose in triumph without losing its distorted quality. "Don't see him again. If you do, you'll be sorry. He's dangerous."

"Who?"

"You know. If I told you what he did to me--"

Heather slammed down the receiver. Her hands shook. *Oh, God, that sounded like a threat! I just got a threatening phone call!*

Chapter 3

She lowered herself into the chair, trembling and gripping the edge of the table. Only when her breathing and heartbeat slowed did she realize what else the call implied. If the person on the phone--surely a woman--warned Heather against her dream-beast, he couldn't be a dream after all. If someone else had seen him, he actually existed.

Hugging herself as if the warm summer evening held a November chill, she walked through the kitchen to the screened porch. The fragrance of honeysuckle perfumed the moist air, but for once the heady sweetness gave her no pleasure. She peered into the darkness under the trees. Was the anonymous caller on her way up here at this moment, planning to lurk outside until Heather fell asleep, then break into the cabin? And what about the dream-man? If he was real, was he truly dangerous, and in what way? After fastening the screen door with the flimsy hook, Heather retreated inside and locked the kitchen door. Then she secured the front door. *Some security! An educated chimp could pick these locks!* She reminded herself to add deadbolts to her list.

She hated surrendering to fear on her own property. She hated feeling compelled to latch all the windows, condemning herself to a stuffy night. *I can't live like a rabbit in a hole.*

She thought of calling Ted. It wasn't that late; he might be awake. *And tell him what? That I'm afraid to stay alone?* Hardly; he would think she was using her fear as a pretext to make advances to him. Then she remembered Ginger and her two half-grown pups. Ted had offered Heather a dog. While she certainly didn't want that burden at this point in her life, it wouldn't hurt to take one home temporarily. *For a trial period,* she thought. Surely Ted wouldn't mind.

To her annoyance, she found her cell phone showed no bars. When she picked up the house phone, she realized she didn't have the number for either the store or his home. *Why didn't the folks ever get a telephone book for this place?* She called Directory Assistance for Ted's father's number.

As she'd expected, Ted still lived in his parents' house. When she called there, Pam answered the phone, responding only with a brusque "Yeah" when Heather asked for Ted. She was rather relieved that the elder Mr. Gaines had not answered, for she didn't want to get sidetracked by polite conversation.

"Hey, Heather." Ted sounded considerably more amiable than his sister. "I'm surprised to hear from you so soon. Anything wrong?"

She couldn't bring herself to mention the anonymous call. She couldn't explain the background to him, and she didn't want to stir his curiosity. "Not really. I just found out I'm a little more nervous about staying alone up here than I expected to be." She forced a giggle. "It's silly, I know, but do you think I could borrow that girl puppy, Brown Sugar, for a few days?"

"Oh, you changed your mind? Great!"

"Oh, no, I said 'borrow'. Kind of a try-out, if that's okay."

"Sure, you can keep her as long as you want to. In fact, just plan on her staying with you until you sell the place." Heather heard a smug grin in his voice. "But I bet after she's been around for a week, you'll decide to keep her permanently."

"Nice try, Ted. I really appreciate the offer, though." She had to stay on his good side, since he was the closest thing she had to a friend in the area.

"I'll drive up there with her right now."

"No, don't do that." She did not want Ted visiting at the cabin; she didn't want to encourage any kind of intimacy. "I wouldn't think of putting you to the trouble. I can drive to your place, no problem."

"Well, if that's what you'd rather do." She heard a hint of disappointment. "Come to think of it, you better meet me at the store instead of home. You'll need supplies for the dog."

As soon as she'd hung up, she scurried to the car, careful to lock the house behind her. She locked all the car doors before starting the engine.

By the time she reached the store, she actually did feel a bit silly for overreacting. Telephone harassers seldom took any action, did they? This one, in particular, could be construed as warning Heather for her own safety, not threatening her. The idea that the caller might lurk in the bushes to jump her as she got in or out of the car seemed ludicrous. Still, Heather knew she would sleep sounder with the dog in the house.

Ted was already waiting at the store, lights on and front entrance unlocked. Brown Sugar waved her plumed tail in greeting when Heather scratched her ears.

"You are a sweetie, aren't you?"

"I told you she liked you." Ted lugged a twenty-five-pound bag of kibble from a lower shelf to Heather's car. "She's used to canned food with that every night." He packed a small box with cans of dog food. "She has a collar, of course. You'll need a leash--and how about something to tie her outside with? Your place doesn't have a fence."

"Okay, sure." She felt bowled over by Ted's onslaught of efficiency. He'd thought of everything. "What, don't you independent mountaineer types believe in letting dogs run free?"

"We don't live in the Dark Ages around here." On the counter he deposited a leash and a heavy-duty chain. "Traffic gets heavy, sometimes, with the tourists, and a few bears have been sighted."

"You're putting me on."

"Fact," he said. "Call the National Park and ask one of the rangers. The black bear population is rebounding. They forage in people's trash, like raccoons."

"All right, you've convinced me. I won't let her run loose." Heather glanced down at the dog that was poking a damp nose into the palm of her hand. "Say, she is housebroken, isn't she?"

"Of course. And she knows a few simple commands, don't you, Sugar?" He bagged the leash and chain, a pair of plastic feeding dishes, a grooming brush, and a can of flea spray. "There, you're all set."

"What do I owe you?"

"Nothing--on the house. Dad wouldn't want me to charge you. He'd like to see you sometime, by the way. He told me to ask you to stop by when you have a chance."

"Sure. Thanks." Heather didn't like feeling obligated to Ted, and the idea of dropping in on his family made her uncomfortable, especially since she'd received the strong impression Pam didn't like her. *Nice as his dad is, I'll still try to keep busy enough that I don't have time to drop by.*

Ted waited in front of the store until the car was loaded, Heather and the pup were locked in, and they had started down the road. Heather felt grateful for his concern and mildly guilty that she couldn't make herself like him more. Still, her nervousness about the mountain night had lessened already.

"We'll have a fun time together, won't we, Sugar?" The dog, who sat politely on her haunches in the front passenger seat, replied with an affectionate whine.

"Maybe I should get the wagon outfitted with one of those gate contraptions, so you can ride back in the cargo area. You'd be safer that way-- I don't know whether they make seat belts for animals." *Hold on, what am I thinking about?* She wasn't planning to keep the dog; they wouldn't be together long enough to warrant spending any extra money on canine vehicular transport.

For the first few minutes, the narrow, twisty road up the mountainside remained deserted. Heather set the radio on "search", looking for a station that played something other than country tunes. She finally settled for a Johnny Cash oldie and sang along, almost cheerfully. That was when she glimpsed a pair of high beams in the rearview mirror.

What's the matter with that idiot, is he trying to blind me or what? She blinked her own lights, with no result. Thinking the other driver wanted to pass, she squeezed as close to the shoulder as possible, grateful for the low stone wall between the road and the steep slope to the valley below. The car behind sped up, but instead of passing, it clung to the station wagon's back bumper.

It's tailgating on purpose! Heather put on a burst of speed but couldn't keep it up. Her tires squealed on the tight curves. The other car matched her pace. She squinted into the high-beam glare in the rearview mirror, trying to make out the other driver's face. No use--she couldn't even distinguish the type of vehicle.

Why is he--or she--following me? Heather thought of the anonymous caller. It would be too much of a coincidence, to have two different people on her trail.

Chill out, she told herself. There didn't have to be any connection; this could be some joyriding juvenile delinquent who thought it was fun to scare people. Still, her heart hammered in near-panic.

The car rocked as she took a curve too fast. The dog emitted a gruff bark. "Quiet, Sugar, don't distract me."

The shoulder was wider and softer here, the stone barrier farther from the pavement. Heather had to concentrate to keep her wheels on the hard surface. She struggled to quell her fear and consider her options rationally. Going home would be stupid; if that driver were chasing her specifically, he or she could ask for no better opportunity than the isolated cabin. *But where else am I supposed to go--crawling back to Ted?* She could appeal directly to his father instead. Mr. Gaines had always welcomed her pleasantly when she'd shopped at the store as a teenager. He wouldn't mind letting her stay at his house a few hours or even overnight.

A scenic turnoff was coming up around the bend. Heather had almost decided to turn around there and head back toward town when a new factor canceled that plan.

Something with wings swooped out of the woods. It swept across the hood of Heather's car, over the roof, and dive-bombed the pursuing vehicle.

Heather caught an impression of a vast, black shadow and glowing red eyes. *It's a bird, that's all--a hawk or an owl. It couldn't be as big as it looked--*

Screeching brakes behind her cut off her mental babbling. She pumped her own brakes and wrestled with the steering wheel. In the mirror, she saw the thing glide over the other car again and vanish into the gloom.

Now the other driver pulled out to the left, crowding Heather to the edge of the road. Sugar jumped up and down on the seat, barking continuously. The wheel spun in Heather's sweat-slick hands. She felt her tires slip off the pavement onto the dirt. She clutched the wheel and slammed on the brakes. The other car roared past her, turned in a tight circle, and careened back down the road. Heather was too busy screaming to snatch a good look at it.

The station wagon bumped to a stop, all four wheels on the shoulder. Heather threw the gearshift into park and switched off the ignition. The headlights showed her that she'd stopped bare inches from the retaining wall.

Shaking, she put her head down on the steering wheel. Air whooshed through the partly open driver's window, and she looked up. She thought she glimpsed a dark, winged shape before the figure coalesced into the outline of a man. Pinpoints of crimson gleamed in his eyes.

Her dream-beast.

Oh, my God, this isn't a dream! This is really happening! She twisted the key to restart the engine. Shifting into drive, she floored the accelerator. The wheels spun in the soft dirt.

The man tapped on the window. "Please be calm, Heather. I'm here to help you, not hurt you."

She turned off the motor and stared up at him. *Might as well listen. The car's stuck, and I sure couldn't outrun him.*

The dog cowered against the far door, growling.

"If I push you onto the blacktop," the man said in his usual melodious voice, "will you promise not to flee?"

"All right," she gasped. If she tried to drive at this moment, she would probably wreck the car anyhow.

"Start the motor again, put it in neutral, and steer."

She obeyed, as he moved to the rear bumper. Seconds later, she pulled smoothly onto the pavement. *How did he get the tires unstuck that fast?* She shifted into drive, but when the man reappeared at her window, trotting alongside, she abandoned any thoughts of breaking her word. Rather than accelerating, she stopped.

"Unlock the door and move over," he said. "I'll drive."

After she obeyed, he opened the door and leaned in, gazing at Sugar, wedged against the passenger door, her ears laid back and fangs bared.

"Be quiet, dog," the man whispered. The growl rumbling in Sugar's throat changed to a whine. "Good girl," he said in a soothing tone. "We'll be friends later." He gestured with one hand.

To Heather's surprise, Sugar clambered over the seat and curled up in the back.

Heather belted herself into the passenger seat. *Am I crazy, giving him the keys? He could take me anywhere.* Yet somehow she felt confident he would only drive her home. If he wanted to harm her, he'd had ample opportunities. *But that woman on the phone said he was dangerous,* an insidious voice reminded her. That he was indeed dangerous in some sense, she had no doubt--but dangerous to whom?

He drove only as far as the next scenic turnoff, where he parked the car and switched on the dome light. His eyes looked normal now.

"I ought to convince you this is your imagination, also."

She hitched herself upright, clutching the armrest of the passenger door as if it could save her from the tornado of unreality trying to blow her away. "Don't you dare mess with my memory again! Thinking I'm crazy is a hundred times worse than anything else you can do to me!"

He lightly touched her arm. "My dear, what are you afraid of?"

Was the hint of sadness in his tone real or another mind trick?

"Have I ever harmed you? Haven't I served as your knight in shining armor?"

She felt herself trembling again. "More like my private dragon."

He laughed, his eyes scanning her with leisurely attention. "A dragon who wishes only to adore this fair princess, not devour her."

She blushed under his blatant examination, imagining that the red glint momentarily danced in his eyes again.

"Let me take you to your home, where we can talk more comfortably. I promise, you have nothing to be afraid of."

Still she shrank from him. "You're real. I saw you in the woods that time--with Ted. What did you do to me? How much of all those nights really happened?" Her voice rose to a wail. "What do you want with me?"

"Not to hurt or frighten you, never that." The man grasped Heather's bare forearm. His flesh felt cool but unquestionably solid. "Let's go to your place and talk, shall we?"

She shivered at his touch, an unnerving sensation that nevertheless ignited a spark of heat deep within her. His eyes held her more firmly than his hand did. A giddy floating sensation displaced her fear--

"Stop that! You're doing it again--doing something to my mind!"

"Only trying to put you at ease." His eyes released hers, and he turned the ignition key.

Neither of them spoke during the drive to the cabin. Parking in the driveway, he opened Heather's door, then released the dog, who slinked onto the porch with her tail between her legs.

I know exactly how she feels, thought Heather.

She unlocked the door and allowed the man to guide her into the living room and onto the couch, where he plucked an afghan from the back of the rocking chair and wrapped it around her shoulders. Meanwhile, Sugar dashed for the bedroom to hide. Heather wished she could do the same.

Turning on a single dim lamp, he sat at the other end of the sofa. "Now I'm not touching you or meeting your eyes. I can't manipulate your mind."

She knew better; the resonance of his voice alone sent a succession of minor shock waves through her bones. "You hypnotized me somehow, didn't you? And that other driver, too?"

"That's the simplest way to put it, yes."

Glowing eyes, dark wings. She felt short of breath, her throat squeezed by a fresh upwelling of fear. "Hypnosis doesn't usually work that way--I've read enough about it to know that. How can you put these illusions in my head?"

"Isn't it enough to know that my--talent--saved you from someone who wanted to terrify you, perhaps even hurt you? And I didn't harm you the night we first met, did I, after that young clod you were with deserted you?"

"Ted." She inhaled a tremulous breath. "No, it's not enough. You've been in my head ever since. How?"

He looked in her direction but not directly into her eyes.

"Do you believe in ESP? Telepathy?"

The question startled her out of the panic that was creeping over her. "Never thought much about it. I wouldn't rule it out."

"Then accept the truth that we have a certain psychic connection. I can't explain further at this time."

Heather shook her head. "Still not good enough." She brushed a ticklish strand of hair out of her eyes. "I saw you in the woods that night--" She suppressed a fleeting queasiness at the memory of what he'd done with the deer. Or was that part real? *I don't think I want to know yet.* "And you came to my room later. You did something to my mind." She blushed, recalling that the first night had ended as enchantingly as the later ones.

Now his eyes roamed over her body, deepening her blush, though he still didn't meet her gaze. "You've changed since then."

"And you haven't changed a bit!" Or was her memory distorted on that point? If this man had actually used hypnosis on her--or some telepathic communion, as he claimed--how much of her perception of him could she trust?

"That's probably why I've enjoyed watching your growth, sharing your life."

"Then all the things I remember telling you--my secrets, things I'd never mention to Mom and Dad--I really did tell you?" Her cheeks glowed with the heat of anger as well as embarrassment, now.

He spread his hands as if in tentative apology. "Whatever parts really happened or not, you may think of each case as you prefer. Does it matter?"

"Darn right it does!" Her fists clenched in her lap. "I talked to you that way because I thought you were imaginary!"

"Exactly what I wanted you to think," he said, "to soothe your apprehensions and protect myself. So if you're angry, I suppose I asked for it."

"Angry doesn't begin to describe--" Her chest heaved. "You took advantage of me! You were no better than a child molester, no matter how you did it!"

"I never thought of you as a child, after our first conversation." The hint of sadness she'd heard earlier softened his voice. "And we do have a psychic link--you must believe that."

"Yeah? How do you explain it?"

He turned away from her challenging stare. "Who knows how these things arise? Nevertheless, it's a fact." Shifting back in her direction, he stretched his arm along the back of the couch. "I want to touch you, but you see, I'm not forcing the issue. I've missed you, these past years. What I said about that, last night, was true also."

"That you need me? Give me a break!"

He laughed softly. Her stomach fluttered. "Sweet Heather, I sensed your approach even before you arrived yesterday. At that moment, I knew I'd been waiting for nothing else but your return. And tonight, when I felt you in danger--"

"Now that you mention it, how did you happen to show up at just the right minute?"

"I was--lurking, you'd probably say in your present mood--in the woods near this house, wondering whether to approach you again. I sensed your fear and came as fast as I could." He leaned over, staring into her eyes for the first time since they'd sat down. "You harebrained female, whatever possessed you to go out alone after dark, when you'd received that threatening call?"

"How did you know about--?" *He reads my mind, that's how. With all these other weird events, why shouldn't I assume that he picks my brain at will?* She tossed her head, eluding the snare of his gaze. "Well, if you want me to hide in the house like a spineless wimp, that's too bad!"

"My dear, there's a fine line between courage and stupidity." His anger seemed to ebb; he relaxed against the cushions. "Well, your spirit attracted me in the first place--the way you resisted my control. I wanted to know you, to share your dreams."

"You created those dreams, didn't you? With that hypnotism or psychic bond or some crazy combination of both?"

"Believe what you like about that," he said. "Whatever makes you comfortable. I couldn't bear to lose you again, now that you've come back."

"Not to stay. I told you that. I'm selling the place. And as for you--"

Again he leaned closer, his fingertips brushing hers. "Please don't shut me out. I've waited so long."

Her hand, resting on the couch under his, quivered like a mouse under a cat's paw. *Shut him out? How could I, now that I've finally got the chance to learn the truth about him?* She fought to hold her voice steady. "I do want to know you better. But I won't stand for any more of that sneaking into my room, or projecting hallucinations into my head, or whatever you were doing."

"You want honesty and openness." Amusement tinged his voice. "How modern." He wrapped his fingers around her wrist, as if taking her pulse. "Very well, when we meet from now on, you can be perfectly sure that you'll be awake."

Tiny electric sparks seemed to dart up her arm.

"You're doing it again--touching me."

"You didn't say that was forbidden." He slid closer to her and cupped her head in his right hand. "You liked it well enough in the past--and even last night." She felt his fingers weave through the tangle of her hair. He lifted his other hand to graze her jawline with his fingernails. Her breath caught in her throat. Her cheeks burned. "Ah, you're glowing--you're like a flame, and I'm the helpless moth."

What a line! she thought, but the attempt at cynicism didn't convince her.

He bent his head, touching his lips to hers as lightly as the wings of that figurative moth.

Heather sighed, the tension in her muscles liquefying into sweet warmth. Hardly conscious of the act, she wrapped her arms around his neck.

Abruptly the contact between them broke. Instead of sitting beside her, he was standing by the front door. She blinked. How did he move so fast? The next instant, she realized with shame that she'd been throwing herself into his embrace all over again.

"No, not this time," he said. "Tomorrow you'd accuse me of subverting your will with my Svengali powers. I'll kiss you again when you can be sure that's your true desire."

"Wait a minute! I don't even know--" A ridiculously inadequate protest; she still didn't know anything at all about her phantom, except that he was flesh instead of dream.

"If you truly want to know me better," he said, pausing in the act of opening the door, "come to the Shenandoah Lounge tomorrow night at eight." Halfway out, he added, "And for God's sake, lock your doors after I'm gone."

She found herself soaring, with a pine-scented wind rushing over her. The darkness melted from her sight to reveal a starry sky and, below her, treetops rippling like waves. Whenever she glided over a clearing, she glimpsed sparks and patches of light, ranging from pale blue to deep rose. She realized she was seeing, through his eyes, the heat that emanated from live creatures.

After a while they swooped lower, hovering above a meadow on a hillside gently sloping toward the valley. Heather rode on his wings toward a pink aura that surrounded a doe pacing delicately across the grass, followed by a half-grown fawn whose spots had almost faded into invisibility. Heather shared his exhilaration as he floated to the ground and coursed after the deer that broke into a run too late to escape the hunter. The landscape of glowing pastel shapes swept past in a blur. They brought down the prey in a final ecstatic surge of speed. Heather felt her hands--his--stroking the animal's muzzle until it ceased quivering in terror and slipped into a trance. He lowered his head to the tender abdomen, and Heather tasted a flood of hot salt-sweetness.

Abruptly she realized what she was relishing. *No, I can't be enjoying this! I'm not a beast of prey!* She wrestled free of his mental snare. *Whatever you are, let me go!*

As the vision faded to gray, she sensed him calling, *No, don't leave me now, I need you.* She summoned the will to cut off the appeal as cleanly as switching off a radio.

Heather awoke late the next morning, her head clogged with the aftereffects of troubled sleep. She brushed away the scraps of dream that clung like cobwebs to her befuddled thoughts and shuffled through her memories in search of something real to grasp. It took her a few minutes to remember last night's wild ride. *My dream-beast scared away whoever was chasing me.* She could no longer deny his reality. But knowing that he actually existed raised more questions than it answered. Why did the mere thought of him rouse an ache of longing inside her? *I wanted him to stay, didn't I? Wanted him in my bed? Girl, have you no shame?* She threw the covers aside and sat up.

Should I call the police about all this? She hadn't even considered that, the night before. That man, whoever he was, had turned her brain to mush. She decided that reporting the harassment would be pointless. She had no clue to the identity of the caller, the driver of the car, or whether or not they were in fact the same person. Actually, the anonymous threat occupied second place on her list of concerns at the moment. She was more interested in her rescuer's last words: *Come to the Shenandoah Lounge.*

You bet I will. Her head whirled at the notion that, all those years, he had exercised some kind of mesmeric influence over her. She'd read enough about ESP, in a casual way, to preclude total scepticism. But admitting the theoretical possibility was a long way from accepting its influence in her own life. And the man's explanation of a "psychic link" between them sounded suspiciously vague. Could all the phenomena she'd experienced, or imagined, have some material cause? Maybe he was a skilled con artist; maybe on the first night he had visited her bedroom so long ago, he had drugged her to make her susceptible to his hypnotic wiles? That scenario sounded more paranoid and far-fetched than ESP.

If I had any sense, I'd report him to the authorities. She paused in yanking a brush through her hair and stared into her own bleary eyes. No misty shape in the mirror behind her this morning. *Report what? That some strange man has been telepathically molesting me? Sure.*

She fed and walked the dog, whose presence gave more comfort than she had expected. Now she had someone to talk to, even if Brown Sugar couldn't talk back, which might actually prove an advantage sometimes. Heather spent several hours sorting food staples in the walk-in pantry and bagging expired canned goods to throw away.

After a sandwich for lunch, she drove down to the village to check out the Shenandoah Lounge, located in the tourist lodge along with the restaurant and TV and game rooms. The sight of it jogged her memory; Heather recalled that her parents had spent many evenings here, listening to the music programs in the bar. She'd never joined them. In her preteen and junior high years, she'd been sent to bed early. Later, she hadn't been invited and had never asked, for she had enjoyed the time on her own. She'd always felt "on stage" in her parents' presence, tiptoeing through her dutiful daughter role. The relaxation of solitude had been a treat.

In the relative dimness of the lodge's lobby, she blinked until the sign at the head of the stairs leading to the basement came into focus. "Devin MacAvoy Performs the Folk Songs of Appalachia and the British Isles." According to the schedule, he appeared from eight to ten p.m., five nights every week throughout the season. Could this Devin MacAvoy be her dream man? The poster displayed no picture of the singer. She walked to the information desk. "Excuse me, I wondered how long Devin MacAvoy has been performing here."

The young blonde woman behind the counter said, "I don't really know. A lot longer than I've had this job." She called over her shoulder to a plump, middle-aged man working at a computer in a cramped office behind her. "Mr. Oakes, this lady has a question about Mr. MacAvoy."

The plump man left his work to come to the front desk. Heather, flustered at attracting more attention than she'd planned, repeated her question. Mr. Oakes said, "Quite a while. About sixteen years, I think." Wearing a courteous but faintly puzzled smile, he waited.

"Thanks. I just wondered because my family used to come here every summer, and..." She let the sentence trail off, hoping the two employees would mentally finish the sentence with their own assumptions. She sketched a wave of farewell and scurried out.

Sixteen years. If that's him, he could've been here when I was a kid. But her dream man looked no more than thirty, at the most. Had Devin MacAvoy started singing in a cocktail lounge at age fourteen? Not likely!

Back at the cabin, she chained Sugar to a tree behind the house, propping the door of the screened porch ajar so the dog could reach the food and water bowls or take a nap inside at will. Fortunately the dog didn't bark, strain at the collar, or otherwise object to being tied out. Sometimes Heather wouldn't be able to keep her inside all day, so she was pleased to see the dog adapted so quickly.

Heather steeled herself for the job she had been putting off: cleaning her parents' room. She knew they must have left miscellaneous clothes and personal items at the cabin.

Come on, how tough could this be, pawing through a lot of old junk? They wouldn't have kept anything important here, she told herself as she dived into the bedroom closet with an empty box.

At first she found nothing she hadn't expected, just a collection of worn-down sandals and tennis shoes and faded summer clothes. She forced herself to ignore the spectral traces of her mother's cologne on some of the blouses. All that could go to charity; she wouldn't have to touch it again. After stuffing the clothes and shoes into the box, she pulled a chair over and clambered onto it to check the shelf. *I hate to think what Mom would say to me about standing on her chair.* Beside a couple of straw hats, she noticed a shoebox. She stepped down with the box in her hands and sat on the bed to open it.

She found a heap of color snapshots. Turning over a few, she found that Mom had labeled each one, according to her usual habit, so that she could annotate them properly whenever she got around to pasting them in an album. The photos showed the family at the cabin and nearby picnic spots. Some of the pictures went back as far as Heather's junior high school years. She gazed into her own green eyes. Already, at that age, her auburn hair had been a shoulder-length mane that her mother had constantly nagged her to get cut. *I'll have to get a scrapbook and arrange these in order.* About to replace the lid, she noticed something else under the pictures--a small book.

She lifted it out. *My diary! The diary I thought I'd lost!*

She had missed the book a few weeks into the summer after graduation. She remembered asking her mother if she had seen it. The reply had lodged in Heather's brain verbatim: "Don't you think I have anything better to do than keep track of your junk?"

She had it all the time. Of course Heather had never done anything so foolish as writing the full truth of her experiences with the dream-man in this fake-leather volume with the flimsy lock. She had recorded only fragmentary phrases about her "dreams", memory triggers meaningless to anyone else. But she still would have collapsed from embarrassment at the idea of a parent's reading her secret thoughts. And come to think of it, right around that time she had overheard her mother and father arguing about whether their child needed a therapist, a notion that had been abandoned by the time the family returned home from vacation. *She snooped! She poked into my private life and lied about it!* Heather was seized by a spasm of anger so intense that her ears rang, and her vision blurred to gray.

Clutching the diary, she stared at the window opposite until her eyes cleared. Her fingers, automatically flipping pages, came upon a folded piece of paper. She opened it--a sheet of the pink stationery her mother had used.

The scribbled phrases in ballpoint pen looked like an unfinished note to her father: "I'm worried about Heather. Diary has something about dreams--strange man. Maybe not all dreams? Something like that happened to me--once--long time ago, when I was pregnant. And again just a few nights ago. When I woke up, I wanted to buy her that computer--what changed my mind?

No--just my imagination. What am I thinking? I can't possibly tell you this." The scrawled words trailed into incoherence, as if the writer had left the message unfinished before tucking it between the pages of the little book.

She saw him too!

Heather dropped the diary, jumping up as if the bedspread were on fire. When her pounding heart slowed, she found herself sitting at the table that held the computer and the telephone. She picked up the slip of paper bearing the name and number of the realtor Ted had recommended, Ellie Norton.

What have I been waiting for? I should have called her already. Heather certainly didn't want to be stuck with the cabin a day or a week longer than necessary. The sooner she arranged to put the place on the market, the better.

Taking a couple of deep breaths to ensure she would be able to speak calmly, she pulled the phone closer and dialed Ms. Norton's number.

Chapter 4

The dim lighting of the lounge, as usual, soothed Devin's eyes. Unlike the raucous crowd one might find in a more typical bar, the patrons here conversed quietly, in a mood of pleasant anticipation. The few who weren't regulars had heard enough about the folk music program to look forward to it. The room smelled comfortably of beer, candle wax, and warm, mostly clean human flesh. No reek of cigarettes, since he'd long ago made it clear that his "allergies" demanded a no-smoking environment.

While setting up his instruments, Devin watched the door for Heather Kincaid. He had no doubt that she would show; her curiosity wouldn't let her stay away. After toying with her for so long, he felt eager to speak with her face to face, open himself to her, and move their intimacy to a new level. Not to mention the more tangible reward he wanted, which he had denied himself on the previous night. He caught his heartbeat accelerating at the thought and had to concentrate to slow it down.

Why does she fascinate me? She's terribly young--and so ordinary. Not ordinary. Intelligent, as her kind went, but intelligent young women weren't that rare.

More significant was the strength of will that had enabled her, at the age of eighteen, to resist his control. That anomaly had drawn him to her. After their first night together, the pleasure of vicariously sharing her life had kept him enthralled. He smiled at the memory of her indignation. *Child molester, am I? Well, she's certainly no child now.* He had to overcome her resistance, preferably by normal persuasion. Of course he could override her will at any time, but he wanted her conscious, voluntary friendship.

Friendship? Dangerous thinking, Devin! Caring for their kind was a trap, a snare he had to avoid. By now he ought to know better than to make any emotional investment in one of them. A similar lapse on his part had drawn him into his entanglement with Judith, a relationship with a catastrophic end. He'd sworn "never again", a vow he'd managed to keep so far. No way would he set himself up for another--*Stop that! Why am I thinking about Judith at all?* He'd dreamed of her, for the first time in longer than he wanted to remember.

Heather didn't even look like her, except for the auburn hair. And the horror that had destroyed Judith didn't happen now, in this "enlightened" time and place. No parallels, and no danger, because he wouldn't fall into that trap. No matter how delightful, Heather was a plaything, a pet.

He positioned the tall stool in front of the microphone and strummed a few chords on his guitar, then adjusted the angle of the mike. The manager, Mr. Oakes, strolled in and watched for a minute, with his usual puzzled frown at the lighting level. Devin knew his preference for subdued illumination onstage set him apart from the average performer, but he wasn't about to endure blinding glare for the sake of apparent normalcy. He compensated with an extra bit of psychic pressure to keep the staff's attention off this oddity, along with his perennially youthful appearance. *If I decide to stay here much longer, I'll have to put some gray into my hair.* And if he could persuade Heather to stick around, he would definitely stay.

He flashed an "okay" signal at the manager, who nodded to him and went back upstairs. The bartender sent a waitress over with a tray bearing Devin's customary pitcher of ice water and a glass. He thanked her, wryly amused at the way she made sure her hand brushed his arm. He sensed her disappointment when he responded to her only with a bland smile. *I'm broadcasting again. Better tone it down.*

The waitress' overture didn't even interest him, a sure sign that he was fixated on Heather. Well, he'd suspected that for a long time. He still didn't have to let the obsession wreck his judgment. And why wasn't she here yet, anyway? Was she so blasé about their meeting that she would wait until the last minute?

A negative surge in the room's psychic atmosphere drew his eyes to the doorway. The turbulence emanated from a young blonde woman. Pamela Gaines. *Good God, not her again!*

She marched over to the low stage. "Devin, I want to talk to you right now."

"Right now isn't good." He gazed into her eyes, striving to project calm. "As you see, I'm busy."

"Well, this is the only time I can catch you. Why do you keep avoiding me?" She hurled the accusation loud enough to be audible throughout the room.

He set down the guitar and moved close enough to rest a hand lightly on her forearm, hoping to quiet her. "Avoiding? I didn't know you were so anxious to talk. But surely this isn't the place for discussion." Her emotions, murky with alcohol, resisted his control. He smelled Scotch on her breath, mixed with the heavy floral aroma of her perfume.

"Damn you, Devin, I'm not letting you get away this time."

He suppressed a sigh. "Very well, I can spare a minute or two, but let's not make a scene, please. Come with me." He guided her into the hallway, where he leaned against the wall and gazed into her eyes. "I'm listening."

The soothing tone had no effect; the combination of alcohol and fury armored her against his influence. "You've been ignoring me! You haven't called me once!"

"I didn't say anything to lead you to believe I would, did I?" He had used her twice, obviously one time too many. In retrospect, he cursed his own laziness. He'd taken advantage of Pamela's convenient proximity. He knew these one-way obsessions could arise with disconcerting suddenness; he should have been more careful.

The girl had shown up at the lounge every night for over a week. Devin's persistent refusal to give her more than a terse greeting hadn't discouraged her. He had finally talked with her two nights earlier, explicitly stating his lack of interest, and even that hadn't worked. "As I told you, my...affections...are committed elsewhere."

"How can you be so cold?" Her face flushed with anger, she stood in the middle of the corridor with her fists clenched at her sides. "It's her, isn't it? You gave me that little lecture the evening Heather Kincaid moved in. And you went to her place that night."

"What?" He clutched her upper arms. When she gasped in pain, he realized how close he was to losing control. He forced himself to relax his grip. Lowering his voice to a whisper, he said, "How did you know that?"

"I was watching your house. I knew you wouldn't talk to me, but at least I could be near you. When you went out, I followed you through the woods."

"You followed me?" He fought to leash his rage. *Steady, Devin, you can't lose it right here in the hallway.* "How long did you stay there spying on me?"

Pam shrugged. "As soon as I saw where you'd gone, I went home. I didn't need to see any more."

He released a long breath, his anger ebbing. "Then it should be perfectly obvious that dogging my footsteps won't get you anything."

"Can't you see how humiliating this is? How much I want you--"

"What do you want from me, Pamela?" He spoke softly, like a man gentling a half-tame animal.

"I don't know!" Her shrill voice grated on his ears. "I want *you.*"

"If you knew me better, you wouldn't." He placed his right hand lightly on her shoulder, trying to establish control with physical contact. "Forget about me. There's nothing between us."

She batted his hand away. "I don't want to forget! How can you say there's nothing after--"

"You're indulging in wishful thinking. On two occasions we took a casual walk together, no more." She couldn't possibly remember anything else, could she? Devin turned cold at the thought that her infatuation with him might undo his blurring of her memory.

Another unwanted memory of Judith assailed him. *That's where involvement leads--to disaster! I have to get rid of this pest.* He glanced at his watch. "I'm sorry, my show's scheduled to start in four minutes. As much as I'm flattered by your interest, I'm afraid it simply isn't mutual."

With a wordless shriek, Pamela swiped at him with her nails. He grabbed her arm before she could connect with his face. She let out a low moan.

Realizing he was hurting her again, he eased the pressure but didn't release her. Out of the corner of his eye he noted the curious glances of an elderly couple on their way into the lounge. "Pamela, be quiet." This time the command worked.

She froze, staring up at him. From the red marks on her bare skin, it was clear that she would have bruises where he'd grabbed her. *Wonderful. Great self-control, there.*

A masculine voice broke his concentration. "Pam, what's going on here? You, what the hell are you doing to her?"

Devin recognized the young man as Ted, Pam's brother.

"You've misinterpreted the situation." He focused on the newcomer, hoping the man might prove more suggestible. "Your sister isn't herself. Maybe you'd better escort her home."

"Just what I plan to do." Ted reached for the girl's free hand. "Come on, Pam. Dad's worried about you. He asked me to find you, and I figured you'd be hanging around here again."

She jerked out of Devin's loose hold and flinched away from the other man. "Stay out of this, Ted. I'm talking to Devin."

"I assure you, we're quite finished talking," Devin said.

Ted gave him scarcely a glance, focusing on Pam. "Don't you have any consideration for Dad? You're driving him crazy, leaving the house without a word and running around at all hours the way you did last night."

A freshly chilling thought hit Devin. Had Pam driven the car that had run Heather off the road? That hypothesis seemed all too likely. Was she only a nuisance, or actually dangerous?

"You can tell Dad I'm not a kid anymore, and I don't have to check in with him."

"Tell him yourself, if you've got the nerve." Ted made another grab for her hand, this time successfully. "Come on, let's get out of here. We're going to have a long talk." He scowled at Devin. "What did you do, brainwash her?"

Breathing harshly, Pam tugged against Ted's grip. "I'm not going anywhere with you!"

Thoroughly exasperated, Devin silenced her with a hard glare. Ordinarily he didn't like to treat the subject too roughly, since psychic bludgeoning could backfire, but he'd had all he could take of this female. And the ridiculous three-way quarrel was about to make him late for his performance. "Listen to me,

Pamela. You will go with your brother, and you will stay away from me. And you will leave Heather alone."

Blank-eyed, like a woman stunned by a blow to the head, she allowed Ted to hustle her toward the stairs. At that moment, Devin sensed someone staring at him. Shifting his attention, he saw Heather standing a few yards away. Her suspicion stung like a slap in the face. *That's all I need! How much of that did she witness?*

Heather stared at the mini-drama before her. Pam lunged at the man, trying to claw him. He caught her arm; she struggled. Ted broke in, and after a brief shouting match, he dragged her away. Heather flattened herself against the wall as the couple staggered up the stairs, still fighting.

Her eyes met the man's. *That's him, no doubt about it!* Heather realized she'd still half doubted his existence. He wore tight black trousers and a white shirt with ruffled cuffs and collar, open at the neck in a plunging V to expose a nearly hairless chest. His silver-gray eyes glittered.

Well, she wouldn't let his ravishing appearance distract her this time. "What was all that about?"

"There's no time to explain now." He strode up to her and lightly clasped her shoulder. "I'm supposed to be onstage already. But I want to talk to you afterward--I need to talk to you. Please don't go."

Pleading? That didn't sound like him. Probably another act. Suddenly short of breath and annoyed at what it implied, Heather said, "Oh, I'm not about to go anywhere. You're not getting away without an explanation this time." She surveyed his lean, sleek height. "You're him--the folk singer, Devin MacAvoy."

"At your service, fair lady." He turned toward the door of the cocktail lounge, his arm slipping down to her waist. "It'll be an honor to have you attend my performance. And afterward, all will be revealed." A wry smile. "Well, a reasonable percentage will be revealed."

"Performance?" She let him guide her to a table for two near the small stage. "I think that's what I've been getting from you all along."

"We'll discuss it later. But this I will say, and please believe it--Pamela and I are not involved." Holding a chair for Heather, he gave her hand a fleeting kiss, then stepped onto the stage.

Among the instruments grouped on the low dais, Heather saw no amplifiers. She was relieved to see that Devin played acoustic only; the pounding of amplified music would overwhelm this confined space. The small, windowless lounge invited mellow rhythms, not a driving beat to rattle the walls.

The bar, located just inside the door, occupied the side of the room opposite the stage. At a right angle to the door was a fireplace of rough-cut gray stone, with an assortment of pewter mugs on the mantle and a rack of antlers mounted above. A couple of dozen circular tables completed the decor.

Heather picked up the menu next to the fat candle burning in front of her. The mixed drinks had fanciful mock-hillbilly names. She ordered a blackberry-flavored concoction called Granny's Home Remedy.

Devin began his show with an instrumental selection on a thing that looked like a xylophone on a stand. The music reminded Heather of a handbell performance she'd once heard at church. His hands made the paired sticks dance with blurring speed, while his eyes lingered on Heather's face as if feasting on her admiration of his skill. When he'd finished, he identified the instrument as a hammered dulcimer and introduced its miniature counterpart, the lap dulcimer.

Heather felt faintly disillusioned, for she'd always visualized the "damsel with a dulcimer" in "Kublai Khan" as playing something more ethereal, perhaps a sort of lute or harp.

After explaining how early Scottish settlers had imported the dulcimer to the Appalachians, Devin picked up a black guitar, decorated with a design she couldn't quite make out from her position. First he sang outlaw ballads: "John Hardy", "The Wild Colonial Boy", "Whiskey in the Jar", "Brennan on the Moor". Most of the Robin-Hood-like heroes fell victim to the betrayal of a "false-hearted woman", she noticed. He encouraged the audience to sing along with the rousing choruses, and despite the armor she wanted to maintain against him, Heather found herself swept away. Never prone to make an exhibition of her minimal vocal talents, she echoed, "Bold, brave, and undaunted, young Brennan on the moor," with the rest of the bellowing group until her throat grew raw.

Sipping her alcohol-laced blackberry juice, she listened with dismay as he switched to "The Great Silkie". How many nights had he crooned that song by her bedside? The selection seemed to mock her uncertainty as to how much of their relationship she had dreamed and how much had actually happened. Yet she couldn't withhold her response to the mortal woman's betrayal and the seal-man's yearning for his half-human son, fated to die by violence. She blinked away tears. *If the Silkie hadn't seduced her in the first place, he wouldn't have this problem. Shapechanging sea monsters should leave human women alone!* She laughed inwardly at her own exaggerated reaction. *It's only a fairy tale, remember.* But was Devin making a special point of singing the ballads he had shared with her in the past? He segued into "House Carpenter", that most durable and versatile of demon-lover ballads, another piece with which he'd often lulled her to sleep. *At least, that's what I think he did.*

Again Devin fixed his eyes on hers while he sang. She suppressed a shudder, abruptly aware of the dark content that had previously slipped past her in her fascination with his voice. The woman chose supernatural over natural love and ended up losing everything--husband, baby, lover, and her life and soul. *Does Devin want my soul, too?* The music seemed to thrum in her veins, making it impossible to shake off the melodramatic fantasy.

Her mind wandered through the next few selections. Finally he finished the set with "The Fair Flower of Northumberland", about an English girl seduced by a Scottish outlaw into helping him escape English justice, and "Bonnie Susie Cleland", the tale of a Scottish border maiden condemned "to be burned at Dundee" by her own father for the crime of falling in love with an Englishman.

"They took their ethnic conflicts seriously then," Devin said in his introduction to the song.

An older woman in the audience asked how picking the wrong lover, no matter how undesirable, could warrant a death sentence.

"Because in the Middle Ages," Devin said, "disobedience to a parent constituted heresy, and heretics were burned." He spoke grimly, the sardonic smile gone.

The ballad ended, not with the gallant rescue Heather expected, but with Susie Cleland's execution. The English lover, despite the heroine's repeated appeals, never showed up. As he let the final chord die away, Devin said with a trace of his previous humor, "Which goes to prove that Sassenachs can't be trusted." Announcing a ten-minute intermission, he set down his guitar and joined Heather at her table.

"What a depressing song," she said. "Why was the Englishman such a rat?"

Devin raised one hand, and the waitress instantly appeared with a glass of white wine. "Maybe he wasn't. Perhaps he did everything he could to rush to her side, and his enemies blocked the way until it was too late."

His serious tone puzzled Heather. "You talk as if you were there."

"Well, I'm used to looking at all angles of a conflict." The smile resurfaced. "I'm very glad to see you here tonight."

"I told you, I'm not about to let you escape again without some straight answers." She lowered her voice. "First, what about you and Pam?"

"Nothing, as I said earlier. She attended a few performances. We saw each other casually, twice. She made more of it than I intended. That's all." He spread his hands in a gesture of innocence.

Innocent? Him? Likely story! Still, Heather decided to believe him. She didn't want to linger on the topic of Pam Gaines any more than he did.

Moving his chair an inch closer to hers, he clasped her hand. "You're the one I want. Only you." He raised her hand to his lips and lightly kissed first the inside of the wrist, then the palm.

A shiver crept up her arm and blossomed into heat in her breast. To her surprise, she felt the warm flicker of his tongue on her palm. She tried to snatch her hand free, but he gripped it tighter.

"Don't fight me," he whispered. "I've waited so long."

The tickle of his breath on her skin made her tremble. "Stop that! People might be watching."

"So?" He turned his head to rub his cheek against her hand, then pressed her fingertips to the side of his neck. She felt the throb of his pulse. "This isn't illegal or even immoral--and it feels so good." He acknowledged her hot blush with a wicked grin.

"What do you mean, 'waited'?" She tried to keep her voice low despite her agitation. "Do you expect me to believe you've been pining away for me all these years?"

"Why not? *You* haven't forgotten *me*, have you?" His level gaze made her flush still hotter.

"If I haven't, it wasn't for lack of trying," she said, flustered into candor.

He released her hand. "We'll talk about it later."

That seemed to be his favorite line. Annoyed, Heather pulled back.

"Walk with me after the show?"

"Sure." Did he plan more than a revelatory conversation? Did he have seduction in mind? And if so, how would she choose to respond? Her stomach fluttered in anticipation.

They sipped their drinks in silence for a couple of minutes, after which Devin excused himself to prepare for the next set, while Heather visited the ladies' room. When she returned to her seat, Devin tuned up a banjo and started off with a selection of songs for the few children in the audience-- awake way past bedtime but clearly enjoying the show almost as much as their parents. When he sang "The Fox Went Out on a Chilly Night", he rendered "A couple of you are gonna grease my chin" with such feral glee that Heather almost imagined she caught a glimpse of fangs.

He's not just a singer, he's an actor! Not too reassuring to a woman already questioning his honesty.

Later he shifted back to ballads of jealousy, murder, and lost love. The always-doomed liaisons between ghosts and mortals stirred Heather most deeply. "The Unquiet Grave", about a young man who wept above his sweetheart's corpse for a year and a day but finally had to release her from the bonds of his grief, brought tears to her eyes. *Crying over a ghost story now? Damn, how does he do that to me?*

He finished the night with "On Top of Old Smoky"--his customary finale, judging from the enthusiastic response of the regulars. Heather, who'd previously connected that song with parodies such as "On Top of Spaghetti", was surprised to discover the original to be another tender, melancholy ballad of lovers parted by adversity.

As the bartender announced last call and the lounge began to clear, she stepped over to the stage to watch Devin pack his instruments. Again she noticed the glossy black guitar. Close up, its painted design resolved into a leafy branch and a white dove. "That's beautiful," she said.

"Thank you. My particular favorite." His hand caressed the polished wood. "A Gibson Dove, made in the sixties."

Heather couldn't help visualizing that accomplished touch on her body once more. And his voice--like hot fudge. Musing over his slight, unidentifiable accent, she linked it with his name and asked, "Are you Irish?"

He didn't seem fazed by the out-of-left-field question. "I was. I've been an American citizen for many years now."

"Couldn't be too many," she said, "unless you're a lot older than you look." When he didn't rise to the bait, she pressed on. "Tell me straight--were you playing here when I was a teenager?"

"You saw me then, didn't you?" He kept right on packing the guitar into its case.

"I thought I did. How much of what I remember really happened?"

Now he straightened up and looked into her eyes. "Why are you so troubled about details?" He spoke softly, forcing her to edge closer to hear him. "I met you in the woods when you were eighteen. I visited your bedroom several times over the next few weeks. We talked. As to what specific memories are real or unreal, believe in as much as you're comfortable with."

Heather shook her head. "Not good enough."

He picked up the guitar case and handed her the smaller banjo case. "Care to help me put away this stuff? Then we'll go."

Silently fuming, she helped him stow the equipment in a closet at the end of the hall. After several trips from the lounge, he locked up and escorted her to the stairs. Only the desk clerk watched them cross the deserted lobby to the exit.

Devin slipped his arm around Heather's waist. "Let's walk a bit. It's a beautiful night." He led her away from the parking lot along one of the paths that wound behind the building.

In spite of her doubts, she leaned into his embrace as they strolled among the trees. Crickets chirped, and a breeze rustled through the branches. The honeysuckle-scented air wasn't quite chilly, just cool enough to make her long-sleeved blouse welcome. After a few minutes Heather realized Devin was guiding her uphill, toward the lookout point above the lodge. There, he sat on the flat stone overlooking the valley, his back braced against a nearby rock, and tugged her down beside him. On that irregular surface, she could hardly help sagging against his side, so she didn't try to resist. She gazed out at the lights in the towns below and the diamond-hard glitter of stars above.

"I'm starting to remember some of the things I liked about this place."

With his arm around her, he stroked her shoulder through the satin blouse. "You know I wish you would stay. But I won't harass you on that topic for the moment."

"If I did--not that I'm considering it, mind you--it would only be for a few weeks in the summer." She absently rubbed her cheek against the silk of his shirt. He hadn't buttoned up the V; with little effort, she could touch his bare chest with her fingertips or even her lips. She resolutely suppressed the image. "What about you? Do you live here year-round?"

"Yes; does that seem so strange?"

"Pretty dead in the winter, isn't it? What do you live on? You can't perform twelve months a year, because the lodge closes November through mid-March."

"I do a few singing engagements in nearby cities," he said. "Mostly holiday programs--traditional English carols and that sort of thing. My main source of income, though, is computer game design. I can do my freelance work anywhere, even snowed in on a mountaintop."

She tilted her head to look up at him. *His eyes do gleam in the dark. I'm not imagining it.* She tabled that realization, certain that he wouldn't enlighten her if she bothered to comment. "Good grief, you're a programmer?"

He laughed. "Nothing so technical. Those complexities are beyond my ken. I create game worlds and design the plots and characters. Someone else translates my concepts into ones and zeroes."

"Yeah? Tell me something you created."

"Lair of the Worm," he said.

"That's yours? I'm impressed." She'd never managed to complete the lethal labyrinth of that game, but she'd enjoyed the challenge. At least until frustration had driven her to drop it.

"Ever thought about writing a hint book? I never did get past the pit of the slime-toads."

"That's the idea."

She couldn't help smiling at his smug tone. Then something clicked in her brain. "You talked to me about computers when you--back then, when I was a teenager. I remember telling you when Mom and Dad agreed to buy my first PC and let me go online."

"I trust you've enjoyed it?"

She stiffened, sitting up straight to break the seductive contact between their bodies. "I'm just getting it through my head that you're really real. You're a flesh-and-blood man with a career and a life. I didn't invent you."

With a soft chuckle, he draped his arm around her shoulders and drew her against his chest. She gave him only token resistance. "Why do you sound so dismayed? Didn't you want an assurance that you weren't losing your mind?"

"If you aren't a fantasy," she said, "then Ted's car hit you, but you were hardly hurt, and that deer--" Her head spun.

"It was dark, and things happened so fast, your perceptions could easily have been distorted." He lifted his hand from her shoulder to caress her hair. "Come, sweet Heather, can't we talk about something else?"

She blinked, fighting his mesmeric touch. "Okay, let's talk about what happened afterwards. You visited my bedroom." She caught herself blushing again. "Lots of times. Somehow you got in without waking my parents. I can accept that, for now, since I can see you aren't about to explain it. But what about those vivid dreams? I never had them anywhere except here. You must have had something to do with that." She wasn't ready to tell him that the lifelike visions had resumed. If he wasn't consciously causing them, if his mere presence had triggered the reaction, she didn't need to give him the satisfaction of knowing his power over her.

Devin sighed. "Very well, I confess. We do have a psychic bond, and I did project dreams into your sleeping mind. It was a way of sharing your deepest emotions. I derived great pleasure from that sharing, and I tried to give you the same pleasure. Can you deny it worked?"

Her face burned hotter at the memories he stirred. "That's beside the point. You got into my head without my consent or knowledge." Why did she so readily accept his bizarre claims to psychic powers? Partly because those Technicolor, multisensory dreams had happened only for a few weeks at the cabin, never any other place or time, a limitation that argued for an objective external source. And partly, she supposed, because she preferred to believe in clairvoyance rather than in her own mental disintegration.

"It was what you needed at that time in your life. Didn't our communion give you confidence and support at some difficult moments?"

She gave a grudging nod. "When I wasn't stewing over whether you were the first step on the road to the loony bin."

"Besides, you did consent." His soft breath ruffled her hair. "You gave implicit permission by the way you welcomed me that first night."

Sizzling at the reminder, she tried to wiggle out of his half-embrace. His arm tightened to restrain her with no discernible effort. "What's the idea of harping on that? A gentleman wouldn't even bring it up."

He said with a velvety laugh that made her insides flutter, "Little one, I'm a gentleman only when it suits me."

"Yeah, you're a regular role-player, onstage and on the computer, I'll bet. And with that weird hypnosis on top of it, how can I trust a word you say?"

"I promised not to lie to you, and I'll keep that vow. I may withhold information, but I'll give you all the truth I reasonably can."

"Want to sell me the Washington Monument, too?"

He only laughed at her again.

I could get tired of that very quickly, she thought.

He stood up, reached for her hand, and tugged her to her feet. "Let's walk."

On the descending path, treacherous with half-buried rocks and protruding roots, she had to cling to his arm. When they reached level ground and she tried to free her hand, he imprisoned it against his ribs. She felt the ripple of muscles.

He matched his pace to her slower walk. "I'd like to think," he said, "that you need me now, in this personal crisis."

"I don't need anybody. I'm an adult, haven't you noticed? I have a career. I have friends back home and at school. I've outgrown you, so thanks anyway."

"Is that why you're in such a hurry to sell your parents' cabin and run away from here?"

"There you go again! I'm not running away; I'm being practical." When she tried to emphasize her point by pulling free of him, she might as well have been handcuffed to his wrist. "Don't go psychoanalytic on me. I already have a counselor--our minister in Arlington."

"Very well, you don't need me," he said. "Then I must fall back on my other argument, that I need--" He stopped abruptly and stood poised like a statue. When she started to question him, he hushed her with a finger on her lips.

Heather obediently stood in silence, listening to the chirp of crickets and the rustle of the breeze in the leaves overhead. Ahead, the trees thinned. She glimpsed movement. A moment later, a doe stepped into view and minced across the path, only a few yards away. Behind her paced a second deer, a half-grown fawn like the one Heather had dreamed of the previous night.

She stole a glance at Devin, who gazed unblinking at the animals. *If he put that hunting fantasy into my head, I don't think I want to know what's going on in his mind right now.*

The smaller deer paused in the middle of the path and turned its head to stare at the human watchers. A glint of moonlight reflected from its eyes. Heather held her breath until the pair of animals vanished into the darkness of the woods.

"Beautiful," she whispered. "They're so bold, not a bit afraid of us."

"No, merely cautious," Devin said. "They seem to know they're protected from hunters in the national forest, and not being aware of human boundaries, they think they're safe here, too."

"How could anybody kill one of those creatures?" she said as they resumed their stroll.

Devin chuckled. "Spoken like a true city slicker. To eat it, maybe?"

"Two hundred years ago, sure. But now, when you can buy meat at any supermarket?"

"It doesn't grow in the freezer compartment, you know. All life lives off other life."

"That's beside the point. Most hunters seem to do it mainly for trophies, anyway--not food."

"There I agree with you," said Devin. "I deplore killing for the sheer fun of it. I can't get terribly upset about deer, though. They're hardly endangered.

As you probably know, in some areas they're downright pests. Harried homeowners whose gardens they nibble call them 'rats with hooves'."

"You sure know how to put a damper on romance. I'd rather keep my image of Bambi's mother, thanks."

"Forgive me." Before she realized what he had in mind, he turned her to face him, wrapping his arms around her to mold her to his tall, lean body. "If it's romance you want, I mustn't disappoint you."

"Devin, please--" Her voice sounded like the squeak of a mouse under a cat's paw.

His left hand cupped the back of her head, while his right tilted her chin up. "Please what, sweet Heather? Please do this?" His lips teased hers, wandered along her jawline, nuzzled her ear.

Chills coursed through her. His fingers felt cool, while his hot mouth branded her skin with each light kiss. Dizziness forced her to cling to his hard body.

"Devin, no--"

Ignoring her whimper, he pressed his mouth to the hollow of her throat, as if savoring the vibration caused by her involuntary moans. After a few seconds, he groaned aloud and raised his head to gaze down at her. Crimson sparks glinted in his eyes.

How does he manage that? Contact lenses? If so, why?

"Ah, Heather, what have you done to my judgment? I should not be doing this."

"That's what I've been trying to say," she whispered. Though she ought to be glad he saw it her way and wanted to put on the brakes, she found herself disappointed. The pulse throbbed in her neck, aching for the interrupted kiss. Contradicting her words, she pressed tightly against him, her breasts hypersensitive to the contact even through clothing.

For a vertiginous instant, she loomed above her own body and stared down at herself, standing with her head thrown back, lips parted, and eyes heavy-lidded. Dry-mouthed, she felt an urgent need burning through her, a wave of lust more intense than anything she'd ever endured. Her stomach cramped with it. Somehow she realized that she was feeling his desire, seeing herself through his eyes. *He was telling the truth; we do have a psychic link!* Her head whirling as if she had just stepped off a roller coaster, she forced herself back into her own senses with a violent lurch.

He unlaced her hands from behind his neck and stepped back a couple of inches. "I don't want to let you go just yet," he said, his breathing ragged, "but I will not stand here fighting a losing battle with temptation. Come home with me, and we'll play around with the computer for an hour or two. Centaur Games sent me a preview of one of my new projects to play-test; maybe you'd enjoy checking it out. A nice, low-key activity for a pair of friends."

Right, I'll bet you kiss all your friends that way. She gulped a deep breath. "At least that's more original than showing me your etchings."

He was already guiding her along the path toward the lodge. "I want you to know me as a real person, not the phantom of your dreams. Then perhaps you'll trust me."

Reserving judgment on that point, she let him lead her by the hand. *I'm halfway to trusting him already. Why?* She could argue that he was well-known to the locals, not a fly-by-night con artist but a fixture at the lodge for over a decade. That wasn't a good enough reason to go home with him, though. Perhaps she felt that, thanks to the psychic bond he claimed, she already knew him on some subliminal level, knew that he genuinely cared for her welfare. Certainly she had been in his power many times in the past, and he hadn't harmed her. *Unless you count the way I lose my grip on common sense and self-preservation every time he touches me.*

"We'll take my car," he said when they reached the parking lot, "and later I'll bring you back to retrieve yours."

"All right." Her voice still quavered. She did want to learn as much as possible about Devin--solid facts rather than fantasies. She didn't have to hurry home for Brown Sugar, since she had left the dog chained by the porch with the screen door propped open. If Devin planned to ravish her, she decided, he wouldn't have cut short their exchange of caresses.

And what if he simply planned to seduce her in a more comfortable setting? *I'll lead that horse to water when the barn door opens. Kind of late to act virginal with him, anyway, isn't it?*

He led her across the half-empty parking lot to a white minivan. As they approached the passenger side, Devin suddenly halted about twenty yards away.

"What's wrong?" She tried to decipher his tight-lipped expression in the anemic light from the nearest lamppost.

"Wait here a minute." He released her hand and disappeared around the van at a brisk trot.

Heather ignored the command, of course. On the driver's side, she found him kneeling beside a figure slumped against the minivan's left front tire. He glanced up, scowled at her, and returned his attention to the unconscious woman. Her head lolled to one side. When Devin gently touched her shoulder, she slipped sideways, forcing him to catch her.

Heather recognized Pam Gaines. *How did he know she was here, before he saw her?*

She noticed an open shoulder-strap purse and an empty flask beside Pam's splayed legs. "Drunk?" she whispered. Somehow she sensed Pam's condition was worse than that.

Devin confirmed her apprehension. "It's not just alcohol. I think she's taken pills, too."

Lightheaded, Heather staggered into the side of the car, leaning on it to keep her balance. "Is she dead?"

Chapter 5

"She's still breathing," Devin said. He looked up at Heather. "I'll stay with her. You go to the lodge and call for help."

Heather didn't argue. She had no desire to be left alone with the unconscious woman. She ran awkwardly over to the building in her open-toed summer shoes.

"Call an ambulance," she gasped to the desk clerk in the lobby. "There's someone passed out in the parking lot." She didn't say "dying"; Devin, at least, seemed to think Pam had a chance of survival.

As she leaned panting against the counter, Heather had a sudden attack of suspicion. Why had he sent her for help, leaving him alone with Pam? Was he worried that Pam would say something to incriminate him, after the fight they'd had only a few hours before?

Like what? Heather chided herself. *He wasn't out of my sight for the past two hours, remember?* If Pam had attempted suicide with some combination of alcohol and drugs, that wasn't Devin's fault. She was responsible for her own actions, wasn't she?

Come to think of it, where was Ted? Wasn't Pam going home with him? *Should I call him?* No, that would be an intrusion, considering their distant relationship; that task belonged to the authorities.

When the clerk picked up the phone to report the emergency, Heather went outside to wait on the sidewalk. From her vantage point she could see the outline of Devin's white van, though the vehicle blocked her view of Devin and Pam. Within minutes she heard the wail of sirens. Soon afterward, an ambulance screeched into the lot and slowed near the curb. She waved to the driver, ran over to him, and called, "She's lying beside that white van over there."

The ambulance backed, spun around, and headed in the direction she'd indicated. Heather hurried in its wake.

Devin stood back from the van and watched the two paramedics strap the girl onto a stretcher and start an IV. The radio muttered cryptic medical phrases in the background. When he caught sight of Heather, Devin reached a hand toward her. She let him clasp hers without stopping to think. His skin felt chilled.

"Is she going to live?" she whispered.

"Looks like it so far," he said. Another siren screamed up the road, and a minute later a car marked "Sheriff" pulled into the lot. "They'll want to interview us."

Heather's pulse quickened at the thought. Of course she and Devin would have to give a statement; why should that prospect worry her? She had nothing to hide. She was just suffering the "wicked flee when no man pursueth" reaction most citizens, however law-abiding, felt at a glimpse of a flashing red light in the rearview mirror. *But what about Devin? Does he have anything to hide?*

Glancing at him, she saw no evidence of nervousness, but how could she tell? She already knew about his acting talents. For the first time, it occurred to her to wonder whether the telepathic bond he spoke of worked both ways. If he could read her mind, why not the reverse?

Feeling slightly foolish, Heather closed her eyes and visualized tendrils extending from her brain to Devin's, like antennae or telephone wires. For a second she sensed a pleasant tingle, like static electricity, but painless. *Well, Devin,* she thought, *are you in there? What about you and Pam? Did you know she was planning this?*

In answer to her probe, shock flared up like a leaping flame. The next moment, a door closed in her face, or so it felt. Opening her eyes, she looked at Devin, who squeezed her hand and gave her a brief smile. *Did that really happen? Did he shut me out on purpose?* If so, she had managed to alarm him. He hadn't expected her to take the telepathic offensive.

A young woman of middle height with dark hair that neatly curled just above her collar walked over to them from the sheriff's car. "I'm Deputy Martinez. If you'll come to the lodge with me, I need to ask you a few questions."

The night clerk offered them the use of a cramped office behind the registration area. The deputy sat in the manager's swivel chair, while Heather took the only other chair in the room, and Devin stood beside her, arms folded, like a bodyguard. Outside, the ambulance siren faded into the distance.

Deputy Martinez took their names and then asked Heather for her version of how they had discovered Pam. Heather told the story as briefly as possible, stammering over the explanation of why she'd accompanied Devin to his van. Going home with him at this late hour to "play computer games" sounded awfully lame. She was careful to mention that she'd been watching Devin's performance continuously since intermission and had stayed with him constantly after that, although she avoided placing exaggerated emphasis on the point.

"Mr. MacAvoy," said the deputy, "you saw Ms. Gaines first, is that right?"

"Yes, when I walked around to open the driver's door." No mention of the fact that he had known, before he got near the van, that something was wrong. Had he expected Pam to lie in wait for him? Or had he merely sensed her presence somehow?

"Did you touch her?"

"Only to make sure she was still alive and keep her from falling over."

"Can you think of any reason why she happened to be sitting on the ground beside your vehicle?"

Without shifting position, Devin answered in the same even tone he had used all along, "I can only guess that she might have been waiting to talk to me. We'd had words earlier in the evening. Her brother arrived to take her home, but apparently she didn't stay there."

"You had 'words'." Deputy Martinez looked him up and down. "An argument, you mean? What was your relationship with Ms. Gaines?"

"No relationship. We spent two evenings together recently. She seemed to expect more. I made it clear that wasn't going to happen." He stared into Martinez' eyes, as if trying to imprint his version of the facts on her brain. "Pamela and I are no more than acquaintances."

The deputy seemed to drag herself away from Devin's intent gaze. "And you, Ms. Kincaid? How well do you know the victim?"

"Victim" made it sound as if Pam had been attacked. But if she had attempted to destroy herself, in a sense that would make her a victim, too. "Hardly at all," Heather said. "We were casually acquainted as teenagers, and I've seen her only once or twice since I came back here."

"When was that?"

"A couple of days ago, for the first time in years." Heather reminded herself not to offer any more extraneous details. If she started babbling, she would sound guilty even though she knew she had no part in Pam's crisis.

"It would be helpful to know whether she had any motive for suicide."

"Then you don't think it's an accident?" Heather couldn't stop herself from blurting out the question.

"She might have gotten drunk and passed out waiting for Mr. MacAvoy to show. It's unlikely that she took the additional drugs by accident. Her purse was open, and I noticed an empty pill bottle inside." The deputy turned her assessing gaze on Devin again. "In your opinion, did she feel strongly enough about this argument you had with her to try to take her own life?"

He shrugged, arms still folded. "How can I give an opinion on that? I'm not a psychiatrist."

Martinez tucked her notebook and pen into a pocket. "Well, her father and brother have been contacted, and when I see them at the hospital, maybe they can shed some light on her mental state. Or maybe she'll be conscious by then."

If the deputy expected Devin to exhibit nervousness at the idea of Pam's waking up and talking, he didn't. He didn't move or speak.

Heather said, "You're sure she's going to recover, then?"

"Can't be sure, but it looks like she'll pull through." Martinez thanked them for their help and dismissed them.

Outside, Devin walked Heather to her car. "I'm sorry for this grim ending to the evening," he said.

"It isn't your fault."

He turned to intercept her gaze. "You're wondering if it is my fault, aren't you?"

Heather turned the question aside with one of her own. "You believe Pam tried to kill herself, don't you? She was delivering a message to you."

Pausing beside Heather's station wagon, he drew her loosely into his arms. "I think that's exactly what it was--a message. She probably didn't mean to die; she wanted to get my attention, knock me over the head with the seriousness of her feelings."

She scanned his shadowed face. "What do you feel, knowing she did that?"

"Pity," he said. "You can't expect me to have any warmer emotions toward her, can you? Not when she's trying to pile undeserved guilt on my head?"

"That sounds very sensible. But still--"

"You're wondering if I asked for it," he said with a sardonic smile. "Would you think that about a female stalking victim? Your sexist double standard is showing, my dear."

Looking down at her shoes, she mumbled, "Maybe you have a point." She raised her eyes to his, half hoping and half fearing he would hug her close and make her forget the events of the past half hour. "I don't want to think about it anymore. I need to get some rest."

"So you do." He stroked her disheveled hair. "Shall I drive you home?"

"Then I'd just have a problem getting my car tomorrow." *And I don't know if I'll be up to facing him first thing in the morning!* "I'm perfectly capable of driving. Good grief, I'm upset, but I'm not an emotional wreck!" She eased out of his loose embrace and unlocked the driver's door of the station wagon.

After she sat down, he leaned into the open door. "Goodnight, sweet Heather." His lips brushed hers like a moth briefly alighting, then flitting away. He closed the door, stepped back, and vanished into the shadows.

Heather woke with her limbs heavy and her brain shrouded in fog. She almost yielded to the temptation to sleep away the morning, but Brown Sugar's damp nose burrowed under the sheet, reminding her of her responsibilities. While walking the dog, she remembered the main reason why she had to dress and face the world. She'd made an appointment with Ellie Norton, the realtor, for ten a.m.

She dismissed the idea of postponing the meeting. This late, a cancellation would be rude, and after last night's ordeal, she needed to keep her mind occupied anyway.

Heather managed to get the floors swept, the dishes washed, and herself clothed in a fresh sundress by the time the realtor knocked on the door at five minutes to ten.

Ms. Norton, a willowy blonde with a French braid, drove a Mercedes and wore a kelly green blazer sporting her company's logo. "This place has a lot of potential. Lovely location," she chirped in a typical salesperson's tone that gave Heather a dull ache behind the eyes.

"I don't want to put it on the market until it's fixed up," said Heather, ushering Ms. Norton into the living room. "I'm in no hurry."

"Good thinking." The realtor whipped out a pen and notepad. "I noticed the roof needs work. Now, why don't we just take the grand tour..." She inspected the four rooms and the bathroom in detail, while Heather trailed after her with scratch paper, jotting down the needed repairs. "Leaky faucet, rust stains--oh, what a pretty dog." Stepping onto the back porch, Ms. Norton held out a hand to Sugar, chained in her usual place by the propped-open door. The dog wiggled and panted in greeting.

So it's just Devin she doesn't like, thought Heather. *I wonder what she has against him.*

"You have to get the door fixed, so you might as well replace all these screens while you're at it," said Ms. Norton. "That seems to be about it. Let's go over some of the details."

Accepting a cup of coffee, she opened her briefcase and spread out a portfolio of forms.

With the acidic coffee resting atop a hasty breakfast in her stomach, Heather tried to follow the realtor's explanations. Finally she signed the listing contract and watched with relief as Ms. Norton packed up her sheaf of documents.

"Once your cottage is spiffed up, we shouldn't have a bit of trouble finding a buyer. I'll get into the computer and print out some compares for you, and we can talk about the asking price. I'll call in a few days." With a hearty handshake, she took her leave.

As the Mercedes drove downhill and disappeared around the bend, Heather scanned the list she'd made. It was a good thing she didn't have a money problem, considering how many hours of labor that slip of paper represented. Luckily, she didn't have to wait for probate to draw on her funds. After her mother's death, her father had added Heather's name to the checking and savings accounts, so that after the "accident" all the ready cash had passed directly to her by right of survivorship. Had he been contemplating suicide, even then?

Stop thinking about that, Heather commanded herself. *It's over; I can't do a thing about it.* Instead, she rummaged through the papers around the computer until she found the number of a handyman recommended by Ted. Catching him on the first try--another pleasant difference from city life--she explained what she wanted and arranged for him to stop by the following afternoon.

Only then did she stop for breath and succumb to memories of the previous night's disaster. What had happened to Pam? Heather telephoned the Gaines' home and got only the answering machine. When she called the store, Ted answered. Of course, she thought, somebody had to keep the business functioning. If Ted was there instead of leaving an employee in charge, Pam's condition must not be critical.

"Ted, this is Heather. I'm sorry about Pam--" She fumbled for words. How could she tactfully discuss such an event? "About the accident." *Now I know why people tried to avoid talking to me about Dad.* "How is she? Will she be all right?"

"Yeah, she'll be coming home this afternoon or tomorrow morning." His voice rasped with suppressed emotion. "I don't know about the rest--her mind. Dad wants her to go into therapy."

"Maybe that would be a good idea."

"Maybe." He sounded dubious. "I just don't understand what's gotten into her lately. She was fine until a couple of weeks ago. It's that guy MacAvoy who's got her head all screwed up. If we can get her away from him--"

"Devin?" She resisted the impulse to defend him. After all, she knew nothing about Devin's relationship to Pam beyond what he'd told her.

"You're seeing him, aren't you?"

"I wouldn't put it that way. I went for a walk with him last night, that's all." And what business was that of Ted's, anyway?

"From the effect he has on Pam, I think you should stay clear of him."

"I didn't ask for advice," Heather said.

"The more I think about it," Ted persisted, "there's something weird about MacAvoy. Keeps to himself an awful lot."

"So? That's not a crime." She couldn't bring herself to say, "Weird? Devin? Where on earth did you get that idea?" Such blatant insincerity would probably make her sprout a nose like Pinocchio's.

"He's performed at the lodge for over half my life, and I don't know a thing about him. Neither does Dad. The guy shows up every night to play his gig, and nobody ever sees him the rest of the time."

Though Ted's statement only confirmed Heather's own impression of Devin's habits, she had no desire to share her misgivings with a former almost-boyfriend. "Since when is that anybody else's business? I don't understand what his living like a hermit has to do with Pam's behavior. If anything, Devin's lifestyle would make him less likely to go around breaking innocent women's hearts. If he never goes out, when does he have the chance to play Casanova?"

"Never mind, it's obvious you're prejudiced--he's got his hooks into you already." Ted lowered his voice. "Can't talk anymore; a customer's coming in. Thanks for calling, and I hope the dog's working out okay."

"She's fine. We get along great. Bye, Ted."

Got his hooks into me? I'm not a trout! Heather shook her head. *Who am I kidding? Devin reeled me in a long time ago.*

She knew she ought to do some more cleaning, but a craving for fresh air seized her. She took Sugar for a long walk instead.

That evening, Heather resisted the temptation to revisit the lodge and watch Devin's show. Of course, he hadn't invited her. If he had, she would probably have agreed without a struggle. Spared the decision, she spent a virtuous few hours packing her parents' neglected summer wardrobes for charity.

Her feeling of revulsion upon reentering the master bedroom soon faded. Handling old clothes didn't bother her, and she took care to avoid any drawers or boxes that might hold more unpleasant surprises. She had stuffed the old diary in the bottom of one of her own drawers, under faded shorts and bathing suits long outgrown. There was no hurry; she needn't face the book and the anger it stirred until she felt ready. *Maybe I'll just throw it away. Why would I even want to read it again?*

At ten-thirty she logged on to join Nightblade in the next installment of their game. Sometimes she wondered why he insisted on such late hours, but she didn't mind. When given a choice, she was more of a night person herself. She had managed to avoid morning classes for most of her college career.

Picking up where they'd left off, Nightblade and Krystal broke camp to travel in the direction the wicked mage had fled. After the simulated "rest period", the were-dragon had regained his full strength. The program steered them--or, as Nightblade put it, the gods guided them--along a sinister road, hardly more than a trail hacked through the trees, into a forest shunned by the local peasants.

While she was admiring the deliciously spooky graphics of moss-festooned trees, eldritch shadows, and swooping bats, a pair of hulking, humanoid figures lumbered onto the path and brandished studded maces. Krystal recognized them at once by their warty green hides and snaggle-toothed snarls.

{Trolls!} she signaled, preparing a flame dart spell. Since these monsters regenerated from normal wounds, even re-growing severed heads, they could be destroyed only by fire. While she launched her first volley, Nightblade shifted into dragon form. The narrow trail barely had room enough for both of them.

The trolls struck by Krystal's darts howled in pain. Nightblade breathed fire on the less injured of the two. It burst into a blaze, rolling on the ground in agony. Whipping his head around, Nightblade roared a warning, then incinerated another troll creeping up from behind. It had two companions.

Krystal sent a second fusillade of flame darts toward the remaining troll in front of her. Confident that it would burn to death, or at least be disabled long enough for her to ignore it awhile, she whirled to face the other two. They were too close to burn safely. As she slashed at one with her dagger, Nightblade felled the second with a swipe of his huge claws. Slimy ichor oozed from the monsters' wounds. Both trolls immediately lurched to their feet, their lacerations beginning to scab already, but the attack gave Krystal and Nightblade time to scramble out of arms' reach. In quick succession, Nightblade set both ablaze. He then engulfed the one Krystal had crippled with her magical flames.

Krystal discovered that a troll's fingernails had ripped open her forearm. She poured healing elixir on the ugly gash. She couldn't wait for it to heal through normal rest, since trolls carried virulent disease. Noting on the bar at the bottom of the screen that her life points had sunk dangerously low, she drank a vial of the potion as well.

{A well-fought battle, dear companion} said the dragon.

{It would be even better if we got something out of it besides experience points.} Krystal searched the crudely stitched pouches slung around the trolls' waists. She found only a few coins, nothing to advance the quest. {Change back and let's get moving.}

A few seconds later, a caption announced {Nightblade's transformation fails}.

{I'm stuck this way} the dragon said.

Heather pondered over this odd development. Since trolls had no magic, what could be inhibiting Nightblade's shapeshifting power? She typed {Krystal casts "detect magic"}.

Instead of finding a magical aura around the dragon, as she expected, she discovered that every object on the screen except Krystal herself shimmered with a violet glow. The caption read {Krystal detects evil magic in the surrounding landscape}.

An enchanted forest, thought Heather. *That figures; it's fouling up Nightblade's innate powers.* She addressed her partner: {Do you think you'll be able to change back once we've left the forest?}

{How do I know?} he said. {We can only hope. Shall we proceed?}

Another hazard occurred to Heather as Nightblade and Krystal marched along the trail. {If you stay in that shape too long, you will revert more and more to the instincts of a dragon.}

He responded, {All the more reason to hurry away from this evil place. Don't worry, my lady}. The creature paused to place a friendly foreclaw on Krystal's shoulder. {No matter how gravely I'm changed, I would not consider devouring you. After all, I'm your private dragon.}

Something about Nightblade's last comment gave her a frisson of mingled excitement and anxiety. Feeling a need to withdraw and think it over, she proposed that they stop for the night.

Her dream-self opened aching eyes upon a dim, chilly room. A glimmer of light softened the fetid blackness to gray. She sat up on the lumpy, straw-stuffed pallet. Her skin crawled with the scrabble of insects' legs, whether real or imagined, she couldn't tell in the near-dark. She heard a rattle at the door. The undulant glow drew nearer, resolving itself into a lantern in the hand of a black-clad man who entered the room. She looked down at her wrinkled, sweat-stained skirt. With one hand she raked through the tangle of her hair.

Heather realized she once again shared the consciousness of Judith. But what was this place?

Judith's memory supplied the answer: She was imprisoned in the cellar of the manse, and the man with the lantern was the vicar.

She didn't consider trying to flee through the door he had left ajar. Where could she go? None of her fellow townsfolk would shelter her; they all believed the tale of witchcraft and fornication with demons. Even her parents had cast her off.

"Well, child? Have you decided to confess your sorcery? If you make full confession, God will forgive your sin." In the lantern's flame, the wispy, white hair that reached to his collar looked like a halo. His thin, compressed mouth and furrowed brow belied the saintly image.

She swallowed to moisten her dry throat, having long since finished the little water they had left her the previous day. "I have nothing to confess. I'm innocent."

He shook his head in a nearly convincing show of compassion. "This obstinacy will consign your soul to Satan." He turned to the door and called, "Come in, Mistress Cooper."

He had brought Susanna Cooper, the midwife. Judith's stomach knotted in renewed fear. She had heard enough whispered rumors about witch trials to guess what this development meant.

Heather, locked inside her head, did not comprehend. A middle-aged woman entered. Her faded brown hair was tucked under a mob-cap. Her expressionless face gave no hint of how she felt toward Judith.

The vicar said, "You must lie down and allow Mistress Cooper to perform her office. We shall need her testimony when you stand before the magistrate." When Judith didn't move, he said, "Defiance will only make this go harder on you."

Judith reclined on the pallet, her heart hammering.

"Proceed," the vicar said. "I shall hold the light."

The girl flinched when the midwife knelt before her and pushed her legs into a bent-kneed position. As the woman arranged Judith's skirt into a decorous drape, what she was doing penetrated Heather's awareness. *She's going to do a pelvic exam in this filthy hole? And Heaven only knows when she last washed her hands.* Judith didn't seem to hear these thoughts; her mind was shrouded in fear and revulsion.

She cringed and involuntarily squeezed her thighs together when the midwife probed under the skirt. Heedless of the girl's discomfort, Mistress Cooper wordlessly forced her legs apart and thrust two fingers inside. Judith moaned in pain. For a few seconds the midwife continued groping. Mercifully soon, she withdrew and stood up, wiping her fingers on a handkerchief from her pocket.

"Her maidenhead is whole. She's a virgin."

The clergyman pursed his lips. Heather thought she heard disappointment in his voice when he said, "Nevertheless, we cannot assume her innocence. Many lewd acts leave no palpable traces. As a virtuous matron, Mistress Cooper, you wouldn't know of such things."

So how does a man of the cloth know about them? Heather wondered.

Judith silently cried in anguish, *No, it wasn't lewd! It was beautiful!* She recalled the ecstasy of his mouth on her throat and bosom, the burning sweetness of his blood on her lips. *It was joy beyond anything I ever imagined.*

The vicar ordered her to stand. She obeyed, though her trembling legs could barely support her.

"Now we must search for witch marks," he said. "Remove your garments."

"What?" She backed up to cower against the damp wall.

"Come, would you rather be stripped forcibly?"

Hastily she peeled off her clothes and stood shivering in the clammy air. Her nipples puckered from the cold. Under the clergyman's glare, she hunched over and folded her arms across her chest, unable to stifle a sob of shame.

The midwife fumbled in a pouch at her waist and brought out a long darning needle. Judith cringed backward until she was trapped in the corner. The vicar set the lantern on the floor, closed on her, and wrenched her arms behind her back. She gasped at the pain.

"Girl, don't you realize that this resistance makes your guilt all the clearer? Mistress Cooper must probe for the place impervious to pain, where the Devil has marked you. If you bear no such brand, you have nothing to fear."

The woman stepped forward, brandishing the needle like a dagger.

"Wait," said the vicar. "She must be blindfolded."

Mistress Cooper produced her handkerchief and tied the musty cloth around Judith's eyes. With her sight cut off, Judith felt panic engulf her. Heather struggled to hold aloof from the smothering blackness in the girl's mind. The needle's point jabbed her shoulder, then her breast, then her belly, then the back of her neck. Judith flinched at each thrust. She couldn't help twisting in the clergyman's grasp, although her movements inspired him to grip her with crueler strength. His hoarse breathing assaulted her ears. The pain of the needle was not severe in itself; her terror sprang from not knowing where it would stab next. She visualized its point penetrating her eyes or the hollow of her throat.

Where is he? Why hasn't he come to my rescue? Perhaps this was daytime, when, he had told her, he customarily slept. In the dark cellar she had no way to judge how many hours had passed since her arrest. Still, she silently screamed to him: *Where are you? Come to me, save me!* She felt not even a ghost of his presence; her call disappeared into an abyss of nothingness.

Heather felt the panic overshadowing her, as well. With a desperate wrench, she ripped herself free of Judith's thoughts and fled into the void.

Heather? Calm yourself; I'm here. His voice wrapped her like a warm cloak. *These visions are only shadows of the distant past; they cannot find you.*

The formless mist coalesced into a new dream landscape. She found herself within the game world, surrounded on all sides by the dark, dripping trees of the ensorcelled forest. Nightblade strode beside her, still in dragon shape, his glittering scales brushing against her silken garments. *Why am I wearing a silk gown in the middle of the woods?* she wondered.

The dragon said, "Danger lurks in this place. You must let me take you away from here."

Understanding that he meant to fly with her, Heather climbed onto the dragon's back. The heat of his scales, as if warmed by the embers of his flaming breath, radiated through her clothes and made her inner thighs tingle. She leaned forward to wrap her arms around the sinuous neck. He broke into a gallop, raising a wind that whipped her hair back from her face. Leaping into the air, he soared over the trees.

"Where are we going?" Heather shouted to him.

"To my castle," he roared in reply.

Glancing down, she recognized the roof of her own cabin and realized they weren't flying over the computer-generated forest. The dragon glided over the mountainous terrain and, minutes after taking off, circled above a cottage not much bigger than hers. He spiraled down and alighted on the driveway.

What kind of cut-rate fantasy is this? We're in the Blue Ridge Mountains, not the Sunstone Quest world, and this sure isn't a castle. She even noticed a mailbox labeled "MacAvoy" beside the drive.

The next moment, the familiar trappings melted into mist, and they were standing outside a castle, after all. It had dozens of turrets, with Gothic arched windows of stained glass. The drawbridge descended, and a second dragon charged across the moat.

In contrast to Nightblade's ebony scales, this dragon was armored in gleaming scarlet. Its mouth, full of dagger-like fangs, yawned in a roar of challenge. Nightblade lunged to intercept it. The new monster belched a cloud of noxious, green gas. Nightblade staggered under the onslaught and coughed out a fireball, which scorched the enemy's hide.

They attacked each other head-on, clashing like a pair of tanks. Teeth and talons ripped, and dark, purplish blood flowed. Steam rose where each drop splashed on the grass.

Heather retreated to cower with her back to a tall pine tree that was overgrown with ivy like any dozen trees within a hundred yards of her cabin. She felt she ought to come to Nightblade's rescue with a spell, but no magic stirred within her. *I'm not Krystal; I'm just me. The game and the real world are all mixed up. What am I supposed to do in this dream, anyway?* It had neither the wish-fulfillment thrill of her teenage fantasies about Devin nor the photographic self-consistency of her two nightmares about the maiden, Judith.

She covered her mouth to stifle a scream as the strange dragon's fangs bit into Nightblade's neck. The black dragon collapsed on his side, panting out irregular puffs of smoke. The red dragon crouched over him, ready to deliver the lethal blow. Nightblade's hind legs curled up like a cat's to rake the other monster's belly. With a single stroke, Nightblade disemboweled the scarlet dragon. Screeching in agony, it rolled over and writhed for several minutes, while Nightblade dragged himself out of its reach.

Heather ran to him and threw her arms around his massive, scaly neck. She heard a harsh rattle in his chest. Together they watched the death throes of the other dragon. When its blood ceased to gush, it began to smolder as if burning from the inside out. Seconds later, it burst into flame. The blaze flared skyward for an instant, then vanished, leaving no trace of the corpse except a black scar on the turf.

Nightblade raised his huge, catlike eyes, filmed with pain, to Heather's. "Help me!"

"How? What can I do?" She longed for the healing elixirs that her game persona carried.

"Elixir of life--your blood."

"What?" She involuntarily drew back but instantly recovered and embraced him again. What did she have to fear? He had promised not to harm her. *But that was the game, and this is a dream. It seems to have different rules.* On the other hand, nothing that happened in a dream could do her any real damage.

"I need to get inside the castle," he whispered hoarsely. "My realm--I'll heal faster there. I'm too weak to move. A few drops of your blood--give me strength."

She held out a trembling arm, folding back the loose sleeve of the silken robe. One of his stiletto-like teeth grazed her wrist. It hurt no more than a razor cut. She felt the cool lash of his forked tongue. A shiver rippled through her body, generating exquisite aftershocks deep inside.

He raised his head. "That's enough. Now let's go inside, where we'll be safe." He struggled to his feet, balancing his weight with his long saurian tail. His wings drooped on either side.

Heather laid her arm across his neck and matched his slow pace. They crossed the drawbridge into a dim, cool great hall hung with tapestries. She tried to focus her eyes to interpret the pictures in the weave, but the outlines blurred.

Nightblade's tongue flicked the back of her neck as he sank wearily onto the stone floor. "My home, sweet Heather."

Heather sat up in bed, staring into the dark. In the shadows at her bedside, she glimpsed the shape of Brown Sugar, who lifted her head with an inquiring yip.

Heather swallowed hard, struggling to control her labored breathing. "Oh, my God," she said aloud. "Nightblade is Devin MacAvoy."

Chapter 6

That devious rat! How dare he!

Once the truth fell into place, Heather felt she shouldn't have needed a message from a dream to clue her in to the obvious. She bent her knees and rested her chin on them as she absentmindedly stroked the dog's head. Sugar laid her muzzle on the pillow, emitting a concerned whine.

Devin had discussed computers with her in those original "dreams". He was a game designer himself. In conversation, he had revealed knowledge of her parents' death, which she had mentioned to Nightblade but not to Devin. Nightblade, in the latest Sunstone session, had echoed the phrase she had used to Devin, "my private dragon". Her gaming partner scheduled sessions for late at night, after Devin would have finished his performances.

All these years we haven't seen each other, he's been watching me. He used the Internet to spy on me! She jumped out of bed, eliciting a yelp from the dog. Heather stormed into the living room and powered up the computer. Her real name and home city were listed for anyone to read. What about Nightblade's?

When she checked his member profile, she discovered, without surprise, that Nightblade's entry repeated his pseudonym and listed only the state, Virginia, as his residence. The online service provider would have the member's complete name, address, and credit card number, but Heather was no hacker. She couldn't break into the files and extract the data.

In her anger, she accepted Nightblade's reticence as proof that he had something to hide. *He's hiding from me! He's got a secret identity, thinks he's Superman.* Still fuming, she switched off the computer and drank a glass of milk to calm herself before returning to bed. She had half a mind to burst in on Devin and demand the truth, right that minute. *Half a mind is what it would be. I'll have a better chance of getting him to talk at a reasonable hour. I'll go see him first thing in the morning.* Satisfied with that plan, she lay down and drifted off to sleep, with no dreams she remembered.

Next morning, thinking about her revelation, she felt like the Old Man of Peru in the limerick, who dreamed he was eating his shoe. "He woke in a fright," she muttered to herself while dressing, "in the middle of the night, and found it was perfectly true."

Her dream was telling her something about Nightblade, beyond the bare fact of his identity. She didn't suppose it was "perfectly true" on a literal level. Devin could hardly be a were-dragon. Yet she had to acknowledge that he couldn't be an ordinary human being, either. His behavior and appearance displayed anomalies she couldn't keep explaining away with vague assumptions about hypnotism and ESP.

So what do I think he is? A mutation? A real superhero of some kind? The advance scout for an alien invasion? Lost in thought, she got the zipper of her shorts stuck and spat a curse or two while struggling with it. Sugar, sitting by the bedroom door waiting for Heather to let her out, looked up and thumped her tail in a worried manner. "What do you think about him, Sugar?" said Heather, finally working the zipper loose. "You didn't like him, I could tell that. Too bad you can't talk."

After the dog's outing, Heather made herself eat breakfast, hoping strawberry yogurt and buttered toast would soothe her jittery stomach. Since she had slept late after the stressful night, it was almost nine-thirty by the time she was ready to leave. *Devin certainly ought to be up by now,* she thought. If he wasn't, he deserved a rude awakening. She considered taking Sugar along but, recalling the dog's nervousness when they had encountered Devin on the road, decided it wouldn't be fair. Why expose the poor animal to a man who frightened her?

Who says I need protection from Devin, anyway? He might be a manipulative snake, but he wouldn't offer a physical threat. Still, she felt reluctant to enter his lair unarmed. If the nightmares about Judith had anything to do with Devin (and two completely unrelated sets of peculiar night visions seemed beyond belief), they offered another name for him--demon. *Come on, I could sooner believe in aliens!* Nevertheless, she searched her mother's jewelry box--relieved to find no ugly surprises amid her mother's costume jewelry--for the amber cross she remembered noticing during her original survey of the room. Hanging the cross on its gold-tone chain around her neck, she braced herself for the confrontation.

Wait a minute--where does Devin live? How do I get there? she thought as she chained Sugar out back. In the next breath, she realized she didn't need to ask that question. The dream, displaying the real-world landscape on the flight to Nightblade's "castle", had shown her a shortcut through the woods to Devin's house. Somehow she did not doubt the accuracy of her mental map. The walk would cover only about two miles.

Striking out from the back of the cabin, she soon picked up a hiking trail that led more or less in the proper direction. Reminding herself that an extra few minutes wouldn't diminish the force of the diatribe she planned to inflict on Devin, she slowed herself to a careful walk. She didn't want to arrive scratched by thorns or bruised and smudged from tripping on the bumpy dirt path. It was bad enough that the humid summer day made her sweat-dampened hair stick to her forehead and neck. Rushing would make her overheat more.

The trail connected with a winding road not much different from the one that led to her cabin, and around a curve she found the cottage from her dream. It looked more substantial than her own place, with a paved driveway and walls of stone rather than wood. It would have to be pretty solid, if he lived here through the winter. The mailbox at the foot of the driveway bore his last name, just as in the dream. She was glad to see the white minivan parked there, as evidence that he was home. Walking past it to the front porch, she noticed the vanity license plate: I BYTE.

"Ha, ha," she muttered. "I bet you do."

The door had a brass knocker, which she banged as hard as its construction allowed. The noise reverberated satisfyingly but produced no response. After trying the knocker a couple more times, she abandoned it in favor of pounding on the door with her fist. "Come on, Devin, you slimy--reptile," she yelled, "I know you're in there. Crawl out of your hole and answer the door."

She paused and sagged against the unyielding wood, panting for breath. *I know you're in there,* she silently repeated, thrusting the thought like a spear into the silence. *Are you too much of a coward to face me?*

She felt something like a warm breeze tickling her cheek, too fleeting for her to be sure it was real. When she heard footsteps approaching inside, she thought at first she was imagining the sound. She straightened up barely in time to avoid toppling over when the door opened.

"Heather." Devin crossed his arms and stared down at her. "To what do I owe this charming interruption?"

"I don't need your sarcasm! About time you answered."

"I take it you're not about to go away." With a sigh, he opened the door wider. "Come on, don't stand there letting in the daylight."

She stepped into a cool, heavily curtained living room. When he switched on a lamp at one end of the couch, she got a good look at him: barefoot, dark hair tousled, wearing a robe of royal blue satin. The casually overlapped V exposed most of his bare chest. She wondered whether the rest of him, under the robe, was equally unclad. She caught a glint in his silver-gray eyes, as if he read her thoughts. Feeling the heat of a blush on her face, she said, "Did I wake you?"

"Yes." His suggestive half-smile raised her temperature another degree or two.

"Good, you don't deserve to sleep."

He sat on the couch, waving her to a chair. "I suppose you're going to tell me what crime I've been convicted of." After a pause, he said in a more serious tone, "This isn't about Pamela Gaines, is it?"

"No, I can give you the benefit of the doubt. I can believe you didn't mean to encourage her. What I can't stand is you lying to me all this time."

"Lying?"

"By omission--tricking me." She drew a long breath. "You're Nightblade."

He maintained silence for a few heartbeats. "So that's why you're angry. I wondered how long it would take you to make that connection."

"Then you admit it?"

"I wouldn't insult your intelligence by denying it."

"Is that all you have to say?" Her anger simmered afresh. "You spied on me--wormed your way into my confidence on false pretenses--"

"Should I have told you, as soon as we met online, that I was your summer phantom? At the time, you believed I was a dream. It suited me to have you believe that, and it seemed better for your emotional equilibrium, too. You preferred it that way."

"Typical--you're off the hook if the victim asks for it." She laced her fingers together to still the shaking of her hands.

"I never saw you as a victim," he said. "When you declared you weren't coming back here, I wanted some way of watching over you. Yes, I 'spied' on you over the Net, but I saw it as guarding you." The insinuating caress of his voice made the claim feel all too plausible.

"From what, online bogey men?"

"I missed you, Heather. Even if I couldn't see and touch you, I wanted-- needed--to know you were well and happy."

"Stop trying to mess with my head. You lied." She closed her eyes to shut out his compelling gaze. "At least, as soon as we met the other night, you could have come clean."

"I suppose I was apprehensive." He sighed. "I was afraid you'd react exactly this way."

"Well, you feared right."

"I'm not lying now, am I? I've promised to deal with you honestly. You're an adult now." His voice deepened, rich as melted chocolate. "Open your eyes, sweet Heather. I have no evil designs on you."

She raised her lashes to gaze back at him. "Yeah? What about Judith?"

He flinched as if slapped. "Who?"

"You said you wouldn't lie anymore. I've been dreaming about Judith. I know she must have something to do with you."

He gave a slow, thoughtful nod. "Yes, and I'll tell you the story, in time. I promise. Heather, we must be more tightly bonded than I thought, if you're picking up all that." His eyes wandered over her. "My dear, must you sit so far away? Surely you aren't afraid of me now? Come over here."

Under the compulsion of his velvet tone, she found herself halfway to the couch before she realized she was obeying. "Oh, no, you don't! You're breaking the spirit of your promise already." She clutched the amber cross at her throat.

He shook his head. "Forgive me. It's a reflex, and when I want you so badly, it's hard to control."

Her stomach fluttered. No man had ever spoken to her so boldly before. And if one had, she would have been offended, not excited. *Yeah, same old line I used to hear in parked cars. You're so desirable I can't control myself--just another way of blaming the victim.* Her breath shallow and irregular with tension, she covered the last few steps to the sofa before she could lose her nerve. Kneeling beside him on the cushions, she thrust the cross into his face.

He shied away, then peered closer to see what she held. He wrapped his fingers around hers and burst out laughing. She tried to retreat, but his seemingly gentle grip proved unbreakable.

"Did you expect me to vanish in a puff of sulphurous smoke?" he said.

She blushed, this time from embarrassment. "It was worth a try. I know you're not an ordinary human being."

She felt a twinge of surprise from him. "Be that as it may, I'm certainly not a minion of Satan. My dear, *if* you had absolute faith in that symbol, and *if* you sincerely wanted to repel me, it might amplify your own psychic strength to serve as an effective barrier. Neither of those conditions exists."

Damn it, he's right, I don't really want to repel him. "Okay, if you're not a demon, what are you? Your eyes glow in the dark. You don't look a year older than you did the day we first met. You have powers and abilities beyond those of mortal man." The flippant phrase took on a loaded meaning as she sensed a tentative exploration inside her head, like teasing fingers under the skin. "Stop that! Get out of my brain!"

The titillating sensation ceased. "As you wish. What do you think I am?"

"The first thing that occurred to me is that you're an alien."

His thumb stroked the hand he still held captive. "I give you my word, I'm not from another planet. I really was born in Ireland."

"Well, you sure aren't a leprechaun."

He laughed softly. "No, I don't have green skin or wish-granting powers."

"Or green blood? Even if you do perform mind melds."

"Not exactly that. But when I told you we have a special bond, I was not lying."

She stared into his eyes, trying to ignore the feathery caress his fingers inflicted on hers. "It didn't happen by chance, did it? Somehow you created that bond."

"Somehow," he echoed. "Yes, I couldn't bear the thought of being cut off from you when you returned home."

"Where do you get that power? Are you some kind of mutation?"

"You may think of it that way." His free hand smoothed the damp strands of hair escaping from the braid at the nape of her neck.

"You're being evasive again."

"I don't want to expose you to so many shocks at once. I want to win your trust."

"You'd win it easier with straight answers." She snatched her hand out of his, and this time he let her go. "You watched me, without my knowledge or permission, over the Net and by reading my mind." With a shaky giggle, she said, "That sounds so silly, but I can't deny it anymore. You used telepathy to--to shadow me. It's like stalking."

"With no harmful intent. You know I only wanted to share your life."

"By strolling around in my head? Since I got here, you've even been scripting my dreams again."

"No, I haven't. If you've experienced any--meaningful--dreams in the past few days, they crystallized from your own unconscious. It's a reaction to our bond." He let out a long sigh. "I do care for you; you must feel that."

She hardened her heart against his pleading gaze. "Why should I believe you this time? How do I know you're not still manipulating me? Maybe this honesty and caring is all an act. How do I know you can't lie with your thoughts and emotions, too?"

He spread his hands as if opening himself to attack. "All I can give you is my word. The truth is, I'm not used to caring for people. I need to learn how it's done."

Heather had read enough paperback romances about reformed rakes to be sceptical of that line, too. In real life, how often did Beauty's kiss actually transform the Beast? "You jerked me around before. How can I get past that?"

"I fervently hope you can."

The simple reply came closer to convincing her than any of his earlier protests. "Okay, show me. Come into my mind." She closed her eyes and imagined herself unbarring a door and inviting him in. In a sudden moment of fear, she added, "But just a little way in. Just to demonstrate."

Very well, my lady.

It took her a few seconds to realize that he had spoken within her mind instead of aloud. Her breath caught in an instant of fear. A cloud of warmth enveloped her, displacing the momentary chill, and she let herself relax. Though she knew he wasn't physically touching her, she felt cool fingers intertwined with hers and a sheltering arm around her shoulders.

I'm here. I won't let anyone harm you. Including myself.

She visualized herself putting her arms around him. He returned the intangible embrace. She felt buoyant, almost as though she were floating. *That's enough, I don't want to lose myself this time.* With a vision of slipping free from his arms and retreating farther into her mental stronghold, she projected a firm *Stop.* Instantly the sense of his presence melted away.

She opened her eyes. He sat a couple of feet away, watching without touching her.

"You see," he said. "I obeyed your command. I won't invade without your permission."

"Yes, you did listen to me. That time." How she yearned to believe him, yet the force of her own desire gave her pause. How much of that longing arose within her, and how much emanated from Devin?

"Won't you give me a chance?"

"I can do that much," she said.

His eyes lit up. "Thank you. That brings us to another question. How can I hope to share your life if you won't be here?"

Heather shook her head, too confused by her recent discoveries to follow the change in topic. "What do you mean? I'm here now."

"Do you still plan to sell your cabin?"

"Oh, that." That practical problem had slipped her mind, overshadowed by the paranormal experience she now had to accept as real.

"Yes, that," he said with a thin smile. "If you get rid of your summer home, you presumably won't come back." He moved nearer and clasped her hand. "Since you don't have financial problems at present, what is your real reason for wanting to sell?"

"I told you." She massaged the tense lines on her forehead. "Partly, I wanted to cut my connection to this place because of you. I thought you were a delusion, and I was afraid of getting sucked down into all that again."

"But now I've set your mind at rest. You know you aren't insane. So that reason no longer holds." When she didn't answer right away, he said, "You aren't afraid of me now."

"No. I'm not sure if I trust you completely, but I know you won't intentionally hurt me."

"Ah, a reasonable start. Then what about the cabin?"

His probing made her stop and think over her reasons for the first time since her arrival. "It isn't just you. It's all mixed up with my feelings about my parents. I saw more of them here than I ever did at home. I want to get rid of those reminders."

"Why are the memories so unpleasant?"

"You know how parents are, always expecting so much. I always felt that I didn't quite measure up, but at home we were all busy most of the time. We weren't hanging around together; I wasn't exposed to it every hour of the day." She met his intent gaze. This time he didn't seem to be working his hypnotic magic, only trying to understand. "Weren't your parents ever like that?"

"No," he said. "I didn't have a family like yours. I was brought up by an uncle."

"Oh--what about your mother and father?"

"She died some time ago. He was--as they say nowadays--not in the picture."

Devin's matter-of-fact tone cut off any impulse to feel sorry for him, but she did feel a new sense of intimacy, knowing they were both orphaned. "Don't you have any other family besides your uncle?"

"A teenage brother. I don't see him often." He shrugged. "I know about high expectations--you should meet Uncle Roderick." He smiled as if contemplating a private joke.

Heather sensed that he was telling her an edited version of the facts, but this wasn't the time to press him.

"I didn't feel about it as you do, though," said Devin. "In our...clan...all children are expected to perform with consistent excellence."

"Well, in my case, I wasn't supposed to exist at all--I told you about that. I was an accident." She surprised herself with her own renewed bitterness. *Shouldn't I have gotten over that by now?* "Half the time, I felt like they thought I wasn't worth the trouble. Especially up here on vacation, when Mom kept after me to do something useful with my time instead of loafing around." She told Devin about finding the diary in her mother's closet. "She didn't trust me, much less think I had any right to my own life. It was her idea for me to stop coming here." The memory of what she'd found inside the diary crashed over her. "Because of *you*. I found a note she wrote to Dad and never finished. She had dreams like mine." Heather recoiled from Devin, who made no move to close in on her.

"My dear, it's not what you think."

"Don't call me that! When did you visit her? On the nights you got tired of me?"

"No! It was very long ago, before you were born--in fact, while she was pregnant with you."

She frowned at him, fighting her own desire to believe every word he spoke. "The way I heard it, you've only worked at the lodge for sixteen years."

"Before I decided to settle here, I made occasional visits. That's how I got to know the area. I...encountered...your mother during one week when she was at the cabin without her husband. That was the only incident. When I realized she was carrying a baby, I stopped. You have my word."

"Yeah, like that means anything." But how she longed to trust him.

He gazed blankly across the room before turning to meet her eyes again. "Heather, I've just realized what this means." He leaned over to reach for her hand, withdrawing when she flinched away from him. "Why I was so drawn to you from our first meeting. It wasn't really the first. I touched you in your mother's womb."

"Come on, how can that--"

"The concept is new to me, too. But why else do we share such a powerful bond?"

"Are you saying we're meant for each other? Sounds like romantic mumbo-jumbo."

He smiled. "Aren't human females supposed to yearn for romance?"

"Not enough that we let ourselves get conned by it." Sharing her demon lover with her mother, even in this tenuous way, undercut the "romance" of Devin's notion of a prenatal bond. "That's one more thing you didn't bother to tell me. Another secret--in a way, you knew my mother better than I did."

"You sound angrier than finding your stolen diary can account for."

"That's just one example. It's--everything! And then Mom had to go and die before I got a chance to prove I could be a competent adult." She wiped tears from her eyes, angry at her own weakness.

Devin's hand cupped her cheek, his thumb brushing away a drop she'd missed. "Your mother did not choose to die."

"No, but Dad did. I told you about that, too. He didn't care enough to stay with me." She summoned the will to pull away from Devin's caress. "I can't sell the house in Arlington right now, but at least I can get rid of this place."

"If I could help you to be cleansed of these emotions," he said, "would you reconsider?"

"Help? How? Now you're a psychiatrist?"

He chuckled at her sarcasm. "I don't need to be. I have skills of my own. Suppose I give you an opportunity to talk with your parents, tell them how you feel?"

She looked at him suspiciously. "I thought we settled that you're not a supernatural entity. And even if you could conjure up the dead, I don't think I could accept that."

"No, I'm not offering to act as a medium. What I can do, through mesmerism, is to create the conditions for you to speak with them inside your mind."

"Kind of a role-playing catharsis? I don't know." The chance to tell Mom and Dad how she felt about them, get the anger out of her system, sounded tempting; however, it would require a deeper mental invasion than anything she had yet suffered.

"I won't prolong the scenario against your will. You can end it at any time."

"How many times have you done this before?"

His half-smile actually seemed to convey embarrassment. "None. But I have seen something like it done by others."

"Great, I'm supposed to surrender my psyche to an amateur." She had to acknowledge, though, that he had projected dozens of elaborate fantasies into her head in the past. *I'm still alive and reasonably sane. And like he said, I can break it off whenever I've had enough.* "Okay. Let's try it."

"Sit comfortably," he said. "Legs uncrossed, hands loose in your lap." When she obeyed, he began rubbing her shoulders. Instantly she tensed, alarmed by the erotic frisson his massage evoked. "Now, now," he whispered. "Relax. Look straight at me. Don't fight."

She gazed into his silver-gray eyes. The crimson gleam flickered in their depths. She fell into those depths, sank into a swirling pool of mist.

He spoke in her thoughts: *See yourself in front of your cottage. Step onto the porch. Walk up to the door and open it. Your mother and father will be waiting.*

The mist faded to reveal the front door of the cabin, just as he described. The paint looked fresh, the porch swept clean of dead leaves. She felt the boards under her sandals, and they didn't groan as she stepped on them. A moment's fear paralyzed her.

Devin's voice reached her faintly, like a radio on low volume: *This scenario belongs to you. Don't be afraid. You may end it when you wish. But now go inside, don't waste it.*

Heather opened the door and walked into the living room.

Her mother sat in the rocking chair, her father on the couch. Both looked younger and healthier than her latest memories of them. No longer thin and pain-racked, Mom, wearing a casual powder-blue pantsuit and matching canvas shoes, had her hair tinted dark brown to cover the gray, trimmed and blow-dried as if she'd just visited the beauty parlor. Dad looked tan and rested instead of haggard, dressed in Bermuda shorts and a sport shirt.

"Come in, honey." He held out his hand. "Sit down. It's great to see you."

"How can you act so calm, like nothing happened? You left me alone!" Heather scanned the room. "Why does the place look so much newer?"

"It's the way we like to remember it, dear," Mom said. "Now that we're not--limited--anymore, we can arrange our environment the way we like."

"I guess that's why you left me. Because you couldn't remold me that easily." She stood with her fists clenched at her sides, feeling the nails dig into her palms. A breeze from a rotating fan on an end table swept past her. *Everything feels so real!*

Dad said with a pained expression, "That's all over now."

"Easy for you to say!" She looked at the braid rug, its colors no longer faded, and the polished coffee table with magazines arranged in a tidy fan shape. "What is this, Heaven?"

"More of a waiting room or lobby," said her father. "We wanted to say good-bye to you before we moved on."

"You should have thought of that first." Heather inched into the middle of the room, trying to work up the courage to sit on the couch.

Mom searched her face with a puzzled frown. "Why are you so angry, Heather?"

"Don't you know? I thought in the afterlife you'd know everything."

"Sit down and tell us about it," Dad said.

Heather perched on the arm of the sofa farthest from him. "You were never satisfied with anything I did. I always had to do better next time to make you happy."

He turned to look into her eyes. "That's not true. We were always proud of you. Didn't we come to all your graduation ceremonies and brag to all our friends about your perfect record?"

"How was I supposed to know that? You didn't brag where I could hear you." Heather was dismayed to hear how whiny she sounded.

Mom sighed. "We thought it wasn't good for a child to hear too much praise. Maybe we were mistaken. But you should have known all our advice and encouragement was for your own good."

"Encouragement? That wasn't what I called it."

"We only wanted to challenge you to do your best," Mom said.

"So I'm supposed to believe you really loved me all the time? You didn't even want me around when you were--" She couldn't pronounce "dying". "In the hospital. At every visit, you always asked me to leave before the time was up."

"Dear, I didn't want to force all that unpleasantness on you. I was trying to protect you from the pain. I didn't want to tear you away from your normal life, your work and friends."

"It never occurred to you that I might have wanted to be with you?"

"I never quite knew how you felt. You were always so quiet and self-contained."

"You mean withdrawn?" A peculiar thought occurred to Heather. "Is that why you snooped in my diary?"

"I never could figure out what you were thinking. That teenage...withdrawal...frightened me. I only wanted to get closer to you. We both did."

"Gee, what a concept. You could've asked." Or could they? In all honesty, Heather doubted that as a teenager she would have answered any intimate questions from her mother. "Okay, I understand, but you were still wrong."

"I know that now, dear. I'm sorry."

The apology left Heather speechless for a moment. *This can't be my parents; they would never think of apologizing to a kid.* Still, the setting felt so lifelike that she could suspend disbelief and accept the conversation as real. The rough fabric of the upholstery made her legs itch, the way it always had. She caught a whiff of her father's Old Spice aftershave. Their voices sounded exactly as she remembered from her teen years, before catastrophe had overtaken them.

"You made me stop coming to the cabin, without one word of explanation. You could have talked to me about it."

Her mother sighed. "I was only trying to protect you. If I went about it wrong, well, I didn't have any experience to guide me."

"You always used to love it here," Dad said, "or so we thought. I hope you can start enjoying it again."

"No thanks to you, if I do," Heather said. "You didn't have to abandon me. *You* had a choice."

"I thought you didn't need me. You'd turned into such a strong young woman. I thought you could do fine on your own." He hid his face in his hands for a second before continuing. "You still can; that's obvious. But I wouldn't have done what I did if I'd been thinking straight. I felt so lost without your mother, and so guilty about letting her die, it was like being cut off from reality."

"You weren't thinking about me," Heather said, thoughtfully rather than angrily.

"I couldn't. I'd lost the power to concentrate on anything, except the minimum necessary to make sure you were provided for." He slid across the couch and reached for her hand. "Can't you forgive me?"

Aware that cherishing her resentment could only handcuff her to a lifetime of bitterness, Heather could give only one answer to his plea. "Of course, Dad." She hugged him, feeling the solid bulk of his chest through the cotton shirt. She flashed on a vague memory of Devin's folk song performance, filled with ghost ballads in which a bereaved person's emotions imprisoned the dead on earth. *Maybe my anger had all three of us in chains, keeping them from moving on to whatever afterlife there is.*

She stood up to meet her mother's outstretched arms. She hugged both of them in turn, then together. Gradually she felt their flesh growing more tenuous. She closed her eyes to avoid seeing them fade to nothing.

She felt cushions and fabric under her. When she opened her eyes, she found herself sitting on Devin's couch.

"Well, my dear, did you find what you were seeking?"

Rubbing her eyes, she nodded. "But it was too perfect. It was all a mental construct you put into my brain."

"I didn't put it there. I couldn't have, because I've never experienced that kind of crisis. I only got you started. You filled in the details and guided the encounter."

"Either way, it was still all in my mind."

"Perhaps," he said. "But so was the other image of your parents, the one that made you so angry."

"You do have a point. Thank you for trying. I don't know if I believe the whole thing, but I do feel...better. Like I could...think...about staying." Suddenly she felt limp, wrung-out. She melted into tears, and Devin drew her into his arms.

Wrapped in his embrace, she felt his breath rustling her hair. His hands stroked her back, generating spirals of heat that radiated to her extremities. Involuntarily, she tilted her head back to gaze up at him. His strange eyes glittered as his mouth descended to hers. His lips and tongue burned, in contrast to the cool caress of his fingers. She parted her lips in a moan, feeling his need rush over her in an irresistible torrent. It would drown her, but she didn't want to fight it; she could only cling to him, answering his hunger with hers.

Abruptly he broke contact. He drew back, his hands firmly gripping either side of her head. "Don't tempt me, sweet Heather." His ragged breathing matched hers. "It would be so easy to take advantage of you. I'm trying to reform, truly I am." He punctuated the vow with a tremulous laugh.

Her heart raced with frustration. "But I want--" *What? It's more than sex; I don't know what it is!*

"So do I, little one. But not now, not until you're properly prepared." He brushed a tickling strand of hair from her forehead. "It's not like me to exercise such restraint. You've no idea what a change you've wrought." He froze, an odd expression of dismay on his face. "Good Lord, this is terrible! I think I may be falling in love with you."

Chapter 7

Her mind reeled with shock at his words. *Love? Impossible. In waking reality, we hardly know each other.* "You think?" she repeated. "You don't know? And what's so terrible about it?"

He released her and sprang up to pace around the room, raking a hand through his hair as if trying to dislodge the idea from his brain. "I've never believed in love. I understand friendship and lust, but I always thought 'love' was a cultural invention. A fantasy of poets."

Chilled by the sudden absence of his touch, she folded her arms and said, "So maybe you were wrong. Is that such a shattering blow?"

"Even if it exists," he said, still pacing, "it should be irrelevant to me. Love is a human emotion."

Half amused and half exasperated by his frank distress, she said, "If you aren't human, what are you? Give me a straight answer this time."

He turned on his heel to glare at her from across the room. "Think of us as a remnant of a long-lived race with certain unusual abilities. We keep to ourselves; we seldom form permanent ties with your kind. That sort of thing just doesn't work out."

Though Heather sensed that he still wasn't telling her the whole story, she believed him. "Sounds like irrational prejudice to me. My kind, your kind-- downright racist. We're inferior? Not good enough for you?"

"That isn't the point." He crossed the room in what seemed like a single stride and gripped her shoulders. "It's not safe for you. Look at Pamela--and I was trying to *avoid* her."

"I'm not Pam. I'm a different person. She doesn't know you." *Do I? Beyond what he allows me to know?* "I have the background to understand you; we have a past together."

"So we do." His hard grasp relaxed. "That makes it all the more difficult to draw the boundaries."

"If you treat me like an intelligent adult, and keep your mesmerism to yourself, we could work on those boundaries like any other couple."

"Confound it, we are *not* just any couple!" His hands slipped away from her shoulders.

Surprised at her own boldness, Heather caught one of his hands and guided it to her cheek. "So? We can improvise. If you lose your nerve and back out, you'll wonder what you missed." She turned her head to brush a light kiss on his palm. *Have I gone crazy? And do I really feel fine little hairs in his hand?* She couldn't resist exploring the silken hair with her lips. The tiny strands bristled as if stimulated by static electricity.

Devin flinched away. "Stop that!"

"Don't you like the tables turned?" she said, gratified that she had power over him instead of constantly playing a passive role. "At least we can be friends, then go from there."

He straightened up. "An excellent compromise. As a friend, you were planning to take a look at my new game, weren't you? Are you still interested?"

Welcoming this face-saving pretext to cool off, she said, "Sure. Lead on."

He showed her into the adjacent room, probably designed as a dining alcove. Instead of a table and chairs, the cramped space held both an IBM-compatible computer and a Mac, two printers, a copier, a tall bookcase, a file cabinet, and a fax machine. A large fan supplemented the cottage's air conditioning, for the comfort of the electronic denizens. Devin pulled a CD-ROM disk from a box on the bookshelf.

"It's called 'Maze of the Morlocks', loosely based on Wells' *Time Machine*. This is only a prototype, of course. Plenty of bugs to work out, and the graphics are primitive." He switched on one of the computers and inserted the CD.

She pulled up an office chair to sit beside him as the drive loaded.

Just as the game's title screen appeared, Devin sprang out of his chair, his face a blank mask.

"Devin, what on earth--"

He dashed into the living room. She followed. At the door, he spun around and snapped at her, "Don't come outside. Stay here." He rushed out, slamming the door.

Heather peeked between the curtains. Devin stood on the front walk, poised like a sprinter at the starting line, turning his head from side to side like a beast sampling the air. After a few seconds of this behavior, he circled the van in the driveway, staring at the ground. He then jogged toward the back of the house, out of sight. A minute later he reappeared at the front and came inside.

"What's wrong with you, Devin? What were you looking for?"

"Never mind, I didn't find anything." He made no move toward the abandoned computer. "Maybe you'd better go home now, after all."

Baffled by the abrupt switch, she glowered up at him, hands on her hips. "If you're going to be that way, I guess I should. The repairman's coming to look at the house today, anyhow." She reached for the doorknob.

"Wait, I'll drive you."

"I can walk just fine!" *How dare he put on a gallant gentleman act now!*

"Please--I want to make sure you're safe."

She didn't bother asking him to elaborate. His gray eyes looked about as pliable as flakes of mica as he put on a pair of mirrored sunglasses and tugged on a baseball cap and lightweight jacket (*In this heat?* she thought).

He helped her into the van and drove her home. Neither of them spoke until they reached her cabin.

"Please believe me, Heather, I don't want to part from you like this. I'm sorry your visit ended so unpleasantly."

"That's an understatement," she said, her suspicions reawakened.

He stroked her hair. "Shall we talk tonight?"

She tried to remain unyielding. "About what? Electronic games? Not much chance of discussing anything important, is there? Not with your 'no trespassing' rules." She opened her door to get out, then paused. "Oh, all right, if you call, I'll answer." She wasn't sure whether she referred to the phone, the computer, or his mysterious telepathic faculty.

He touched her lips in a quick kiss before he drew back, both hands firmly on the wheel. "Good day, sweet Heather."

With her stomach twisted into knots, she brought the dog in, then retreated to her bedroom. She flopped onto the bed in front of the fan to mull over her meeting with Devin. *Do I really believe all that weird stuff? That he's not quite human?* If she had been told a week previously that a race of people with superhuman powers existed on earth, she would have thought the notion belonged in a supermarket tabloid. Yet she did believe Devin's account of himself. It explained so much, without requiring her to assume she'd been delusional all these years. But what more did she still not know about him? What facts was he still withholding?

And what had caused that outburst of weird behavior? *Why wouldn't he tell me? Why does he have to keep being so evasive?* After his speeches about caring, he couldn't wait to get rid of her, instead of sharing his problem. *He claimed he was protecting me. Typical male chauvinist, human or not.*

She sat up and lifted her hair away from her neck, turning her back to the breeze from the fan. *I'm not letting him get away with it. If he really wants me around, he'd better start treating me like an adult.* She realized her attitude about staying in touch with him and keeping the cabin had shifted. Devin's role-playing therapy had served its purpose; she already felt a long-unfamiliar contentment. While not yet ready to make a firm decision, she wasn't ready to close out her options, either. If nothing else, she had to resolve things with Devin first.

She phoned Ellie Norton and asked her not to list the property. "I haven't really decided against it, but I want to put the process on hold for now."

Meanwhile, the cabin still needed fixing, if only for her own comfort. After an unenthusiastic lunch composed mostly of cottage cheese, Heather tidied up before the handyman, Marty Bernstein, arrived.

Tall and lean, about thirty, with reddish hair drawn back in a stubby ponytail, Marty jotted down Heather's repair list and penciled in estimates as she showed him around the cottage. "It'll take over a month to get all this done," he said. "I got other jobs lined up."

"That's okay, I have plenty of time." She just hoped he wouldn't turn out like the contractor who had replaced the master bath fixtures at home a few years before; that one had hauled away the old tub and immediately vanished for two and a half weeks.

"Want me to start right now? I got an hour or so to spare."

Taken aback by an offer she couldn't imagine hearing from a repairman in the city, she said, "Sure. Maybe you could do something about those leaky faucets."

When he carried his toolbox into the kitchen and got straight to work, she had no trouble overlooking the reek of cigarette smoke that emanated from his clothes.

While the pipes banged in the background, she scribbled postcards to the few people who might wonder why she hadn't written. She had difficulty figuring out the appropriate phrases, since she couldn't mention the things that weighed heaviest on her mind. *Having a wonderful time. I'm falling for this alien or something like that...*

She didn't consider dropping in on Devin's performance that evening. Let him make the next move, as he had promised. What he chose to do would reveal how sincere his protestations of honesty were.

Instead, she went to bed early and dreamed of the dragon Nightblade, bleeding on the stone floor of the castle's great hall. Labored breaths hissed from his nostrils. His wings trailed like broken kites. When she asked why he was still wounded, he said, "Only you can save me, my lady. Your love can restore me to wholeness and transform me into what I should be."

In the dream she covered the hot, dry scales of his muzzle with frantic kisses. "I do love you. Please don't die!" Like the Beast in the fairy tale, the dragon changed into Devin, standing healed and strong before her. He drew her into his embrace, and convulsions of ecstasy annihilated reason.

In the cool sanctuary of his dark living room, Devin collapsed on the sofa, his head pounding from the brief exposure to daylight. The shaded, filtered sunlight he could normally have handled with little discomfort hit him harder because of the emotional hammering he'd taken from Heather. How much longer could he put her off with half-truths and sketchy answers? More important, how could he share his life with her and yet guard her from the dangers he represented?

Too late to pull out; we're already fixated on each other. Whatever her conscious mind thinks about me, she wouldn't let me send her away if I tried. Yet the example of Pamela proved to Devin how hazardous such a fixation, whether mutual or not, could become. Even in this modern age, a catastrophe like Judith's wasn't impossible.

He was still worried about what he'd heard while starting the game to demonstrate to Heather. He'd rushed out front to investigate a rustle of movement. Too late to catch the prowler, he had heard the faint sound of breathing and footfalls receding into the woods. It didn't take much thought to guess who had left the fresh, just-fading heat traces on the ground. Pam. Suppose she got tired of stalking him and decided to take out her frustration on Heather?

Devin sank into a restless sleep, far removed from the restorative coma he needed. He dreamed of Judith, hanged by the neck until dead while he lay helpless, paralyzed by multiple wounds and the searing heat of full daylight.

He woke, unrefreshed, at sunset and tried to distract himself with the computer until he had to head for the Shenandoah Lounge. As much as he longed to speak to Heather, he decided to wait until after the performance, when he might feel less agitated. Music relaxed him, and the psychic energy emitted by the audience provided at least a little nourishment. Meanwhile, he kept his shields firm against the possibility that Heather might try to reach him. Her telepathic probe that morning had come as a surprise, but not an entirely unpleasant one. How many human females would dare that, or even think of it? *How can I let her go? What am I going to do about her?*

Cybernetic entertainment couldn't keep his mind off Heather. He needed advice from someone who could provide the necessary perspective. He rejected the idea of calling his Uncle Roderick. Like most of the elders, Rod viewed with pity and disdain anyone weak enough to care for an ephemeral. So what if the girl was in danger, he would say. Ephemerals all died eventually; that was one reason not to get involved with them. Caring for a human being held the same risk an ephemeral would face in getting passionately attached to a pet hamster.

As for Devin's contemporaries, he couldn't think of anyone likely to show much sympathy. *There's Claude Darvell, of course.* Only about a century younger than Devin, Claude had actually married a human female and seemed to be managing fine in that scandalous predicament. Claude, though, was hard to get hold of, a frequent traveler who kept erratic hours even if one were fortunate enough to track him down. A typical lifestyle for an actor, the profession Claude had followed for over a hundred years under one name or another.

And then there's Roger. Roger Darvell, Claude's half-brother, lived close by, in Maryland, practicing psychiatry, of all things. He, too, had a human mate, and despite his youth, Roger had a unique perspective on the problem, since he had grown up with human foster parents.

He decided to phone Roger. They had met only a couple of times, but maybe the resultant objectivity would be a plus. Devin felt uncomfortable needing someone to confide in, like some confused human male with romantic difficulties. He dialed the number before he could change his mind.

Annoyed at getting the answering machine instead of a live voice, Devin growled at it, "Roger, this is Devin MacAvoy, in Virginia. Think you could take a minute to call me back tonight? I'll be out from--"

The receiver clicked, and Roger's voice came on the line. "Hello, Devin, what can I do for you?"

The crisp New England accent sounded so competent that Devin felt irrationally reassured already. He settled into a chair with the phone on his lap. "I need advice."

"From me?"

Devin could almost see Roger's eyebrows arching.

"I don't usually psychoanalyze people over the phone."

"I'm not interested in being psychoanalyzed. Silly human fad." As medical fashions went, Devin preferred phlebotomy to Freud; at least the former had a practical use. "I said advice, not headshrinking."

"Why me instead of one of the elders? I'm not only ludicrously young by your standards, I'm tainted by human values."

"That's exactly why I called you. I want the human viewpoint. I'm...involved...with an ephemeral. A girl, barely grown. What should I do? How do *you* handle it?"

"Good God, do you really expect me to advise you on your love life? I'm not suicidal." Roger sighed audibly. "How long have you known this young woman?"

"Since she was eighteen. I bonded with her around that time, but she doesn't remember it--not in detail, anyway."

"That's awfully young."

"Not by the standards of my birth century. Back then, she would have been married and probably a mother by that age."

"Beside the point, I suppose," said Roger. "The damage is done. Have you told her anything at all about yourself?"

"Some. She knows I'm not exactly human, but she doesn't know...other details."

"In other words, you haven't gotten around to explaining your liquid diet." Roger sounded mildly irritated. "Devin, I don't know what to tell you. Britt"--his lover--"figured out my...secret...on her own, and she made the advances.

There was never any question of dishonesty between us. If you want a complete, open relationship with this girl, you have a lot of deception to undo."

"I'm not sure I want that. It's dangerous for her. But the only other choice is to break it off. I don't know if I could stand that." He hesitated, wrestling with the outrageous idea he had blurted out to Heather that morning. "Roger, how can I be sure whether I love her?" He felt like an idiot, asking such a sentimentally human question.

"First, are you addicted to her?"

"I'm afraid so."

Roger said, "I suspected that. The fixation makes it difficult to separate genuine emotion from biochemical need. Next question--when did you last feed?"

Devin realized he'd been so preoccupied with Heather that his physical need hadn't even registered in his consciousness. He'd been brooding over his desire for *her*, not for what she could give him. "I had her the night she arrived, Sunday. That was the last time."

"You've left her alone for her own good, I suppose?" Roger said.

"Well, yes." Devin wasn't accustomed to thinking of himself as altruistic.

"And you haven't sought an alternate donor?"

Thinking of Pamela, Devin swallowed a spasm of queasiness. "No."

"Then my first suggestion would be that you find one. You can't think rationally when you're thirsty."

"You may have a point." Animal blood and milk provided bulk nourishment, supplying their night-to-night physical needs, but they couldn't thrive without the essence of occasional human donors. Devin had already abstained for a dangerously long stretch. He could feel his nerves fraying and his vitality wearing thin.

"Once you're properly fed, you'll be clearheaded enough to decide whether you value her welfare above your own, which is the foundation of love." Roger turned away from the receiver to speak to someone in the background. "Britt says I've inflicted enough pompous philosophizing on you. She also says you owe it to the girl to tell her the full truth and trust that she's intelligent enough to know her own mind. My colleague forgets," he added dryly, "that the addiction works as powerfully on your donor as it does on you. Nevertheless, I think she has the right idea."

"All right. I'll try those suggestions. Thanks."

Makes sense, in theory, Devin thought. *But suppose I come clean to Heather, and she decides she loathes the sight of me?*

By the end of the evening's gig, Devin decided to follow part of Roger's advice immediately. He had to feed. He couldn't think straight, and the constant, dull ache in the pit of his stomach, along with the dryness in his throat that no amount of water or other liquid could alleviate, reminded him of how long he'd neglected his body's demands. Since he had sworn not to prey on Heather again without her informed consent, he had no choice but to search elsewhere.

The prospect seemed so dreary, though. He packed up his instruments feeling an unaccustomed apathy toward the night's hunt. *There's always Pamela.* She would provide an easy way out, with her established interest in him--an interest he dared not encourage. He'd had a narrow escape from her obsession already.

He headed his van down the mountain, to the nearest large town along Route 29. Even on a Wednesday night, the place he had in mind would be open at this hour and patronized heavily enough to serve his purpose.

A few decades back, the Sunset Cafe would have been called a roadhouse. It featured drinks, snacks, a small dance floor, a jukebox for off hours, and live country music all evening. Not that Devin classed the Stetson-clad quartet entertaining tonight as "music" in any meaningful sense, but he hadn't come to listen to them.

The scent of beer enveloped him as he entered the dim lounge. The air conditioner blasted away, augmented by a pair of noisy ceiling fans. He took a stool at the bar, ordered a beer more for show than consumption, and surveyed the potential prey.

Eliminating the men instantly diminished his prospects by over fifty percent. Though he wouldn't disdain a male if left with no other choice, sexual polarity enhanced his satisfaction. Several tables were occupied by clusters of women giggling together and eyeing the men. Devin didn't feel up to the challenge of cutting one of them out of the herd. Two unattached females remained. One sat at the other end of the bar, trading repartee with the bartender. The second occupied a table in a corner near the band.

Devin studied her over the rim of his glass. Almost as young as Heather (*Can't you forget about her for a few minutes?* he admonished himself), with platinum hair in a loose French twist, she wore a white satin blouse buttoned in a plunging V. After about half a minute, she glanced up to meet Devin's eyes across the room. Picking up his drink, he strolled over to her, holding her gaze. When his need became this acute, women gravitated toward him like filings to a magnet with little effort on his part.

"Are you alone?" he said, bending over so that she could hear him through the lugubrious caterwauling of the lead vocalist, who sang something about alcohol and adultery.

She gave him a quick, nervous nod, nibbling on her lower lip.

"I can remedy that," he said, placing his glass on the glossy, laminated wood tabletop. The aroma of her drink identified it as a weak gin and tonic. No tobacco smoke hovered around her, and her aura glowed a healthy rose pink. Devin scented a cloying floral perfume, distasteful but not strong enough to kill his appetite. "What's your name?"

"Norine." An anxious flicker of her tongue between glossed lips accompanied the word. "What's yours?"

"Don't worry about that." He stared into her hazel eyes and ran a fingertip along her bare arm.

She gazed back at him, her respiration slowing as she drifted into a light trance. Neither resisting nor responding, she let him clasp her hand and stroke the palm.

Good, I don't feel like dragging this out. Devin dismissed the nagging reminder that this reaction was abnormal in itself; ordinarily, the game of seduction lent spice to the meal. "It's too loud in here. Come outside with me."

She stood up and let him lead her by the hand like a pet on a leash. Outside, the night had cooled down. He smelled rain in the air. Away from the noises of the lounge, the girl's heartbeat drummed in his ears. His stomach cramped in anticipation. He put his arm around Norine's shoulders and guided her to the van.

She gave him a faintly puzzled look as he helped her inside and led her to the bench seat in the rear. After taking a few seconds to reinforce the tenuous trance, Devin eased her onto the seat and drew her into a loose embrace. With a wordless purr, she cuddled up to him. The bench could fold down into a double bed, but he didn't consider using that option. He had no desire to spend a minute longer than necessary with this anonymous ambulatory snack bar.

What would Heather say if she heard me thinking that? He shook off the uncomfortable reflection. *This is what I am; I have to do this to survive.* It wasn't as if he harmed his donors. He drained less than a blood bank donation, and he repaid them with pleasure, even if he allowed them to remember only a vaguely sensual daydream.

He brushed his lips across Norine's mouth and cheek, skimming along her jawline to the side of her neck. She sighed, closing her eyes and lolling against him. Her perfume clogged his nostrils. She tasted like talcum powder.

His stomach churned with conflicting thirst and nausea. He inched away from her, leaving her slumped half-conscious in the corner of the seat. *I can't do it! She's not Heather.* He couldn't bear to taste anyone else. He was already addicted beyond redemption.

"Norine," he said softly. Her eyes opened. "Go back inside. Find someone else. Forget you met me."

She replied with a dazed nod.

He hustled her out of the van, locked the doors behind her, and roared out of the parking lot before she'd reached the front door of the bar. He drove home at twenty miles over the limit, half hoping to encounter a highway patrolman to vent his frustration on. Anger might give him the incentive to feed, even on a male, where lust couldn't. *Just my luck, the road will probably be deserted.* He couldn't conjure up the energy to hunt lesser game tonight. He'd have to fall back on the unappetizing alternative of his frozen emergency supplies, with a mug of brandy-spiked warm milk for a chaser.

What the devil is the matter with me? If this discomfort was an unavoidable consequence of love, the ephemerals could keep it. Would he have to choose between seducing Heather or starving? *What has the wench done to me? I'm trapped!*

Chapter 8

A disembodied voice shattered Heather's dream of the dragon-knight's kiss. She opened her eyes to the clatter of rain on the roof and the grumble of thunder in the distance. Curtains flapped in the damp wind blowing through the open window.

Stumbling across the room to close it, she heard the voice in her head again. *Heather, please answer me. I must talk to you.*

She leaned on the window sill, shaking the fog out of her brain. *Devin, is that you?* Well, who else, for heaven's sake? With a glance at the bedside clock radio, she added, *It's one in the morning!*

The desperation in his tone yielded to wry amusement. *Sorry, little one, but this is like high noon for me. I'm nocturnal; get used to it.*

She felt an intangible caress, like cool fingertips running down her spine.

Besides, I couldn't wait any longer. I need you.

Oh, yeah? For what? *All right, I'm awake anyhow. We can talk. But not like this.* She staggered back to bed to wrap herself in the covers. Since sunset, the temperature had been falling until it was almost chilly.

How, then?

The diffident question threatened to soften her even more than the erotic resonance he usually projected. *Not on the phone, either. I don't want to hear your voice. You keep trying to distract me with--*

You insist on a non-distracting method of communication? He sounded amused again. *How about the computer? Thoroughly objective.*

Though she doubted she could listen to Devin objectively in any circumstances, she welcomed the suggestion. *Sure, we can talk online. Just give me a couple of minutes.* She tossed aside the bedspread and reached for her robe. *Now get out of my skull!*

She was sure she heard him chuckle as he obeyed.

Ten minutes later, with her hair tied back and a cup of instant coffee next to the keyboard, she watched Nightblade's greeting scroll across the monitor.

{What's with the screen name? I know who you are now} she keyed in.

He responded: {For this, I want to be Nightblade a while longer. You wondered why I got rid of you so abruptly this morning. I'm ready to attempt an answer.}

{Great.} She still had reservations about his sincerity.

{I shall start by telling you a story.}

What's this, some new evasive tactic? {Fine, go ahead.} She leaned back in her chair to watch the message appear, line by line, on the screen:

{"This tale concerns a young woman named Judith who lived in a village north of London over three centuries ago. She was the oldest of five children of a respectable shopkeeper.

"Just outside the town stood a manor house that had been purchased by a wealthy stranger from Ireland. This man, whom we may call Nightblade, had lived there for three years but was practically unknown to the local populace. He never darkened the door of the village church. He employed only a few servants, who could not be persuaded to gossip when they ventured into town on market day. Their master left the house only after dark; he was sometimes glimpsed riding his horse on moonlit nights.

"Judith began to dream of a pale, dark-haired man--breathtakingly sensual dreams that she would have been ashamed to confess to anyone. After several such dreams, though, she began to suspect that the assignations were real meetings, not visions. She began to recover fragmentary memories of rising from her bed to open the window, then lying down to await her lover.

"When she challenged him on this point, he was impressed by her audacity and admitted that he was more than a dream. Only then did she learn that he was the mysterious, wealthy gentleman, Nightblade.

"This went on for almost two months, nocturnal visits two or three nights a week. Judith remained a maiden. Her lover kissed and fondled her until she burned with a passion she could never have imagined, but she never disrobed for him or saw him unclothed. Still, she had few illusions about the sinfulness of her deeds. To make matters worse, she was realistic enough to admit to herself that she had no prospects of marriage to this landed gentleman. She had long been betrothed to the son of one of her father's friends, but she became more and more obsessed with her secret paramour. Finally she told her young man that she could not marry him.

"Noticing her strangely languid, indifferent behavior, her fiancé consulted with Judith's parents, who confided their worries about her. She had grown pale, lost her appetite, and lacked energy for ordinary household tasks. The physician could offer no help. The young man began watching Judith's home by night. Eventually he went to the vicar with a report of a black-winged shape hovering over the house, changing into a patch of fog as it floated to the ground, then assuming the shadowy form of a cloaked man, who entered through Judith's window.

"The vicar and the magistrate together arrested the girl and imprisoned her in the cellar of the rectory. They drew up an accusation of witchcraft. Since

Judith did not deny her nocturnal meetings but persisted in claiming that her lover was no demon, her parents declined to interfere. They feared that defending their daughter would doom the whole family. The town was too small and the case too insignificant to merit the visit of an official witchfinder. The vicar examined Judith for devil's marks--either a spot insensitive to pain, or any skin blemish he chose to consider abnormal. He found several partly healed wounds, resembling superficial scratches or bites, on her bosom.

"All this happened very quickly, over the space of a few hours. Judith cried out silently, in her thoughts, for her lover to come to her aid. After dark, when she had nearly abandoned hope, she sensed his reply. Because they were bonded, he shared her pain.

"He came to her at midnight. The house had no armed guard. The maiden, after all, was locked in the cellar, and the crosses at every door and window ought to prevent demonic interference. Of course, those symbols had no effect on Nightblade. He broke in through the front door, knocked out the servants who tried to block his path, and did the same to the vicar. Later I wished I had killed them.

"*He* wished, that is.

"When he emerged, carrying the half-conscious girl, a mob of several dozen village men thronged the street, led by the magistrate and Judith's former fiancé. Confident in his inhuman powers, Nightblade had taken no precautions against being watched in his approach to the vicarage, nor had he suspected anyone would have the courage to challenge him. Before he could summon the power of transformation and leap into flight, three musket balls struck him, two in the right leg, one in the ribs. A fourth hit Judith in the shoulder. Putting her down, he faced the attackers. They shot him twice more, wounding the other leg and his chest. A few of the men fled when they saw Nightblade rise to his feet and charge them, when he should have been dead or dying. But enough stood their ground to overwhelm him by force of numbers.

"Faintly aware of the clergyman snatching up Judith and rushing her back to her prison, Nightblade collapsed under the fists and knives of the villagers. When he lay barely conscious in the middle of the street, someone shot him through the heart.

"He awoke near dawn on the heath outside of town where the men had dragged, as they supposed, his dead body. No doubt they planned to bury him with proper rites of exorcism later, under the protection of daylight. In agony, he dragged himself into the nearest woods. By the time he reached that shelter, the sun had been up for almost an hour. In his weakened condition, its direct rays seared his skin, doubling the pain.

"In the deepest shade he could find, he slept until nightfall. Turbulent dreams haunted him, visions of Judith hanged in the village square. When he woke, he knew she was dead. He lured several rabbits to his hiding place and fed on them. Once he had healed enough to move, he returned home and took refuge there until he recovered completely. His servants, well-paid for their loyalty, kept out hostile visitors, and in broad daylight the town officials were not bold enough to accuse a wealthy landowner of being the 'demon' they had tried to slaughter.

"Over the succeeding weeks, using stealth rather than open violence, shrouding himself in the psychic veil that prevented human eyes from noticing him, he executed the vicar, the magistrate, and Judith's betrothed one by one. He left enough time between killings to allow their vigilance to relax. He would have liked to exterminate the entire town, but he decided that would pose an unnecessary risk, and it would not alleviate his pain.

"He closed up the house and returned to Ireland. Later he sold the property and traveled throughout Europe and the British Isles, but he was never seen in that village again."}

Heather stared at the screen in stunned silence for a minute. She believed the story, for its events and her dream fragments corroborated each other. But could she accept that Devin was the "Nightblade" of the tale, over three hundred years old?

She typed: {I dreamed part of this.}

{I know.}

{But why?} she asked. {I don't believe in reincarnation.}

{Nor do I. You picked up the memories from my mind. You and I are bonded, as I was bonded with Judith--except that the communion between you and me has greater depth. Judith was hardly more than a child and only half aware of what was happening to her.}

Heather still wasn't sure she was fully aware, herself. {I would really like to believe that you're talking about an ancestor of yours. A family legend.}

{But you don't believe that, do you?}

She had to acknowledge that she didn't. {You slipped and wrote 'I', and you didn't delete it. You wanted me to know.} How could Devin have projected such vivid memories into her sleeping mind, unless they were his own?

{Exactly when did this happen?} she typed.

{In 1649. I was very young then, born in 1602.}

For fear of overloading her "impossible things before breakfast" file, Heather postponed considering his casual claim that he was four centuries old, and his dismissal of forty-seven as "very young". But: *Hold on, if he's the "demon" in the story, he's just admitted to killing at least three people.*

Devin answered the unspoken question. {Yes, I have sometimes had to kill in self-defense, or to protect others. For what it's worth, that was the first and last time I've killed for revenge.}

It happened a long time ago. He said he was young; he must have matured since then. If his kind grew and changed the way human beings did. If he was telling the truth.

{We can't communicate anything but the truth mind to mind. I can shut you out, but I can't lie to you.}

{You read my thoughts} she typed, hoping he sensed the annoyance that accompanied the words.

{Forgive me. I can't help it, when you project so strongly.}

So he killed for Judith. Would he do the same for me? Heather didn't find the idea entirely comfortable. {Did you love Judith?}

{I didn't believe in love then. Even for middle-class Englishmen, marrying for love was a new, untested fad at the time. I cared about Judith--more than I wanted to.}

Reflecting on his restrained account of "Nightblade's" suffering, Heather typed: {You risked your life for her.}

{Not as great a risk as it would have been for an ephemeral--one of your kind. But I could have died, if that last bullet had shattered my skull instead of lodging in my chest.}

Heather felt sick at the image. {Most people would call that something like love.}

{It was youthful recklessness. My elders would have considered my behavior sheer madness. Judith should have been no more to me than, at most, a pet. I took care not to get involved that way again.}

A pet? Is that how he sees me? Disillusion soured her response: {I see. Getting involved with me was a mistake. That's why you sent me away this morning.}

His emotions flared up; his anger and passion heated her flesh like a tangible flame. {No! That is not the point I'm trying to make. Judith died because of me and her would-be lover's jealousy of me. My kind are always potentially in danger from human enemies. I don't want another woman hurt by someone out to get me.}

{What brought this on at that particular moment?} she typed. {Why were you acting as if somebody hit you over the head?}

She felt his hesitation before the next message appeared.

{Pamela was watching my home this morning. I sensed her presence. If she decided to confront me, I didn't want you in the line of fire, so to speak.}

Indignation sparked within Heather. {Wake up, this isn't the seventeenth century. I'm not about to hide behind the castle gates while you fight the dragons. You were going to treat me like an adult, remember?}

{A sensible adult doesn't throw herself into harm's way for nothing. There's not just Pam to consider. There's her brother.}

She had no patience with that line of argument. {If Pam keeps hanging around you and gets violent, or if Ted decides to fight for his sister's honor, I might possibly be in danger. Sounds awfully hypothetical to me.}

Sensing Devin flinch as if she'd hit a tender spot, she added {You know what I think? I think you're putting me off because you're afraid. Afraid of being hurt again if you get attached to one of us inferior human females.}

{Inferior? Not you. Afraid? Damn right I am. She tried to run your car off the side of a mountain, remember?}

{She was just trying to scare me. I don't believe Pam's a murderess.} Heather decided that his armor was softening, and this was the moment to strike. {Tell me straight--do you really care for me? As more than a pet?}

{You know I do. Why else would I reveal so much?}

{Then we have to share things. If you keep me at arm's length now, you can forget about making it up later.}

A flood of warm sweetness washed over her. Instead of answering on screen, he spoke telepathically: *Lovely Heather, you have a talent for tempting me to things I desperately want to do anyway. May I see you tonight?*

How strange, that she already considered this silent communication as natural as a phone call. *That sounds good, but only if you stop dodging around the facts.*

Agreed. Come to the lounge tonight, and after the show I promise to spend as long as you like giving full and candid replies to any questions you ask. The vow held a flavor of sincerity.

Okay, it's a date.

She went back to bed and fell asleep with his affection wrapped around her like a fur coat in a snowstorm.

The telephone interrupted Heather's breakfast the next morning. Her heart fluttered before she realized it could hardly be Devin. He slept during the day and would not bother with the phone, anyhow. *I'm reacting like a teenager with a crush. I'm obsessed with him.*

"Good, I caught you at home this time," said the female voice on the other end. "At least you haven't moved in with him. I saw you at Devin's yesterday."

"Pam. What do you want?" Heather's stomach tightened. She'd had almost no experience in dealing with hostility.

"I'm calling for your own good. Ted likes you, so I don't want you to get into trouble." Her tone sounded more threatening than concerned.

"I don't need advice, thanks. I know what I'm doing."

"You're going to get hurt. Devin hurts people. He hurt me."

She's jealous. What am I supposed to do about that? It's not my fault Devin rejected her. Heather felt sorry for Pam but knew better than to say anything so condescending. "You don't want me seeing him. I understand that, but I have to do what I feel is right."

"You don't understand." The other woman's voice turned shrill. "I'm not threatening you; I'm trying to get you to see the facts! Devin did something to me, I can't remember exactly what. He made me sick. And now I can't get him out of my mind. There's no reason for you to end up the same way. There's still time for you."

Swallowing a nervous lump, Heather tried to speak calmly. "How could Devin possibly make you sick? Your own emotions did that. If you don't make sense, why should I listen to you?"

"Oh, why do I bother talking to you? I guess I have to do something about it!" Pam hung up.

Heather gazed at her bowl of granola, her stomach heavy with anxiety. The dog stared at her and whimpered expectantly. Setting the half-empty bowl on the floor, Heather stroked Sugar's silky back and mulled over Pam's message. The original impulse to ignore it was probably sound, since Pam spoke out of jealousy. She had turned hostile to Devin and resented any other woman he paid attention to. Still, Heather couldn't suppress the doubts aroused by the call. Pam claimed Devin "made her sick". Was she speaking literally instead of figuratively? Ted had mentioned that Pam behaved strangely, sleeping late, showing a loss of vitality. Nightblade's story reported the same of Judith. He had undermined the girl's health somehow; he'd admitted it himself. Could she have suffered only from lovesickness, or something more tangible?

Before accusing Devin (*of what, exactly?* she wondered), Heather wanted a second opinion. She decided to speak to Ted again, to ask for more details on Pam's personality change, find out whether she'd been physically ill. After that, Heather could face Devin with concrete facts. He had promised to answer all her questions tonight. Fine, she would insist that he tell the full truth about Pam.

Early in the afternoon, Heather drove to the store to see Ted. Luckily, she found his father tending the cash register along with him. The questions she wanted to ask Ted would have been awkward over the counter. After exchanging greetings with Mr. Gaines, she asked Ted whether they could talk in private.

"It's our busy time of day," he said, glancing around at the four customers browsing the shelves, a veritable crowd for this place.

"Go ahead," said his father with a grin, "I can handle it. I'm not completely over the hill yet."

Heather said, "Please, could we just step outside for a few minutes, Ted?"

"Okay, why not?" Now that Heather showed a preference for Devin, Ted seemed distinctly less interested in her company.

They stepped onto the porch and sat on the bench next to the wooden Indian.

"It's about Pam," she said. "I'm sorry to bother you with more bad news, but I thought you'd want to know." She summarized the "warning" phone call.

"God, what's wrong with her?" he said. He hunched over, glaring into the distance with his elbows on his knees. "I can't figure out what that guy's done to her."

"Devin? How can you blame him for Pam's obsession?"

"Don't give me that amateur shrink jargon. I know her a lot better than you do. She never acted like this until she came home for this visit and saw MacAvoy's show at the lounge."

"Does that make it his fault? What do you think he did, put some kind of spell on her?" Heather kept her tone light, but she knew something like that had actually happened, whether Devin had intended it or not.

"I don't know, but it sure wasn't normal for her to forget all about the man she's going with in Richmond. Heck, the last time she phoned home, she was talking about getting married. Now she won't even return his calls. I mention the guy's name, and she acts like she never heard of him."

"That is strange," Heather said. *If Devin has that effect on a woman who barely knows him, how can I trust my own feelings? Maybe he's put a spell on me, too, even if he's not aware of it.*

"Thanks for telling me about that call," said Ted, straightening up and turning to face Heather. "She's worse off than we thought. Not that she'd hurt you or anything, don't think that. But we have to get her away from here--away from MacAvoy."

"That sounds like a good idea. Will she go?"

"I'll talk to Dad as soon as we get a free minute. Maybe what Pam needs is therapy--I've never put much stock in that stuff, but Dad and I sure can't handle this. I'll get him to convince her to go back to Richmond--I'll drive her if I have to. And I'll make sure she finds a shrink."

"I hope it works out," Heather said. "I saw a counselor after Dad died, and I think it helped." She sincerely wished the best for Pam. She didn't want her newfound feelings for Devin clouded by guilt over the other woman's unhappiness.

While getting dressed for that night's show, Devin brooded over his latest conversation with Heather. He had promised to tell her the whole truth about himself, and he had to follow through on that promise. Tonight presented his last chance to win her without coercion. If he reneged on his word, she would justly reject him.

Or try to. *She doesn't know it, but she can't break away from me, any more than I can from her. If we stay together much longer, the only choice will be whether she stays as a conscious decision or as a compulsion.* Sure, such addictions could be cured, but only by permanent separation. *Not much chance of that, if it depends on me--I don't have the will to leave her.*

After the previous night's rainstorm, the weather had turned pleasantly cool. Devin paused on the porch to savor the pine scent of the evening air. The low-lying sun didn't bother him as long as he stayed in the shadow of the house.

A rustle in the trees attracted his attention. *Too clumsy for an animal,* he thought. "Who's there?"

Pamela stepped out from behind a tree at the foot of the driveway.

He hadn't seen or heard a car; she must have walked all this way through the woods to avoid making her family suspicious. A shift in the breeze carried her perfume to him. Her aura looked murky, with dark streaks tainting the pink. He noticed that she wore a hip-length denim jacket with the too-long sleeves rolled up. *It's not all that chilly, even for an ephemeral. Hasn't she recovered physically yet?*

"What is it now, Pamela?" He chose rudeness over any hint of encouragement. "I'm on my way to the lodge."

She walked up the driveway toward him. "My father wants to send me back to Richmond. He thinks I should get into therapy."

Devin stepped off the porch. As the distance between them lessened, he heard the racing of her heart. "That sounds like a good idea. You'll feel much better once you get away from here."

"Only one thing could make me feel better." She scurried up to him and clutched his sleeves. "You know what I want."

"Believe me, that's out of the question."

"Because of Heather."

Her bitter tone alarmed Devin. "Among other reasons," he said. "Go back to your fiancé, Pamela. And get the help your father suggested." He reinforced the words with a psychic nudge.

The girl shook her head. "I don't need that kind of help. I'll go to Richmond with Ted tomorrow, if you let me spend tonight with you. It's our last chance. My last chance to make you forget Heather."

"Pamela, nothing could do that." Her insistence chilled him. Would his rejection drive her to attack Heather with something worse than threats?

As if he hadn't spoken, she persisted with, "We'll share tonight, and tomorrow I'll leave, to get Dad and Ted off my back. Then, a few days later, I'll come up here again to be with you. They don't have to know."

Her desire was genuine enough; its aroma assailed his senses. Against his will, his half-starved body responded with a tingling at the roots of his teeth. *I could take her, just this once. She'd be easier to control after that, anyway.*

He cast off the temptation. Even if his hunger could override his revulsion toward her, preying on Pamela would constitute a betrayal of Heather. *I couldn't face her after that. I couldn't hide it from her, and she would loathe me for it.* "That is pure fantasy. Now please go; I'll be late for the performance."

His icy tone had no effect. Instead of backing off, she wrapped one arm around his neck and stood on tiptoe to press her mouth to his. She tasted like Scotch; she must have taken a drink to fortify her nerve. For an instant Devin's lips involuntarily parted to accept what she offered. When her tongue skimmed his incisors, he almost broke down. It would be too easy to let the razor edge of his teeth nip the unguarded flesh--

"I said no!" He shoved her away and glided out of reach. "I'm leaving now. Stay here for the rest of the evening, if you wish. It will be a waste of time."

She whirled around to watch him stride to the car. "Don't you walk away from me!" she shrieked.

To Devin's inhuman perception, rage seethed from her like steam from a cauldron. He paused to fix her eyes with his hypnotic gaze. "You mustn't excite yourself, Pamela."

In her hysterical state, she was beyond his influence. "Stop right there, Devin." She pulled a handgun out of the jacket's side pocket.

"You don't really want to shoot me," he said softly.

"I gave you a chance. I would've taken you back, no matter what you've done to me. But I'm going to make sure you don't do it to any other woman." She fired.

He hadn't really believed she would do that. If he'd been more alert, he might have dodged the bullet. As it was, he flinched just in time to catch the round in a shoulder instead of his chest. The fiery pain roused memories of that other time, almost four hundred years ago.

Blindly he lurched toward the girl, intent on ripping the gun out of her hand.

She fired again. That bullet slammed into his breastbone. He fell back onto the sidewalk.

He heard the gun land on the ground. With his eyes closed, he lay paralyzed with shock, struggling to suppress the pain. Pamela emitted a cry that would have been a scream if she'd had the breath for it. Sensing her drop to the pavement beside him, he retarded his heartbeat and respiration to an imperceptible slowness. Pamela's fingers poked at his wounded shoulder and the bloodied gash in the front of his shirt. Curled within himself, distant from the agony of her touch, he waited for her to leave.

"Oh, God," she whimpered, "I killed him!"

Devin felt her back away, heard her scramble to her feet. A few seconds later, her running footsteps faded down the drive and into the woods.

The sun hadn't sunk behind the trees yet. Its rays, though not as fierce as at midday, beat on his unprotected face. Weak from hunger and his injuries, he couldn't tame the pain of the wounds or even roll over to shield his eyes.

He took refuge in the only alternative, a deliberate plunge into unconsciousness.

Chapter 9

Pain lanced through Heather like a bolt of lightning.

Crumpling onto the living room rug, she buried her face in her arms until the aftershocks dissipated. The dog's wet tongue laved her ears and neck.

She levered herself up on her elbows. "Okay, Sugar, I'm all right."

What was that? She examined her arms, half expecting to find the skin charred. A moment's thought suggested only one source for the convulsion of agony. *Devin's hurt!*

Heather silently called to him through the void. No sign of Devin, not the slightest echo of a response. *Dear God, he isn't dead, is he?* The horror that suffused her at that thought astonished her, but she had no time to sift through the implications. She had to find out what had hurt Devin.

What--or who? She realized the danger might not have passed. The assailant might not have left yet. *Better take along reinforcements.* Heather scrambled into her tennis shoes and light jacket, snatched up purse and car keys, then leashed the dog and hustled her into the station wagon. No time to waste on a two-mile walk through the woods.

She drove to Devin's house with her head buzzing, thankful she met little traffic on the way. At twilight, in her agitated condition, she couldn't have handled the challenge of a congested road. She avoided thinking too hard about whether the dog would provide enough protection if Devin's visitor still lurked nearby. She didn't even let the other logical question rise to the surface of consciousness--where she would search next if Devin weren't home. *He has to be there, and he has to be alive. I can't lose him when I've just found him!*

Screeching to a stop at the foot of Devin's driveway, she instantly saw a body sprawled on the sidewalk. Forgetful of possible danger, she jumped out of the car and slammed the door behind her, leaving Sugar in the front seat.

Heather almost flung herself on Devin before she remembered the rules for handling an injured person. Remnants of a long-ago first aid course rattled in her head. She mustn't jostle or move him until she checked his condition.

He lay with his eyes closed, arms and legs flung at random as if he hadn't moved from the position in which he had landed. Blood stained his shirt at the shoulder and near the center of his chest. The latter wound made Heather feel sick and faint. *None of that, I can't help him if I lose it!* He couldn't be beyond help; he had to be merely unconscious.

At least the blood no longer flowed, so she didn't have to worry about pressure points. She ran her hands over his limbs, checking for broken bones but not sure she would recognize a fracture if she found one. The only concrete advice she recalled was a scrap of doggerel about treating a patient in shock: "Face is red, raise the head; face is pale, raise the tail." Before that rule could apply, she had to decide whether it was safe to move him.

What am I thinking about? I'm no medic. I should have called 911 the minute I got here.

But first she had to satisfy herself that he was alive. She fumbled for the pulse at the side of his neck. His skin felt feverishly hot, despite the coolness of the evening. *Then he can't be dead.* Yet she found no heartbeat when she explored under his collar. Encircling his wrist with her other hand, she couldn't feel it there, either.

Don't panic. I don't have the training. I could just be missing the spot. Her eyes prickled with tears. *Damn it, Devin, you can't die! Don't you dare be dead!*

Tone it down, will you? My head hurts like the devil.

The silent voice pierced her forehead like a stiletto of ice. "Devin? Is that really you? Are you alive?"

I think so. His eyelids fluttered.

She squeezed his wrist. "Don't move! I'll call an ambulance."

No! The command stung like a slap. *No doctors, no paramedics. Just get me inside.*

"But, Devin, moving you will make things worse--"

No, it won't. Do as I say. Please.

His pain twisted like a snake inside her own bosom. She couldn't defy his appeal. "Okay, but I can't carry you, and even if I could manage to drag you, you might start bleeding again."

Probably wouldn't. But there's no need. Lend me your strength, and I think I'll be able to walk that far.

Dubiously she inched her arm under his shoulders, eliciting stifled groans. "I'm hurting you."

Never mind. He clasped her free hand, his fingers interlacing with hers.

A painless spark sizzled through her flesh into his. For a second her head spun with dizziness.

"Thank you."

His voice surprised her, even if it was only a harsh whisper.

"What was that?" she asked as he clutched her sleeve and gathered his legs under him.

"I borrowed energy from you."

She hoisted him upright, with his arm draped around her shoulders. He leaned most of his weight on her, but somehow they managed to stagger onto the porch without falling. Devin sagged against the wall while Heather opened the door, glad to discover it wasn't locked. She guided him across the room and lowered him onto the couch. He lay back, his breathing labored. His gray eyes flickered over her before closing again.

"Many thanks, my brave lady. Maybe you should leave now."

"Don't talk like an idiot. What if the person who did this comes back?"

"She won't. She thinks I'm dead."

So did I, but this is no time to quiz him about it. "She?" An image flashed in Heather's mind. "It was Pam, wasn't it?"

Devin gave a minute nod. "Did you notice if the gun's still out there?"

"I didn't see one."

"Go look, please."

Running outside, she scanned the sidewalk and driveway. No sign of a weapon. She realized she had left Sugar in the car. Opening the door to pick up her purse and the dog's leash, she said, "Come on, you can protect us if Devin turns out to be too optimistic."

On the threshold, Sugar hunched down and whimpered. Heather had to yank on the leash to pull her far enough inside to shut and bolt the door. As soon as Heather unhooked the lead, the dog made a dash for the hall.

Devin's lips curled in a ghost of a smile. "Smart animal."

Heather dropped her things and pulled up a hassock to sit beside him. "I didn't find a gun."

"Took it with her. Too bad--she's a menace as it is."

"What now? Why won't you let me call 911? I sure can't extract bullets."

"No need. Only one lodged--in the chest. Missed my heart, thank God." He heaved a long breath. "I'll heal around it. Eventually it will work itself out-

-or not. Not important." He turned his head to gaze at her. "Plastic bags in the freezer. Thaw one--microwave--then heat it until warm to the touch. Pour it into a mug and bring it here."

Heather walked through the computer den into the kitchen. She padded over the flagstone floor, skirting a circular redwood table and a freestanding food-preparation island on her way to the fridge. Devin seemed to take little advantage of the luxurious facilities. The counters were bare except for a blender, coffeepot, and microwave; no carving knives or copper pans hung on the paneled walls, and the stove looked as if it had never been used.

Out of curiosity, she took a quick peek in the refrigerator first. It contained only two cartons of milk, a box of eggs, and a bottle of white wine. She couldn't guess what to expect in the freezer.

She found dozens of plastic bags stacked on the freezer shelves--flask-shaped sacks that reminded her of her last visit to the Red Cross bloodmobile.

She picked up one and studied it in disbelief. The frozen lump of reddish-purple fluid looked exactly like what she feared. *Blood--the sun--born in 1602--Devin is--*

Never mind that; she could deal with the shock later. More important, he was hurt and needed this right now. Laying the bag on the microwave's turntable, she punched in the defrost setting.

After shaking up the thawed liquid, she warmed it slowly, to avoid overheating. *I guess he wants it at body temperature. Lord, this is surreal.* She tested the bag's heat on the inside of her wrist. She had no trouble finding a tall pewter mug in a cabinet, but then she wondered how she should open the sack, without making a mess. *Bela Lugosi never had this problem.*

She found a pair of shears in a drawer, clipped off a corner of the bag, and poured the contents into the mug. She carried it out to Devin, holding it in front of her in both hands as though it were a ceremonial chalice. She tried to ignore the faint metallic odor.

Devin tried to sit up as she entered the living room.

Quickly setting the cup on the coffee table, she crammed pillows behind him to support his back.

"All right." His voice rasped like sandpaper on metal.

Heather placed the mug in his hands, made sure he had a firm grip, then hastily stepped back.

Rather than watching him drink, she shifted her eyes to survey the room, which she hadn't examined closely on her first visit. The Victorian claw-footed couch and matching armchairs formed a grouping around a deep fireplace faced with gray stone similar to that on the exterior of the house. Opposite, a stereo system and wide-screen TV dominated another wall. A picture window would have offered a view of the woods, if forest-green drapes hadn't hidden it. Wall-to-wall carpet in a lighter green covered the floor.

Suddenly aware that the deepening twilight forced her to strain to see details, Heather clicked on a lamp at one end of the sofa, hoping the dim light wouldn't aggravate Devin's headache. As she did, she heard the mug thunking onto the coffee table. She looked around in time to notice him licking his lips in an oddly feline gesture.

"Thank you." He sounded less frail already. "Now you really must leave."

"Leave you alone in this condition? Are you out of your mind?" His eagerness to get rid of her distressed her; she'd thought they had passed beyond that stage.

Claiming the spot on the couch he cleared by sitting up, she started to unbutton his shirt. "Let me look at that." The sticky cloth made her feel more queasy than heating his drink had, but she needed to check the severity of his wounds. She still had trouble accepting that he didn't need a doctor.

He winced as if her fingers scalded him. "Don't touch me. My condition is the problem. A few minutes ago, you could have fought me off, if necessary.

Now you couldn't--and in this condition, once I started, I wouldn't have the willpower to stop."

Stop what? Stop feeding on my blood? The idea didn't repel her as much as it should have. Recalling the content of some of those adolescent "dreams", she suspected he had already sampled her vital fluid more than once. "I'm not afraid of you. I know better than to think you'd hurt me."

He retreated to the end of the couch. "You don't understand, Heather. I wouldn't be able to help myself. I would drain more than you could spare, and you wouldn't even want to stop me."

Ignoring the words as well as the tremor they inspired in her nerves, she pursued him and continued peeling off his shirt. He sat rigid, as if afraid his control would snap if he moved. She essayed a tentative probe of his mind. For an instant she stared down into a bottomless well of hunger/thirst/lust. The contact ignited a flame of answering need within her. She couldn't bear his anguish; she yearned to relieve it.

Then he slammed down his shield, locking her out. "See what I mean?" he whispered.

Feeling heat flood her cheeks, she dropped her gaze from his silver-gray eyes to his chest.

With stiff movements, he cooperated in stripping off the shirt. Random flashes of pain leaked through his mental armor.

"Sorry," she said. "But you need to get cleaned up, if nothing else."

Her stomach churned at the sight of his injuries, obscured though they were by clotting blood. She mumbled an apology and hurried to the kitchen, partly to snatch a minute to calm her nerves. She grabbed a handful of paper towels and dampened them.

Devin hadn't changed position when she returned to the living room. With clenched jaws, he endured her sponging the blood from his skin. When she'd cleaned off as much as possible, she saw with surprise that the bullet wounds looked half-healed. Admittedly, she had no previous experience for comparison, but from the size of the bloodstains, she had expected worse.

"We heal fast," he said. "The drink helped. Do you see why I couldn't let a doctor examine me?"

Heather nodded. Running her fingers over his shoulder near the thin gash, she found that his flesh now felt cool. "You were hot before, outside."

"That came from the sun shining right in my face. Think of it as a form of heatstroke." He shivered as if her hand were icy instead of warm. "Heather, *please* stop touching me."

He allowed her a few seconds' access to his mind. She sensed that holding himself immobile under her attentions added to his pain. Reluctantly she backed off, collecting the red-stained paper towels and the mug to take into the kitchen.

As soon as she rejoined him, he asked, "Are you leaving?"

"Not when you're in this shape. I don't care if you do have a constitution like Superman."

"Then you have to do as I tell you," he said in a voice taut with strain. "Shut your dog in one of the back rooms."

Heather found Brown Sugar trying to wedge herself under the bed in the smaller of the two bedrooms and closed the door. *What's the point? She sure isn't about to get near Devin, unless I force her.*

"No problem, she was there already," she told Devin when she returned. "Now what?"

"Open the front door. Then get out of the way and don't interfere, whatever you see. Is that clear?"

She wanted to say, "No, it's not. Why can't you explain yourself instead of making me take everything on trust?" But she said instead, "I guess so."

"Not guess--give me your word, or you leave."

"All right." Grinding her teeth in frustration, she propped the door ajar and retreated to the entrance of the computer den, where she could watch without getting in Devin's way. A cool breeze swept into the house, along with the chirping of insects.

Resting his hands limply, palms up, on his knees, Devin closed his eyes and breathed in a slow, meditative rhythm.

What's he doing, self-hypnosis? Heather felt his guard drop. Enticing waves of warmth radiated from him. She caught herself edging in his direction and dug her nails into the doorjamb to keep from breaking her word. His emotional broadcast promised shelter, satisfaction, rest. Although devoid of the erotic heat he usually stirred within her, it was still nearly irresistible.

After a few minutes of this silent emanation, she heard a scraping shuffle on the porch. *That sounds like--claws?* A gray ball with a long, nude tail and pointy snout crawled in through the front door. An opossum. *So that's why he wanted the dog locked in.* Canine whimpers leaked from behind the bedroom door.

Devin opened his eyes, revealing minute flecks of crimson in the silver. He bent over, beginning a low, tuneless hum. The animal inched toward him. Heather watched its creeping progress in silent amazement. When the opossum crawled within Devin's reach, he ran the palm of his hand down its back. It flopped over on its side.

I've heard of playing possum, but that's the first time I've seen it.

Devin picked up the prey and cradled it in his arms. His brow shadowed his eyes as he lowered his mouth to the exposed abdomen.

Swallowing hard, Heather looked away from him to a pair of bronze dragon figurines on the fireplace mantle. It wasn't long before she heard Devin rise from the couch and walk toward the door. She watched him step outside with the opossum's flaccid body.

Still clutching the doorjamb, she felt as if her emotions had been shredded in a Cuisinart.

When Devin reentered and bolted the door, he gave her a long, searching stare.

"You're a vampire."

"Yes, that word is the closest approximation to what we are." With his mental shield blocking any hint of what he might be feeling, he turned toward the hallway. "Excuse me, please."

A minute later, she heard the shower running. She seized the opportunity to let Sugar out of the spare bedroom and walk her once around the yard. She then hunted up a soup bowl in the kitchen and gave the dog a drink of water. Once Sugar had finished with that, she took refuge under the table, against the wall.

Heather wandered from the kitchen into Devin's office to wait for him. Both computers displayed the same screen saver: a moonlit scene of a ruined castle, with drifting clouds and fluttering bats. *Wonder where he got that? Maybe he had it custom-made.* She knew she was focusing on trivia to distract herself from the question of why she didn't run screaming for home. As unsettling as Devin's diet was, she still found him enthralling. More important than her infatuation was pride. She had demanded the truth; how could she cower in fear from it now that she had it?

"Heather." He stood in the doorway between the office and the living room. His bare feet on the carpet had made no sound. "You're still here." His bushy eyebrows arched in apparent surprise.

She brushed the surface of his thoughts, getting no response. "What did you expect me to do, desert you? By now I ought to have better tolerance for weirdness than that."

He relaxed his barrier, radiating warmth at the same time that he opened his arms in invitation. "It's safe now," he said. "I'm not back to normal yet, but I'm not starving anymore."

With no sense of movement, she found herself snuggled against him, her arms wrapped around his waist. His hard body shuddered in her embrace. Pressing her cheek to his black satin robe, she inhaled soap and the peculiar metallic tang of his skin. He tilted her head up to give her a quick kiss, as if he still didn't trust himself. She tasted mint toothpaste.

"God, I've been aching to do that for so long."

"Me, too," she whispered into the fabric of the robe. "Why did you stop?"

"We have to talk. I promised not to take advantage of you again, and I won't."

He led her to the couch, where they sat close, his arm around her shoulder, her knees tucked up so that she reclined against him.

"You know I'm not a demonic entity or an escapee from a coffin, don't you?"

"I understand that much. You're a different species."

He nodded. "Quite so. Can you accept that?"

"I'm trying. It'll take me a while to get used to--" She gestured toward the door.

With no trace of humor except around the eyes, he said, "What? You have ethical objections to hunting?"

Laughing, she started to punch him in the arm but remembered his wound in time. "You know darn well what I mean. Most people hunt for trophies or meat."

"Broaden your mind, my dear. Blood is used as an ingredient in many ethnic cuisines. Haven't you heard of black pudding? Blood sausage?"

"Well, yes, but--"

"Victorian ladies and gentlemen often visited the slaughterhouses for a dose of beef blood, because they believed it was good for the health and complexion. The Masai warriors of Africa imbibe the blood as well as the milk of their cattle."

"All right, I get the point! I guess from a certain angle, it's no worse than raw oysters--which I can't stand, either."

"Instead you eat burned animal flesh." He shook his head. "No accounting for taste."

"What about human blood? You can't expect me to accept that so easily."

"Granted, that's a little more complicated." He absently rubbed her shoulder as he continued. "Animal blood and milk provide bulk nourishment, but we can't thrive on that alone. We have to feed on live human donors at regular intervals. The amounts need not be large, but without the psychic energy we absorb with the vital fluid, we would sicken physically and disintegrate emotionally."

"Regular intervals? Like how often?" She remembered his frequent visits to her bed during that dream-haunted summer.

"Normally, at least twice a week. Four days of abstinence is pushing it. But I know a few of our people in long-term relationships who stretch it to five or six days. Otherwise the human partner's health couldn't stand it."

Heather sat up straight. "So that's what I am to you, dessert?"

He gently pulled her back into the circle of his embrace. "Much more than that, sweet Heather. Pamela was dessert. You are a necessity."

"You probably say that to all the women. What *about* Pam? She said you hurt her."

He sighed. "I can't understand why she remembered even the vague bits she did, much less why she got fixated on me. That happens sometimes. I did my best to discourage her. As for the two occasions when I fed on her, I can assure you that she thoroughly enjoyed it."

The words sounded so smug that she felt like slapping him.

He winced as if she actually had. "Please, Heather. Your anger stings. I'm not gloating, simply stating a fact. That's our survival mechanism, to keep the prey coming back for more."

"And if we--" She couldn't manage the phrase "fall in love", not with her brain a buzzing hive of confusion. "If we stay together, I'm supposed to sleep alone while you flit around seducing other women?"

"No." He squeezed her so hard that she gasped. "Sorry. I have no desire to drink from anyone else. In fact, I can't. I'm addicted to you."

She looked up at him, her head on his chest. "Addicted?"

"I've dreaded explaining this part." He paused as if groping for words. "It's a real, physical phenomenon, a biochemical addiction. It tends to develop whenever we return over and over to the same donor. With you and me, it's even stronger because we're bonded."

"You've said that before. What, exactly, does it mean?"

"My people sense the emotions of others; that follows naturally from our need to absorb emotional energy--which we can do to a limited extent without drawing blood, the way I did a little while ago, from you. When we bond with someone, though--whether human or our own kind--we can read thoughts, communicate telepathically."

She felt his hesitation--embarrassment?

"We create the bond by mutual blood-sharing."

She had to mull that over for a few seconds before she realized what "sharing" meant. "Wait a minute, are you saying I've drunk your blood?"

"Well--yes. I had you taste it for the first time the summer we met. Even after a few encounters, I couldn't bear to leave you without forging a link between us."

"Devin, you--" She felt as if tiny explosions were detonating behind her eyes. "What else did you do to me that I don't know about?"

"Heather, please don't." He rubbed the nape of her neck until she succumbed to the ripples of warmth and relaxed against him again. "We both enjoyed it."

"That's no excuse. You can't treat people like puppets. You have to start thinking in moral terms."

"You mean human terms, don't you? Perish the thought." He laughed quietly. "I'm not human; you may as well get used to the fact. I can't risk my survival to obey the rules of your species. I do have ethics, but they aren't the same as yours." He sounded completely serious now. "I have promised not to lie to you or manipulate you any longer, and I'm keeping that promise."

"So if you treat me with respect, it doesn't matter what you do to other people?" She had to keep cudgeling her brain with the fact of his morally dubious behavior. Her body and emotions wanted to melt into his arms and forget the rest of the world. "Who else have you bonded with?"

"My younger brother, Brendan, and Uncle Roderick, our adviser. As for human companions, before you there was only Judith. I experienced her fear and hurt when they arrested and tortured her. She thought I'd deserted her."

"Oh, Devin--" Heather reached up to touch his face. He turned to kiss her palm, setting off sparks along her nerves.

"The superstitious idiots buried her at a crossroads with a stake through her heart. If only I *could* have raised her from the dead!" He sighed. "As I said, I was very young. I had no idea what agony could result from entering into the emotions and senses of an ephemeral."

"You said you weren't in love with her, so why did you do it?"

"Bond with her? Because I'd heard that it produced ecstatic passion beyond imagining."

"Was that true?"

He said with a weak chuckle, "Yes, indeed. It never occurred to me that all the negative emotions would be transmitted with equal strength. Human youths have no monopoly on recklessness and libido-driven stupidity." His lips touched her forehead like a hot ember. "Nor how the bond would intensify the addiction, so that losing her tore me apart. I vowed I would never go through that again. Until you."

Heather didn't want to know, but she had to ask. "If we're chemically addicted to each other, how can I be sure my feelings for you are real?"

"I wish you'd ask easier questions, my dear." He hugged her closer to his side. "How can I answer that when my judgment is as clouded as yours, maybe more so? But I can say one thing--normally, one would expect the magnetism between us to have faded years ago. Time and distance should have extinguished the dependence. Since it still exists, I like to think it's genuine emotion, not biochemistry."

I want to think so, too. She knew she ought to resist the conclusion purely because it harmonized so well with her desire. But she was tired of fighting for one night. "Let's take that as a working assumption," she said.

Devin gently turned her in his arms and nuzzled her hair. They both flinched when the phone rang. He growled a curse, freezing through the four rings until the answering machine picked up.

Heather heard a man's voice shouting on the other end before the beep had barely sounded: "MacAvoy, if you're there, pick up! You're half an hour late, damn it!"

"Oh, God, it's Oakes, at the lodge. I forgot to call in."

"Gee, I wonder why?" She felt a sudden chill when Devin disentwined himself from her to go to the phone in the office.

Picking up the receiver, he cut off the manager in mid-rant. "Sorry for the inconvenience. I'm sick, and I've been asleep most of the day. Would've called earlier, but I just woke up." After listening for a half minute or so, he added, "Yeah, the fever medication put me out like a light. I should be okay by tomorrow, though." After another minute or two, he murmured a good-bye and returned to the couch.

"He was mad, huh?" said Heather, rather enjoying the spectacle of Devin caught off guard.

"Not once I gave him a reasonable explanation--which fortuitously even happens to be true, more or less." Devin let his head loll on the back of the sofa, his eyes shut, as if walking across the room had revived his pain.

"I hate to think how he'd react if he knew what kind of medication you take."

"Considering that this is the first night I've missed due to illness during the sixteen years I've performed there, he can hardly make a fuss about it."

"Sixteen years." Heather shook her head. She felt as befogged as if this were the middle of the night instead of only eight-thirty. Certainly she'd already gone through enough upheaval for an entire night. "Unless my memory is distorted, you haven't changed since I first met you. You don't look anywhere near as old as you claim. Isn't hanging around one place that long dangerous?"

"Could be, but I'm careful." He opened his eyes and resettled in their earlier cuddling position. "I can age my physical appearance when it becomes necessary. So far, I haven't deemed it essential. Cosmetic age doesn't vary as radically for men as for women, and anyway, few people see me up close--only Oakes and some of the other lodge staff. The audiences view me under stage lights. And people expect performers to do vain things like dye their hair."

"Ted has some suspicions about you." The outside world just wouldn't leave her alone, as much as she yearned to forget about Devin's not-quite-human "ethics" and their consequences.

"No wonder, with the way his sister acted. He's only one man, though; I can handle him. And now that Pamela has tried to murder me, I doubt he'll pay much attention to any accusations she'll make. She's obviously mentally unstable, or so he'll think."

"I don't know about that." Heather wondered what it said for her morals, that she worried more about Devin being exposed than about the way he'd treated Pam. "She's his sister, after all. He might think her shooting you was justified. Blood is thicker than water." She winced as she heard herself blurt out that cliché.

Devin groaned softly. "Please, no puns. I can't take them in this condition."

"It wasn't intentional." She reached up to rub the back of his neck. "You're still hurting, aren't you?" She hardly needed to ask, for a nagging ache oozed around the edges of his lightly-held mental shield. "Don't waste energy trying to hide it from me."

Taking her at her word, he dropped the barrier altogether. An eddy of pain/thirst/emptiness washed over her, like high tide submerging a sand bar. Fighting to keep afloat, she felt sharp tuggings in her breast and diaphragm. She yearned to fill that void in him. *What is this, some kind of test?* She visualized herself stepping back from him, untangling herself from the net of his craving.

You don't have to overwhelm me, she told him. *I want to help you already, without that.* The feeble word "help" scarcely covered what she wanted to do for him. The need to satisfy him constituted a hunger in itself.

The tide receded a fraction. "You're very strong, Heather." He removed her hand from the nape of his neck. "Yes, I still need you badly. I can't control it very well--I didn't *mean* to override your will. It's a reflex." His gleaming eyes met hers, but without compulsion. "You see the problem we face? It's terribly hard to separate genuine emotion from physical need."

"I don't quite understand the...urgency. You had a lot to drink already." It would be a while before she would feel comfortable discussing his appetite without euphemisms.

He sighed heavily. "I tried to explain that. Live human blood and the life-force that flows with it is the only thing that can completely satisfy me--or complete the healing. That's why I couldn't just get into the car, drive to the lodge, and put on my usual performance."

Heather's mind boggled at the thought. By rights, he shouldn't even be able to sit up; he should be hooked to monitors in an intensive care unit. He acted so nearly normal that she kept forgetting he'd been shot in the chest less than two hours before. "You said the--the amount doesn't have to be large?"

Am I considering offering him my blood? she thought. *Well, why not? Classic case of locking the barn door too late--heaven knows how many tastes he's already had.*

"No, but that small amount is vital to me. And I can't take from anyone else. I'm fixated on you."

In a sense, he's in my power, she thought. If he kept his vow not to force himself on her, he remained at the mercy of her decision. With that thought, a cramp wrenched her stomach. *I can't reject him. I need it almost as much as he does!*

She lightly touched his cheek to turn his head so that their gazes locked again. She felt him tense in resistance. "Don't," she said softly. "I'm not teasing. I'm ready for you."

Once again the whirlpool of need swirled around her. Clinging to him as her only support, she felt his arms wrap her in a cocoon of heat. She heard/felt a pounding like the vibrations from a heavily amplified bass guitar, reverberating from her feet up through all her internal organs--the thunder of his heartbeat in sync with her own. His lips seared her throat.

Chapter 10

Blinded by an iridescent scarlet mist, she felt her essence pouring out of her like a pent-up river cascading over the ruins of a broken dam. *I'm drowning!* Yet the thought didn't terrify her. She willed the torrent of life-force to flow on and on and on.

When the fog melted from her vision, she found herself supine on the couch, with Devin's weight pinning her down. His fingertips gently pressed the side of her neck.

"Sweet Heather, you frighten me." His voice trembled.

She could barely whisper a retort. "Isn't that supposed to work the other way around?"

"You've wrecked my self-control."

"I don't care." Involuntarily her hips arched against him, straining to intensify the contact between their bodies.

"I do. I didn't mean to submerge your senses. I want you fully aware." He eased his weight off her, lightly kissing her throat as he withdrew. "We can take our time about this, and in decent comfort." Before she could catch her breath, he cradled her in his arms and strode down the hall so fast the walls seemed to spin around her.

Beside the bed he paused, his face close to hers. "What just happened makes me afraid for you. I have to restrain myself. Use some of that peculiar human strength of yours, and stop me. I don't want to annihilate your consciousness again."

She rubbed her cheek against his smooth black robe. "I don't think I could stop you. I wouldn't want to."

"Then we must restrain each other." First bending to flip back the covers, he laid her on the bed.

Somewhere in the process of walking the dog, she had shed her jacket. Now she pulled off her shoes and socks while watching him turn on a small lamp on the dresser. It took her a second to identify the muted, otherworldly illumination as emanating from a blue light bulb. "You can see in the dark, can't you?"

"You can't," he said. "I told you, I want your full awareness."

"Don't worry, I don't plan to miss a thing." She squirmed on the satin sheets, cool against the feverish skin of her arms and legs.

He closed the bedroom door and sat beside her on the mattress, his left arm reaching across her to support his weight, while he bent over to smooth her hair with his right hand. The dim azure glow from the lamp didn't conceal the red gleam in his eyes. "You must have bewitched me," he said. "I've never done this before--shared my bed with anyone."

Not even Judith? No, of course not, she realized; Devin had visited the maiden's home, not vice versa. "What about female vampires?"

"Never. In fact, if you're jealous--dare I hope so?--I've never mated. After all, I'm not quite four centuries old. Females prefer older sires for their offspring, if possible."

"You're a virgin?" She blushed at her own tactlessness.

Laughing, he said, "It's not that uncommon. We seldom breed. Our women freely choose their mates, and only a few of the males ever get chosen. Since a male becomes fertile and potent only in the presence of a female in estrus, the rest of us don't miss what we've never had."

"But you're--" She trailed off in confusion, unable to think of a graceful way to ask how he'd become such an irresistible seducer.

He caught her meaning without words. "Reproductive sex holds little importance for us. We don't marry; the father's role is purely genetic, so we don't need to form long-term ties. Our erotic drives focus on blood--with the life-force it carries, it fulfills all our hungers, not just the appetite for bodily nourishment."

"The blood is the life."

"Your scriptures got that right," he said, "and it's much truer for us than for you. Therefore our libido is almost exclusively directed toward human targets, not our own kind. So you don't have to feel jealous." He planted a light kiss on her forehead. "No female of my own species will ever rival you."

"I'm not jealous." She shifted restlessly on the slippery sheets, wishing he hadn't stopped with a token kiss and fighting the urge to grab him and force the issue.

Clearly reading her mind, he caressed her jawline with his thumb and said, "Don't rush me. I've waited too many years for this." His hands skimmed down the front of her T-shirt, instantly rousing her nipples to hard peaks. She raised up momentarily to let him peel the shirt over her head and toss it aside. Since she hadn't planned on going out, she wore no bra. The caress of his eyes felt as sensual as the rhythmic stroking of his fingers. Inner heat welled up to suffuse her bare skin.

Twining her arms around his neck, she urged him toward her. His tongue teased the hollow of her throat, then danced over each of her breasts in turn, swirling around the nipples without touching them. She couldn't suppress a moan of frustration. His soft chuckle woke a flare of anger in Heather; she dug her nails into his shoulders.

"Careful," he murmured into the ticklish spot just above her waist. "I don't want to lose control again. I'm helpless against you."

"Helpless? You?" With her eyes closed and her head thrown back on the pillow, she luxuriated in her own surrender as he unzipped her shorts and discarded them, along with the panties underneath.

Yes, he silently replied. *I have never shown this much of myself to anyone. Never.*

"Neither have I," she whispered. The brief affair with her college boyfriend had consisted of hasty back-seat couplings or the snatching of a few minutes in a dorm bed while a roommate stepped out. Heather realized that never before had she let a man view her entirely naked.

Devin spoke aloud again. "With other donors, I could hold back. Not you."

She opened her eyes. "Then why don't you take this off? Equal exposure." She fumbled at the sash of his robe.

She sensed a tinge of anxiety in his thoughts. "I customarily don't. Seems superfluous. But if that's what you want--" He untied the knot for her and allowed her to slip the robe off his shoulders.

Kneeling beside her, Devin looked down at her with an almost defiant expression, as if expecting her to dislike what she saw. He was greyhound-slim but tightly muscled, not scrawny, and as far as she could tell in the weak, blue light, very pale. To her amazement, the two bullet wounds had closed to half-healed pockmarks. A light sprinkle of dark hair formed an inverted triangle on his torso, the apex trailing down below his navel. Running her fingers over his chest, she found the hair fine and silky compared to an ordinary man's. Though his skin felt cool, he shivered at her touch, as if *her* flesh were cold.

"You don't like that?" she said.

"Oh, no, I like it very much. Thirst makes my whole body hypersensitive. Anything you do to me is almost--too much." His voice dropped to a husky whisper, conveying the strain of leashing his passion.

The pleasure of exercising this power over him bubbled through her. Guided by the arrow-point of hair, she let her eyes trail lower. Her blush deepened, but she squelched her shyness and followed her gaze with touch. He shuddered again when her fingers curled around his shaft. Though more slender than she'd expected, it stirred and sharpened to a dart in her grasp.

"I thought you said you didn't get aroused this way."

"I can't become fully erect or...consummate...the act as you would normally expect. That doesn't mean I can't enjoy this." A moan escaped from his lips. "But I told you, it isn't any one spot--what you'd call an erogenous zone. It's *everything*." He clasped her free hand and opened his, palm up.

In response to the wordless invitation, Heather traced his palm with her fingertips. Fascinated, she smoothed the delicate hairs in the center, then felt them bristle like a cat's fur under her caress.

Devin gasped. "Easy." His hand closed around hers, and he raised it to kiss the inside of her wrist. "They're like miniature antennae, designed to react to heat and magnetism. They're also extremely sensitive to light touch--to what you were just doing."

"*That's* an erogenous zone for you?" *Hey, this has possibilities*, she thought. An image of teasing him that way in the middle of a crowded room stirred a delicious flutter in the pit of her stomach.

"You'd torture me that way? You wouldn't dare!" With a mock growl, he nuzzled her neck. "God, you taste wonderful!"

Her stomach clenched with desire. "Then what are you waiting for?"

"I want to give you ecstasy. I need that, for my own satisfaction." His hand swept down her body to the hot, molten center. Writhing and arching her back to meet him, she retaliated by stroking his half-erect shaft.

With her eyes closed, in a whirlwind of sensation, she felt him bend over her, felt his breath on her neck and bosom. His tongue flicked first one nipple, then the other, while his fingers explored her inner softness. She cried aloud when he found the focus of her need and caressed her with as much certainty of aim as if he'd been inside her, sharing each pulse of her excitement. *But he is, isn't he?* a voice whispered from the heart of her arousal.

Convulsions radiated from her core to every inch of her body, while a painless sting pierced her throat, followed by the swirl of his tongue tasting her, urging her to an ever-higher pitch of frenzy.

His hands moved to her shoulders, and without breaking off the exquisitely tender lapping at her neck, he shifted position to lie on top of her. His hardness slid into the aching hollow between her legs. His mouth caught her moans for a few seconds, before he returned to feasting on her. Momentarily she felt the heat of her flesh through his nerve endings and tasted the salt-sweetness of her own blood on his lips, shared the warmth that spread through his vitals as he drank.

A long time later, she spiraled down to normal consciousness. The bed seemed to rock. She felt the way she had in childhood when, after hours in the surf at the beach, the waves still seemed to pound her when she tried to sleep that night.

Devin lay upon her, his mouth still touching her throat. She sensed his reluctance as he drew back, pressing gently on the spot to staunch the trickle of blood she barely felt.

After half-dozing for a few contented minutes, she said, "Are you...uh...okay now?"

He shook with silent laughter before answering, "Sweet Heather, do you have to ask?" He raised his head to meet her eyes.

She saw no bloodstains on his mouth, no movie-monster stigmata.

"I still need to rest, but you've basically healed me."

She fingered his parted lips. "No fangs."

He made a disgusted face. "Movie cliches! I don't need them; my incisors and canines are razor-sharp. And think how conspicuous we'd be if we looked like wolves or rattlesnakes, and how hard it would be to hide our feeding, if victims really had those silly double punctures."

Feeling for the wound at her throat, Heather couldn't find a scab, only a damp spot from his prolonged kiss.

"It's tiny," he said, "like a shaving cut. Because of the secretions in our saliva, it can't get infected, and it will heal faster than a normal incision."

"Convenient," she said. "I don't have to go around with marks for vampire-hunters to notice."

He laughed. "I trust you won't meet many of those nowadays. Anyway, if that becomes a problem, I can always choose a less visible spot." He caressed the curve of her breast. Incredibly, she reacted with a surge of arousal. Devin withdrew his hand. "Me, too--unbelievable, isn't it? But we're going to be strong and wait a while."

"Yeah, who says?" She guided his hand to her lips and tickled the fine hairs with her tongue.

He sighed with pleasure and allowed her to continue a few seconds before pulling away. "I'm trying very hard not to overdo this," he said. "The weakness you feel comes mostly from the energy drain; the volume of blood loss is negligible. But if we do it too often, it adds up." Turning on his side, he drew her head onto his shoulder. "That was a new and strange experience for me. Almost frightening, the way I enjoyed it so much."

"Not so different from any other man--scared of commitment." She only half teased. How far could she trust his fidelity, once the novelty wore off? True, he'd spoken about "addiction", but could she accept that as a substitute for love?

"My dear, you don't grasp the extent of it. I hardly know what commitment *is*. It's not part of our culture. All I know about love, I picked up from your songs and stories."

"That *is* pretty scary." Much as she wanted to reach an honest understanding with him, she almost wished he hadn't shadowed their pleasure with that statement.

"Heather, I'll do my best. You must correct me when I go wrong. My only models for relating to donors consist of 'victim' and 'pet'. You're the first human friend I've ever had." He shook his head with an ironic smile. "And most of my people would think I'd lost my mind, to make friends with a donor at all."

She relaxed and snuggled into the curve of his arm. On reflection, she had to admit his honest bewilderment held more promise than the slick lines she'd too often heard from human males.

Heather woke three hours later, by the digital clock, surprised to realize she'd slept at all. *Deep down, I guess I do trust him.* Reclining on one elbow, she gazed at Devin, who opened his eyes as soon as she moved.

"I've been asleep, too," he said. "That never happens in the middle of the night, unless I'm exhausted, like now--but never with an ephemeral in the room!"

"So you do sleep during the day. What, no coffin?"

He grinned up at her. "No, but the day-sleep--suspended animation--does look remarkably like death to the untrained eye. I wasn't asleep that deeply, just dozing." He sat up. "You're hungry, aren't you? And you need fluids." He left the bed and gathered some clothes from drawers. "I don't keep much food around, but I can find something for you."

She hugged her knees, staring bemused at the blue light and listening to water running in the bathroom. When she heard Devin walking into the kitchen, she collected her own clothes and snatched a quick shower before dressing. She wished she had something clean to put on instead of the wrinkled shorts and T-shirt.

Entering the kitchen, she found Devin spooning vanilla ice cream into a bowl, while Brown Sugar still cowered under the table, whimpering and trying to merge with the wallpaper.

Heather crouched down and rubbed the dog's bristling fur. "Oh, gosh, I forgot all about you. Bet you want to go out, right, girl?" Sensing Devin's eyes on her, she shot an accusing look at him. "She's scared to death of you."

"Yes, and I can't let it continue. Move over."

When Heather got out of the way, he knelt by the table and stretched one hand toward the dog. Motionless except for the vibration of his parted lips, he crooned a wordless hum.

Heather watched Sugar's pelt smooth down. The half-aggressive, half-fearful whine ceased, and the dog inched away from the wall. Her jaws went slack, allowing her tongue to loll in the canine "smile" of greeting.

"That's right," Devin murmured. "Come out, I won't hurt you." He resumed his tuneless lullaby. Sugar crept on her belly from her corner to Devin's hand. He tousled her ears and massaged her neck until she let out a gusty sigh and laid her head on his lap. "Good girl," he said. "I won't hurt you or your lady. I'm a friend." He eased away from the dog and stood up. "There, that should do it."

Heather blinked. Despite the shower, she didn't feel quite awake. "Well--sure. Guess I'd better take her out." Hooking on the leash, she walked Sugar twice around the cabin. Reentering the kitchen, they found a bowl of milk on the floor. Sugar slurped it down, then curled up for a nap with apparent unconcern.

Devin had the ice cream and a glass of orange juice waiting for Heather on the redwood table. "I don't encourage people to drop in," he said, "but once in a while someone on the lodge staff does, and it would look odd if I never offered refreshments. And I like ice cream myself sometimes--but not now." He flashed a rakish smile that hinted at why he didn't need any more dessert.

Blushing, Heather picked up her spoon. "I thought you didn't eat food."

"I can consume liquids," he said, "though most of them don't do me any good. Things like gelatin and ice cream are liquids, in a sense--that helps when I get stuck with a dinner invitation I can't turn down. And I do get nourishment from milk." He had poured himself a glass, which he sipped while watching Heather eat.

"What we just did," she said, irritably sensing his amusement at the way she groped for words. "We did that when I was eighteen, when I thought I was dreaming?"

"Not like *that*, dear one. It's incredibly different when you're fully aware of me." He reached across the table to squeeze her hand. "So much better--I had no idea."

"But it couldn't all have been real. Some of it had to be just dreams, fantasies. Zorro and Lancelot and all that."

"I drew upon whatever scenes would please and excite you the most," he said. "Manipulative--that's what you're thinking, isn't it? Well, yes, but I also aimed to enhance your pleasure."

"You did that, all right." *Good grief, why can't I quit blushing?* "I remember flying. In fact, I dreamed that again recently. Now, that can't have been real-- unless you're holding out on me. You can't turn into a bat, can you?"

"Certainly not. Where do you think the extra mass would go?"

What little she knew of nuclear physics made Heather cringe at the thought.

"However," Devin went on, "we can fly, in a sense. Levitate, actually--even though our bones are a bit lighter than yours, true flight is impossible for a human-size creature. And we do transform into a winged entity. The wings are needed for gliding and steering."

"A giant bat?" Heather rubbed her eyes. "That's even weirder."

"Our scholars believe it's an ancestral form imprinted on the DNA, a shape we discarded as we evolved to mimic your species in every outward respect. One of our psychic gifts involves resuming that shape. The older we grow, the better we can do it, and the longer we can maintain it."

She swallowed a cold lump of ice cream, chasing it with a gulp of juice. "Show me. I'm tired of blundering around in a fog about what's real and what's not."

He finished his milk and gazed thoughtfully at her. "What the observer sees depends a great deal on what he or she expects to see. We can project illusions of whatever monstrous shape we want to assume. But yes, I can show you--without clouding your mind."

Her eyes challenged him. "No illusions."

"No. You'll see only what physically exists."

They cleared the dishes into the sink. "Shall we use the living room?" he said. "More open space there."

"You mean you aren't going to fly with me?"

That remark evoked a rueful laugh. "You flatter me, little one. I'm not Superman. Thanks to you, I've recovered most of my strength, but I'm not up to *that*." His amusement faded. "Anyway, considering what happened a few hours ago, I think I'd better keep my transformations behind locked doors tonight."

Following him into the living room, Heather wished he hadn't brought up Pam's attack. She had temporarily forgotten about it and had no desire to remember. The unease soon faded, however, in the pleasure of watching him move chairs to the edge of the room and strip off his shirt.

"I'm not old enough to include clothing in the change, as a rule. I can manage it briefly, with deep concentration, but it's so much trouble I don't bother. The elders have the ability to shapeshift garments as if they were part of the skin--I'm a long way from that."

Assuming a stance in the middle of the rug, he held both of her hands. "Watch closely," he said. "I'm not mesmerizing you. This is a physical transmutation."

Electricity tingled from his cool fingers up her arms, making her hair bristle, like static on a cold, dry day. Violet sparks danced over his chest and shoulders. His eyes glowed red. She saw a shadow spreading down his cheeks and torso, a black velvet growth. *Fur!* she thought. He had a sleek covering of ebony fur.

His ears elongated to points. At the same moment, a pair of pale green wings blossomed from his back. When he smiled at her astonishment, she saw pointed teeth.

"Your mouth--" She brushed his lips with hesitant fingers.

He nipped her without breaking the skin. "This is the only time after childhood that we actually have fangs." He drew her into a close embrace, his lean body hard against hers.

The floor melted from beneath her bare feet. A giddy floating sensation possessed her. She glanced down. *Oh, God, I am floating!* She clung to Devin in a spasm of panic.

His warm breath stirred her hair. "You're perfectly safe."

Together they drifted toward the ceiling. She risked another look down. At least three feet separated her from the rug. *We really are levitating!*

Devin spun in a slow circle, making her lightheaded. Gradually he floated down again, while she hugged him so tightly her arms ached. "When I was much younger, I wouldn't have had the power to lift you as well as myself. I'm glad I can do it now."

She burrowed her face into his shoulder, feeling as if she'd just stepped off a Ferris wheel. "You actually flew with me, back then, didn't you?"

The wings draped around him like a cloak. "A few times. More often, I let you share my sensations while I hunted from above the trees."

She looked up into his eyes. "Sounds like an awful risk. Somebody could have seen you."

"I stayed away from populated areas. The few people who might be roaming the woods at night never noticed me. We can make ourselves--well, not literally invisible, but unnoticeable."

She didn't want to pursue that comment. *Too many impossible things in one night.* Instead, she reached up to finger the curve of a wing. Veined like a dragonfly's wing, it felt as light as parachute silk. The delicate membrane quivered like a leaf in a breeze.

"Careful," he whispered. "In this state, with my cells in flux, I'm extremely sensitive."

"It doesn't hurt, does it?" She couldn't resist stroking the satiny surface.

"You could very easily hurt me there," he said, "but this doesn't. Quite the opposite." With a sigh, he kissed her ear, teasing the lobe with his lips and tongue. His skin felt hotter than usual.

Answering the unspoken question, he said, "The change generates energy. Ah, Heather, you'll have to stop that." But he made no move to retreat from her caresses. His mounting excitement tingled through her own body.

"Please, Devin--" She sank her teeth into his neck.

"Yes--" He lifted his right hand to his mouth and bit his wrist.

She saw and felt his shape melting back to fully human form, just as he pressed his wrist to her lips.

In response to his silent urging, she sucked the tiny cut. The blood had no particular taste, only a faint saltiness, but the surge of energy that pulsed between them made her head whirl with rapture. She felt as if he caressed her from the inside out. The pressure built unbearably, then exploded.

She came to on the couch, reclining in Devin's arms. "That was--incredible." Her voice shook.

"That is how our bond was formed and nurtured, by the mutual sharing of life-force." He sounded no steadier than she felt. "I'd forgotten how--cataclysmic--it can be." He sat up part way, shifting Heather to a more comfortable position. "Now do you grasp what I've been trying to tell you? We have to be very cautious. It would be all too easy to get swept away. I can't bear to think of endangering you like that."

"We'll manage," she murmured, her lips brushing his chest. "We have to." She couldn't stand the thought of giving up that ecstatic experience. *Is this what he means by addiction?*

"The only way we can hope for any restraint," he said, "is to stop lingering in these tempting situations." He got up, tugging her unwillingly to her feet. "We have to distract ourselves with an activity that's a little less...incendiary."

"Oh, all right." She ran her fingers through her tangled hair. "Like what?"

"You wanted to try out my new game, didn't you?" He took her into the office, where he booted up the rough version of his latest design. After watching the introductory material and his demonstration of "Maze of the Morlocks", she walked through a few scenarios herself. With Devin to extricate her from the unavoidable wrong turns and dead ends, she enjoyed the program without the usual frustrations of learning an unfamiliar game.

"I have a lot of bugs to work out, as you notice," he said when they got tired of exploring the maze. "The encounter with the Riddle Robot doesn't play as well as I hoped."

While he turned off the computer and put away the disk, she scanned some of the shelves. Several of the CDs had Devin's name on the labels. "I didn't have any idea you recorded professionally."

"Semi-professionally, at most. I sell them at clubs and by mail order. It's not as if I have a huge fan following."

She picked one off the shelf. "Mountain Memories, by Devin MacAvoy," she read aloud.

"That's basically the same material you hear at the lodge--or the more serious ballads, anyhow. It has a companion tape featuring the humorous pieces and children's songs. I also have albums of my other repertoires. Take one of each home with you--it's a small gift, after what you've given me tonight." Standing behind Heather, he reached over her shoulder to pick out two more dics. "This one includes the traditional carols I perform for the holiday season. And this--well, I play these in bars and pubs with a more adult orientation."

"Merry Jests and Bawdy Choruses," she read. "Devin, you sing dirty songs?" She giggled at the image.

"Not dirty," he said. "Bawdy. PG-13, suggestive--no four-letter words or anatomically accurate terminology. Not that I could ever grasp this human obsession with reproduction, not to mention the peculiar patchwork of standards about what's polite and what's taboo. If you're going to talk about the subject at all, why shroud it in euphemisms?"

Heather had trouble imagining a race of people for whom sex was less emotionally loaded than eating. She studied the titles on the label. "'The Cuckoo's Nest'? Does that mean what I think?"

"Sure. Freud didn't invent sexual symbolism. It goes back to the Middle Ages and probably back to the beginning of language. 'The Blacksmith', 'The Coachman's Whip', 'The Threshing Machine', 'Wanting Seed'--the list goes on and on. In some audiences, I've seen it reduce strong men to helpless blushing."

"I remember this one from a Buffy Saint-Marie record Mom used to play. It's not exactly bawdy."

"'Johnny Be Fair'? Just a variation on the perennially popular theme of cuckoldry." He picked up a guitar standing in a corner--not the black Gibson he played at the lodge--strummed a few chords, and sang the concluding verse in the persona of the mother:

"Daughter, haven't I taught you to forgive and to forget?

I let your father sow his oats, e'en so you needn't fret.

Your father may be father to all the boys in town, but still

He's not the one that sired you, so marry whom you will!"

She laughed along with him as he returned the guitar to its place. "That doesn't mean a thing to you, does it? You don't have marriage, so you don't have families or incest."

"An unwarranted conclusion, my dear," Devin said, putting an arm around her shoulders and guiding her back to the living room. "The sibling bond remains important throughout life, and we depend on the mother's brother or sister, if any, for guidance." Pulling her down on the couch, he kissed the top of her head, and she snuggled closer. "As for incest, we have no rules against mating between close relatives, but the elders strictly enforce the rule against not producing offspring that way. Our gene pool is dangerously small as it is; we can't afford inbreeding."

Heather stifled a yawn. *Good grief, what time is it, anyway?*

Hesitantly, not wanting to tread on sensitive ground, she asked, "Your mother--is she really dead?" At his affirmative murmur, she said, "How? If you don't mind telling me? I mean, you don't get sick or old, do you? And from the way you healed, you're hard to kill."

"That's true." He sighed. "She died in a traffic accident when Brendan--my brother--was seven. She was driving a sports car, and a semi totaled it at freeway speed. Her skull was crushed. Destruction of the brain kills us as quickly as anybody else."

"I'm sorry." The lame condolence was all she could think of to say.

He rubbed the nape of her neck under the tousled hair. "Enough of this. You need to sleep, and I don't want to send you to bed with nightmares. Come on."

He picked her up, evoking a squeal of pleasure from her, but if she hoped for a repeat of the earlier part of the night, she had to accept disappointment. He did deposit her on the bed and help her out of her clothes, but instead of lying down with her, he pulled up the covers and turned off the light.

"You rest. I'm staying up until it gets closer to morning." He kissed her lightly on the lips.

A minute later, she heard one of his ballads playing on the stereo, accompanied by the beep of a computer switching on. She drifted into sleep, wondering how she could feel so secure here.

The weak light of dawn, filtered through thick drapes but still perceptible, woke Heather. She rolled over to find Devin asleep beside her.

As far as she could see, with the sheet pulled up to the middle of his chest, he slept naked. She rested tentative fingers on his breastbone. He felt as cold as marble and didn't react to her touch in any way. His chest didn't rise or fall with inhalation and exhalation. She probed the side of his neck and found no more hint of a pulse than she'd felt the previous night, after he'd been shot.

Her heart leaped with alarm. Then, remembering something he'd said about "day-sleep", she drew a long breath to calm herself. He'd mentioned suspended animation. Hearing about it wasn't nearly as great a shock as seeing it. A glance at the clock showed it was five-seventeen a.m., which qualified as day by some people's standards.

Heather visited the bathroom, took the dog out as far as the sidewalk, then returned to the bedroom and lay down to sleep again.

A sound from outside roused her a short while later. It took her a minute to wake up enough to recognize the noise as a car pulling into the driveway. *Who would come to visit Devin at dawn?* She checked the clock, which now read a little after six. Scrambling back into her rumpled clothes, she hurried to the living room and twitched aside the heavy curtain over the picture window.

A car marked "Sheriff" sat in the driveway behind the van. Ted sat at the wheel of a green sedan parked under a tree in the lane; though the early-morning shadows made him difficult to discern, Heather thought she recognized Ted's father in the passenger seat.

Heather rushed back to the bedroom and shook Devin. His eyes flew open, and he grabbed both her wrists painfully hard. An inarticulate snarl burst from his lips.

She involuntarily tried to pull away, then relaxed when his eyes lost their feral glare and focused on her.

"Damn it, Heather," he said, "what did you do that for? I might have hurt you."

She drew a tremulous breath. "There's a police car out front."

Devin sat up, then bent over to rest his head in his hands. "What the devil--" He swung his legs over the side of the mattress, swaying as if dizzy.

"Devin, are you all right?"

"Just the shock of getting yanked back to life, so to speak. I'll be fine." He slowly stood up. "If you could get me a glass of milk? And coffee would help--very strong, please."

She scurried to the kitchen to follow his instructions. *What does he mean by strong?* She decided to double the amount she normally used per cup. As she filled the coffeemaker, the front door knocker reverberated. "Just a minute," she called.

"Is anybody home?" a male voice shouted through the door. "Open up, please--sheriff's office."

She darted into the living room to yell, "Hang on, I'll be right there," then returned to the kitchen to start the coffeemaker and pour Devin's milk. By the time she reentered the living room, Devin, in jeans and T-shirt, had drawn the drapes to admit a grudging ration of sunlight and was opening the door. She handed him his milk, from which he took a long swig.

"What can I do for you, officer?"

A short, stocky man in uniform, with brown hair meticulously combed forward over a bald spot, stepped inside, leaving the door ajar. "I'm Deputy Maslow. I called a few minutes ago but got no answer. I'm looking for Devin MacAvoy."

"Well, you found him." Devin moved over to sit on the couch, waving the deputy toward an armchair.

Deputy Maslow ignored the invitation. Standing in the middle of the room, he glanced dubiously from Devin to Heather and back again. "We received a report of a shooting, sir."

Devin said with an expression of blank innocence, "I beg your pardon?"

The deputy flipped open a notepad. "Did you receive a visit from a Pamela Gaines yesterday evening around seven?"

Heather eased herself onto the opposite end of the sofa, wondering, *What happened? Did Pam turn herself in?*

"Yes, what about it?" said Devin.

"According to Miss Gaines, she shot and severely wounded you."

The door behind him opened wider. Ted appeared, followed closely by his father. Ted gave Heather a long stare and looked away, flushing a deep red.

Heather felt herself blushing in response, although she had no reason to feel guilty about Devin in front of Ted.

Ted glared at Devin. "You look awful healthy, MacAvoy."

"What is this nonsense all about?" said Devin in a convincing imitation of an unfairly put-upon citizen.

The deputy exchanged an uneasy look with Ted's father. Fishing a set of keys out of his pocket, Maslow said, "You'd better come with me, Mr. Gaines. Your presence might help calm her."

They had to shove past Ted, who blocked the doorway. Arms folded, he scowled at Devin, who volunteered no comment.

A minute later Pam slouched in, supported on either side by her father and the deputy. Wearing a wrinkled sundress, with her hair tangled and purple shadows under her eyes, she stopped short and choked off a shriek, then stared at Devin like an avenging spirit from one of his revenant ballads. "Devin? You're supposed to be dead!"

Chapter 11

Pam swayed like a sapling in a high wind. Maslow grabbed her by the elbow and steered her to the nearest chair. "Take it easy, ma'am. It's obvious that Mr. MacAvoy isn't dead."

"But I shot him!" she wailed.

Looking discomfited, the deputy patted her hand. "Then you missed and didn't realize it. You must have been real upset."

"I *know* what happened. I felt him--he didn't have a pulse." She stared wild-eyed at Devin. "I shot you in the chest. How did you get--like this?"

Devin spread his hands in a pose of utter bewilderment. "Will someone please tell me what she's talking about?"

"You tell me," said Ted, while his father listened with a stunned expression. "What have you done to her this time?" He turned on Heather as if to blame her, too, for Pam's hysterics. "What *is* going on? Pam stayed out for hours last night--"

"I was walking in the woods," Pam interrupted. "Seeing Devin dead scared me out of my mind. I threw the gun away--I don't remember where--"

"And she came home around midnight," Ted broke in, "all dirty and scratched up from thorns and branches. She hid in her room and wouldn't say a word to us. Then, a little while ago, she woke up Dad with this story about killing MacAvoy." He glared at Heather as if waiting for an explanation.

"I have no idea," Heather said. "As you can see, Devin's fine."

Pam twisted her fingers in her lap, head down, muttering, "I couldn't stand it anymore. I had to tell somebody."

"Yes, ma'am, we understand that," the deputy said in the soothing tone used to humor someone mentally deranged. "Mr. MacAvoy, for the record, did Miss Gaines in fact shoot you?"

"Deputy, do I look as if I took a bullet in the chest last night?"

Clever answer, Heather thought with a touch of acid. *He didn't even have to lie.* Little as she wanted Devin's inhuman powers exposed, she felt sorry for Pam, forced to doubt her own sanity.

"No, sir," said the officer, deadpan. "Did this young lady threaten you with a firearm at all?"

"Certainly not. We argued, I admit, but then she left without further incident."

"Then you don't wish to press charges against her?"

"No, why would I?"

The older Mr. Gaines visibly relaxed, doubtless relieved that his daughter wasn't a murderess. But his face plainly showed his sadness and confusion as he crouched beside her chair. "Let's go home, honey. Everything's going to be all right."

"But, Dad, I know what I saw!" Nevertheless, she let her father take her hand and help her up.

"Don't worry," he said, "we'll work it out. We'll get you some help."

Devin stood up, too, the courteous host ready to show his visitors out. "That's a good idea, Mr. Gaines. You'd better take both your children home."

Ted's frown showed that he hadn't missed the insult. He glowered at Devin and Heather in turn, evidently still more than half convinced that one or both of them had caused Pam's delusions. "MacAvoy, I'm not sure this is finished." He stomped out of the room.

Mr. Gaines guided Pam to the door. He paused to cast Devin an apologetic look. "I'm sorry about this."

"Me, too," Maslow said, pocketing his notepad. "I won't waste any more of your time, Mr. MacAvoy."

They all walked out, and Devin bolted the door behind them. Only after both cars started their engines and drove away did he return to the couch. He leaned back with his eyes shut. "Good Lord, I never expected that. No accounting for the effects of a guilty conscience."

"Now everybody thinks she's crazy," Heather said, haunted by the image of Pam's tear-streaked face. "She thinks so herself."

"At least that means if she comes up with any more wild tales about me, nobody will listen." He opened his eyes. "Look, my dear, that may sound callous, but after all, she did try to kill me."

"Yeah. As healthy as you look now, that's hard to remember."

"What I hope," he said, "is that her father will follow through on sending her back to Richmond, preferably to a psychologist. She hinted at that last night." He glanced toward the kitchen, inhaling the aroma drifting through the house. "I think that coffee may be ready."

Hearing the fatigue in his voice, Heather hunted up a pair of mugs and poured them each a cup of coffee, which they drank on the couch. She could tell from the aroma alone that it had turned out "strong", as he'd requested. She consumed hers in tiny sips, grimacing. Though she didn't use sugar, for this brew she could almost make an exception.

"Not bad," Devin said. "I have a feeling I'd better not sleep too deeply today."

"Coffee affects you?"

"Most drugs either have no effect or make us sick," he said. "Caffeine and alcohol do work, if ingested in quantities far greater than most ephemerals need for the same result. Even so, if I overdo either one, my body will reject it." He grinned. "Sometimes I find it very inconvenient to have trouble getting drunk."

The subject of drinking reminded her of the bags in his freezer. "I've been wondering--where do you get your...provisions?"

"I don't steal it, if that's what you're thinking. Not exactly, anyway." He draped his arm around her shoulders. "Blood banks, like supermarkets, use expiration dates with a generous margin of safety. I bribe employees to divert supplies that would be discarded anyway. None of my contacts know my name or why I want the stuff."

They probably imagine he's into satanic rituals, she thought. The mundane explanation reassured her, though. *Viewed from the right angle, it's not much different from any other restricted diet or special medical need.*

He gulped half his coffee, set down the mug, and said, "Now I think you'd better go home. It's been a strenuous night."

She flushed, from annoyance as well as embarrassment. "There you go again. I don't want to leave you. Suppose Pam gets away from her keepers and decides to come back?"

Devin smiled wryly. "And what would you do, throw yourself in front of the bullets?"

Heather mumbled into her coffee, "Well, I could talk to her."

"That's moot, because she won't be here. Her father and brother won't let her out of their sight." He stood up and loomed over her with arms folded. "I'm much more concerned about Ted reappearing to finish that conversation. His last words were practically a threat."

"You're still trying to protect me!"

He started to make a grab for her, then ran one hand roughly through his hair instead. "You exasperating female, what the devil is wrong with that?"

"You act like you think I can't take care of myself. You're treating me like a kid--or a pet."

"I told you, I do not think of you as a pet!" He clenched his jaws together as if fighting the impulse to take a bite out of her.

She stood up and planted both hands on his chest. "Then why are you making such a fuss about having me hang around?"

His fingers dug into her shoulders. "Ordinary caution is not overprotectiveness. I simply want to keep you out of the way until I'm sure Ted's given up any thought of striking at either of us."

"I understand how you could feel that way. Personally, I don't think Ted would ever hurt me, but you don't know him that well."

Devin relaxed his grip. "Then you'll go home until it's safe?"

"Not on your life! I said I understood, not that I agreed." She wiggled away from him. "By that reasoning, you could keep me away indefinitely. This world is full of risks; there's always another one around the next curve. If you're so afraid of getting involved with a weak, incompetent human female who might die on you, why did you ever start this?"

His blank stare told her she had chanced on the truth. After a long silence, he grazed her cheek with the fingertips of one hand. "I started because I couldn't resist you. Given a choice, I would never make myself so vulnerable."

She wanted to hate him for the admission, but the near-sob in his voice disarmed her. She flowed into his arms, leaning on his chest and listening to the eerily slow beat of his heart.

"Little one," he rubbed the nape of her neck under her hair, "see what you've done to me." His other hand crept under the hem of her T-shirt.

She sighed with pleasure as she felt the rhythm of his heart accelerate to a gallop. Brushing hair out of her eyes, he tilted her face up and captured her mouth in a fierce kiss that made her head reel, forcing her to cling to him for fear of falling.

He pulled back, saying with a shaky laugh, "Forgive me. My people tend to a high degree of possessiveness." A crease appeared between his thick eyebrows. "Shall we start over? Let me put it this way: I would feel better if you returned home now. The choice is yours."

His tone mollified her. Maybe he really *was* trying. "Well, when you put it as a request instead of an order, that's different. No reason I can't humor you." She leashed the dog and headed for the door.

He mimed an exaggerated sigh of relief. "There, I feel better already." He walked her outside and down the driveway, lingering for another long kiss.

"Shouldn't you go in?" she said in a breathless whisper. "Isn't the sun bothering you?"

"Holding you, I hardly notice it."

The gallant fib made her pulse race.

He released her and stepped away from her car. "You had better go home, though. May I come to you tonight?"

As if I could stop him! "Sure. You know I want you to." She fumbled behind her for the door handle.

"I can't get enough of you. I've never wanted anyone the way I want--*need*--you." He reached for her once more, then flinched away as if her skin burned him. "Not now. Tonight, my love."

He disappeared into the house with a speed she still wasn't used to. Only after she'd pulled onto the road did his words sink in: "my love".

Does he mean that? And do I love him? Can I?

The telephone woke her from the nap that had been her first priority after walking and feeding the dog. Fuzzy-brained, Heather stumbled out of bed, speculating about the call. *Devin?* Not likely; why would he use the phone, even if for some reason he wasn't sleeping off the excitement of last night?

She next thought of Ted, whom she had considered calling to ask about Pam. But Heather suspected she was the last person Ted would want to communicate with, given the hostile way he'd confronted her at Devin's place.

The woman on the line was one whose voice she had never heard before. "Ms. Kincaid? I hope you'll forgive my calling out of the blue like this. My name is Britt Loren; I'm a psychiatrist in Annapolis. Devin MacAvoy asked me to speak to you."

Heather struggled to shake the cobwebs out of her skull. *Devin thinks I need to talk to a shrink? That doesn't make sense.* "You're a friend of Devin's?" The surge of jealousy that accompanied the thought jolted her awake. *Good grief, am I that nuts over him?*

"Only an acquaintance," the woman replied. "Actually, I'm in a relationship similar to your bond with Devin--have been for over twenty years."

"Twenty *years?*" Heather feared that, at her and Devin's current pace, the intensity would drain her to a wraith after twenty days. "Wait a minute. You're human, and you're in love with a--" She couldn't say the word, not to a stranger.

"One of Devin's people, yes. You see, it *can* work. Devin thought you might have some questions."

"He told you about us? Just like that, without my permission?" Heather plopped into a chair beside the desk. Her indignation evaporated quickly, when she realized what this call meant. She could finally get solid information from an objective source. "He thought it would help if I heard it from somebody else?"

"I suppose so," the woman said with a throaty chuckle. "That wasn't his first request, though. He mainly wants me to talk you into keeping your distance until he's settled this crisis he's involved in."

Oh, no, they're ganging up on me. "Dr. Loren, I'm not about to--"

"Please, call me Britt. Heather, I know perfectly well how you feel about his overprotectiveness. I deal with the same thing constantly."

"What, it's a racial characteristic?"

"I'm afraid so, and I have no intention of advising you to cater to it. Give in to that nonsense, and they'll smother you. They think we're fragile."

"Compared to them, we are, aren't we?"

"In some ways," Britt said. "Look at their disadvantages, though--the restricted diet, the way they react to the sun, their constant need to hide what they are. And Devin's dependence on you--he can't help recognizing that as a weakness."

"He talks about addiction," said Heather, twisting the phone cord around her fingers, "but it works both ways, doesn't it? I'm just as trapped as he is."

"Devin probably won't tell you this, but in a word, no."

"Huh?"

"Keep in mind that he needs you a heck of a lot more than you need him. For him, the addiction is both biochemically and emotionally exclusive; no donor except you can satisfy him. For you, the emotional attachment is exclusive, but as far as your body's need for the chemicals transmitted by a vampire's bite is concerned, any vampire would do."

"I don't want anyone else!" Heather nibbled on her lower lip while Britt waited in silence on the other end. "I think I love him. But how can I possibly know? He's so--"

"Intoxicating?" She heard a wry smile in Britt's tone. "Don't I know it. If your attraction has remained strong over all these years of separation, that suggests something deeper than chemistry."

Heather found comfort in hearing a more experienced woman echo her own thoughts. "But how can I *know*?"

"You can't, no more than you could with an ordinary man. We all take our chances in love."

Thanks a bunch, Heather thought. On the other hand, did she really expect someone she'd never met, even a psychiatrist, to read her mind long distance and straighten out her feelings when she couldn't untangle them herself? "I'm not sure I'd dare to let myself love him. He's killed people."

"He told me about that," said Britt. "He was protecting a woman he cared about, wasn't he?"

"Well, yes, but..."

After waiting a few seconds for Heather to continue, Britt said, "Suppose he did something similar for you? Saved you from a mugger or a rapist? Would you have these doubts?"

"I guess not." Heather mulled over this angle for a minute. "It's not just the action, Britt, it's his attitude. I think what bothers me is how cool he is about that kind of thing. As if he has every right to dispense his private justice."

"It's true, his people aren't human. You mustn't lull yourself into thinking they are. It's sort of like living with a domesticated tiger. If he loves you, he'll try to abide by human ethics for your sake. That's the most you can expect."

"That sounds like an awful responsibility. Are you saying I'll have to be his conscience?"

"He may see it that way," Britt said. "Don't let him con you into accepting blame for his choices, though."

Still light-headed with fatigue, Heather giggled at the image that leaped into her mind. "I really can't see myself as Jiminy Cricket."

Britt laughed, too, but quickly sobered. "Do remember what I said about his needing you more than you need him. If you decide you can't handle the relationship, break it off quickly, and get as far away from him as possible. Don't prolong the agony."

The solemn tone of the warning frightened Heather. Was Britt referring solely to Devin's potential suffering, or implying that he would resort to force? Heather decided she didn't want an answer to that. "I'll remember. Thank you for talking to me."

After hanging up, she paced around the living room, brooding over the conversation. Sugar watched this unaccustomed behavior with a troubled expression in her brown eyes.

Finally Heather returned to the desk and called the realtor, Ellie Norton. She was relieved to get the answering machine, ducking the necessity for another verbal confrontation. "Ms. Norton, I apologize for taking up your time, but I've decided not to sell the cabin after all. If I ever change my mind in the future, I'll let you know." She hung up the receiver with a euphoric sense of release.

What would Mom and Dad think about this? I'm sticking around for a man--who's not even human. Like a crisp autumn breeze, the thought swept into her mind that she didn't have to worry about her parents' hypothetical opinion. Even if they'd been alive and in the room with her, she wouldn't. *I'm grown up now. I don't have to be afraid of memories. I don't have to worry about measuring up to what they wanted from me six years ago!*

She leashed the dog and went out for a run, as buoyant as if she were four-footed and carefree, too.

After bolting the door, Devin went to his bedroom to undress. Heather's scent hovered in the air. Grazing the edge of her mind, he discovered that she, too, was preparing for a nap. The temptation to invade her dreams and share ecstasy that could do her no physical harm teased him. *Absolutely not--too distracting!* If danger approached, he couldn't risk having his brain clouded with passion.

To his amazement, the very thought made hunger stir in the pit of his stomach. His teeth tingled, as if he hadn't spent the night satisfying his desire--and hers. He resolutely clamped down on the self-indulgent reverie that memory inspired.

With a final check on Heather--just to make sure she was safe, he told himself--he invited sleep.

An indeterminate time later, Devin snapped awake, alerted by some change in the atmosphere that his conscious mind couldn't identify. He sprang out of bed and stood rigid, listening. A car rumbled on the gravel road out front. Maybe the vehicle would pass by without slacking its speed.

No luck--the engine decelerated to a stop.

Good God, what now? Surely the sheriff wouldn't have returned? Could it be Pamela's nuisance of a brother?

Someone knocked on the door. Inwardly fuming, Devin stalked into the living room. *Why didn't I bulldoze Ted into submission and order him to stay away? It would have saved us a lot of trouble.* He knew Heather would find that attitude repugnant, but under this kind of stress, he couldn't force himself to think in human terms.

When he opened the door, Ted stood on the front porch. Devin folded his arms, blocking the entrance. "What do you want now? Aren't you supposed to be taking care of your sister?"

The young man's mouth twisted in a grimace of disgust. "Don't jerk me around. She told me what you did to her--what she thinks you did, anyway. You sick bastard."

Oh, damn, the memory block I put on her is coming unstuck. "Come on, you know she isn't...herself, lately. You can't rely on what she says. I think you've made a mistake in coming here, don't you?" Devin stared into the intruder's bloodshot eyes. *He's exhausted.* Ted's overwrought condition might make him suggestible. Devin brushed his fingers lightly along Ted's arm. "You need to go home and rest. Don't get entangled in Pam's delusion."

Ted twitched away from Devin's touch.

Why doesn't he succumb? The powerful emotions driving him, no doubt, helped shield him against hypnotic influence. Devin glimpsed a fine gold chain around the young man's neck. *So that's it. He must be wearing a cross.* If the subject cherished a strong faith in a religious symbol, it could serve as psychic armor.

A pistol sprouted in Ted's right hand.

Devin's eyes flicked toward the muzzle pointed at his chest. *Oh, no, not again!*

Ted rooted in his left jacket pocket and pulled out an atomizer bottle. "I'm sick of this runaround! Back up and let me in!"

Raising his hands, Devin obeyed. Ted kicked the door shut behind them. "I'm not saying I believe you're some kind of supernatural monster. But if half of what Pam remembers is true, you're pretending to be one. Maybe you even believe it yourself."

"One what?" Devin stopped his retreat in the middle of the room, leaving himself space to maneuver.

"Don't play dumb." His voice rasping with exhaustion, Ted nevertheless held the gun steady.

"There's still time to avoid trouble. Just go home."

"I can't walk away and let you do that to other women." Ted brandished the small atomizer bottle like a weapon.

Devin suppressed a sigh. *Deja vu all over again, as Yogi Berra said. And what's he got in that vial, anyway?* "If you leave now, I won't file assault charges."

"I haven't assaulted you yet. I have to test you--find out if you really think you're a vampire."

"How? Throw holy water on me? Drag me into the sunlight and wait for me to shrivel up? You'll have a long wait."

"Maybe, but first--" Ted squirted the atomizer in Devin's face.

Devin's eyes stung, and he choked as if a hand clutched his windpipe. He doubled over in a spasm of nausea. *Garlic!*

Ted looked wonderingly at the bottle he held. "How about that, it works."

On his knees, Devin clamped his jaws tight until his stomach stopped heaving. "Idiot. Anybody would choke, if you sprayed that right in his nose."

"Not like that, they wouldn't. Oh, hell--maybe you aren't just crazy. Maybe you really--" Ted broke off as Devin struggled to his feet. "Oh no, you don't." He squeezed the rubber bulb again to discharge another puff of reeking vapor from the bottle.

Cramps seized Devin. He collapsed, retching, and banged his head on the coffee table behind him.

Distantly, Devin sensed Heather's thoughts. He grasped the tenuous thread of support she extended to him, then regretfully released it. *No, Heather! There's nothing you can do--stay away.* A mental wail of protest emanated from her. *I said, stay away!* He had scarcely enough strength to fight her appeal.

Meanwhile, over her telepathic call and the pulse throbbing in his skull, he heard Ted reopening the front door.

Devin hitched himself sideways and rose on one elbow. His hope of catching his attacker unawares died quickly as a third dose of garlic hit him. While he fought the fresh convulsion of retching, Ted flipped him face down and handcuffed his wrists together behind him. Devin barely recovered enough to reflect that his legs remained free before Ted snapped a second pair of cuffs around his ankles. Flexing his legs, he discovered that a short chain joined them, allowing a few inches for movement.

Ted grasped Devin's bound hands and dragged him like an overloaded sack out the open door.

In the back of his mind, Devin heard Heather's mental voice: *What's going on, Devin? I'm coming to help. You can't stop me.*

It wouldn't do any good, he replied as Ted opened a car door and rolled him onto the floor behind the front seat. *I won't be here. And I won't let you look for me.* The thought of her throwing herself into danger for him made Devin sicker than the garlic. He shut her out of his mind with a barrier like a stone wall.

Not that the telepathic silence encasing him like ice made him feel much better. That he'd ensured Heather's safety was his sole consolation in his misery. Confident that she couldn't rush to the rescue now, he concentrated on conserving his energy until an escape attempt had some hope of success.

Gritting his teeth while the car jolted over the gravel road, Devin tried to relax rather than make the bone-jarring sensation worse by fighting it. The garlic fumes didn't help. They pervaded the vehicle's interior, worse than the vapor on his clothes could account for.

"Where are you taking me?" he said after about five minutes. Though without eye contact he couldn't hope to mesmerize Ted, any loosening of tension he might induce could increase his chance of catching the man off balance.

"You mentioned the sun. I'm going to find out what it does to you. Depending on how you react, that'll prove whether you're human or not. Hard to believe--but if it turns out you're a monster, I'll get rid of you and do the world a favor." His voice took on an earnestly persuasive tone. "I'm no murderer, MacAvoy. Even if you conned Pam, I won't hurt you any worse than I already have--if you're an ordinary man. Looks bad for you so far." He punctuated the last sentence with a humorless chuckle.

Shortly Devin felt the car jounce off the road and slow to a stop. "No court would accept what you call proof," he said as Ted opened the rear door.

"All I'm interested in is proving it to myself," said the other man. He panted and strained to haul Devin out and dump him on the grass. "I know nobody else would believe this stuff, no matter what I showed them. I'm not crazy."

That's debatable, thought Devin. He rolled onto his back, tensing his leg muscles to kick up at Ted. If he could knock the man out, he would gain time to recover his strength.

Ted clearly anticipated resistance, though. He gave Devin another blast from the atomizer, then looped a pendant of irregular lumps strung on what felt like fishing line around Devin's neck.

Oh, Lord, garlic bulbs! Ted had planned better than Devin had suspected. *And I thought nobody would listen to Pam, even if she did remember. Damned overconfidence!*

Dizzy, his stomach churning, Devin didn't resist when Ted manhandled him upright.

"Clever, huh?" said the young man, waving the bottle in Devin's face before returning it to a pocket. "I dissolved garlic powder in warm water. Never expected it to work that well, though." He unlocked the car's trunk to pick up a coil of chain with a padlock. "Okay, get moving."

With his ankles linked together, Devin could take only mincing steps. Ted had to half drag him. Several times, he had to catch Devin when he tripped.

Glancing back, Devin noticed that the car was parked far enough under the trees that it wouldn't be obvious from the road. Not that its visibility mattered much; a casual passerby would assume the vehicle's occupants were picnicking or hiking.

For ten weary minutes he stumbled through the woods, choking on the aroma that oozed out of the slashed garlic bulbs. How could ephemerals enjoy *eating* the stuff? Swallowing hard, he said to his captor, "Garlic's easily available, but where did you get the other equipment on such short notice? I can't believe you kept a vampire-hunting kit in your closet, just in case." There, he'd said the V-word.

"A friend," said Ted. "He runs a shop for wannabe detectives and vigilantes. Those are police-quality cuffs, not S and M toys."

"I'm flattered."

Ted gave Devin a hard shove, laying him flat, face down, in foot-high weeds. Devin felt direct sunlight scorching the back of his neck. He heard the length of chain clanking and wondered what purpose it served. He got the answer to that question in the next minute. Ted yanked him to his feet and dragged him to a dead tree near the center of the clearing where they'd stopped.

"I picked this spot before I went to your place." Ted aimed the gun at Devin's chest. "Stand with your back against the tree." He had already wrapped the chain around the trunk. When Devin backed up, the other man completed the loop, secured the padlock, and pocketed the key. He'd carefully chosen a leafless tree away from the forest proper, unreachable by any shade.

"How far do you plan to take this farce?" Devin said. "You can see the sun isn't making me melt or explode."

"For all I know, that's strictly from the movies. Like I said, this is a test." He tucked the handgun into his belt and extracted a pocket knife from his jeans.

What's the knife for? I don't think I even want to guess. The chain's links dug into Devin's bare forearms, and his wrists were becoming cramped. His stomach still churned from the garlic. The sun, though not at noonday strength, thank God, still gave him a pounding headache to complement the nausea.

"I haven't seen you turn into a bat. But it's obvious you don't like daylight much. Next test--does this hurt you like it would a normal man?" Ted unfolded the knife. Inching closer to Devin, as if afraid of him even weakened and chained, he scored Devin's left arm with the blade.

Devin reacted automatically to block out the sting of the cut and suppress the bleeding.

Ted stared at the gash with an indrawn hiss of excitement. "Pam claimed she shot you yesterday. Then there you were this morning, not a mark on you."

"You believe that?" Devin said.

"That's what I'm trying to check out." Ted jabbed the knife's tip into the incision. "Sure looks like you heal fast. Want me to try again?"

"Torture me all you want. I can hardly stop you." *So I have a choice--either control the bleeding and confirm his suspicions, or leave it alone and have my energy drained by blood loss.* He softened his voice to a persuasive croon. "Come now, you don't really want to do this, do you? You aren't that kind of man. There's still time to go home and rest. That's what you really want, isn't it--rest?"

For a few seconds Ted gazed into his eyes, actually listening. His lids drooped as if the frantic pace of the past few hours had caught up with him. But then he shook his head, growled a curse, and slashed a deeper cut across Devin's other arm.

Deciding that his only chance lay in conserving his strength, Devin halted the bleeding as efficiently as his stressed condition allowed. "Have you thought about the consequences of what you're doing?" he said. "If you let me go, I'll forget about all this. I know you're a sick man; I won't hold it against you. But if you kill me, you're sure to go on trial for murder. Did you think of that?"

"I'll take that chance. I know these woods well enough to stash your body where it won't be found anytime soon. And nobody saw us driving off together."

Devin winced as the blade cut him again, this time a shallow line on the side of his neck. *How long can I stand this?* Eventually his energy level would drop low enough to interfere with his ability to fight off an attacker, even if free to do so. *If this demonstration keeps him entertained until dark...* Under cover of darkness, he might risk allowing Heather to intervene. If nothing else, she might summon the police to catch Ted in the act. At this time of year, sunset was a long way off, though. Before then, Ted might decide he had enough "proof" and proceed to the execution. Devin suppressed a shiver at the thought of the best-known methods of vampire-killing. Although Ted didn't have a stake or a decapitation implement in sight, he might well have both stashed in the car's trunk.

"God knows how many girls you've treated the way you did Pam. If they do catch me, it'll be worth it." Ted flashed a grimace meant to pass for a smile. "The way the law works nowadays, by the time the appeals are used up, I'll probably get off with time served. Especially if the autopsy shows you're what I think." He unhooked the gold chain from his neck, brandished a crucifix, and moved in for another cut with the knife.

Chapter 12

Heather curled up on the couch in her living room, racked with cramps that reverberated from Devin's mind to hers. The dog, her muzzle resting on the cushion a few inches from Heather's nose, whined in concern.

Heather stroked Sugar's head with a trembling hand and fumbled for Devin's mental embrace. When she flung the net of her love over him, he slipped free and thrust her away. A wordless cry burst from her. *I have to get to him, have to save him!*

With a final harsh roar of *Stay away!* he locked her out. Further effort felt like battering against a wall of ice.

Sliding to the floor, she wrapped her arms around Sugar and rocked on her knees, sobbing until her throat turned raw. Finally, drained of emotion enough to think rationally again, she staggered to the bathroom to wash her face in cold water. Scouring away the tearstains with a hand towel, she took stock of what she'd gleaned from Devin's mind.

Somebody had attacked him; the shock of pain made that fact clear. And he'd ordered Heather not to come to him. In the instant before he had slammed down the barrier, she had glimpsed the inside of a vehicle. A man whose face she couldn't see had loaded Devin into the back seat of a car. So he probably wasn't at his house anymore.

Why kid herself? She didn't need to see the attacker's face to guess who it was. Ted had come back alone. *I can't let him hurt Devin!* But if she couldn't even find Devin, how could she rescue him? *Damn him for trying to protect me.*

Clutching the edge of the countertop and closing her eyes, she extended her telepathic antennae in Devin's direction. Nothing. With his power and experience, he'd shut her out so thoroughly that she hadn't a clue where to search for him.

Unable to stay home doing nothing, she decided to check Devin's house, however far-fetched that chance might prove. Maybe Ted would bring Devin back for some reason, or maybe he had left some physical traces. With a vague idea of using the dog as protection, she led Sugar to the car and drove to Devin's cottage.

As soon as Heather pulled up and scanned the house, she noted that the front door stood ajar. Devin would never leave it that way, especially in daylight. In the back seat, the dog shifted restlessly from one window to the other, her claws scrabbling on the upholstery.

"It doesn't look right to me, either," said Heather. Leaving Sugar in the car, she tiptoed up the driveway. When she paused on the sidewalk, straining her ears, she heard no sign of life. *They're gone, all right. It was a slim chance anyway.*

She crept onto the porch and sidled in through the half-open door, alert for any noise that indicated the cottage wasn't deserted after all. The living room had the lifeless atmosphere of an empty dwelling. She immediately noticed that the coffee table had been knocked out of its usual space, and a lamp at the end of the couch had a crooked shade. No other signs of a struggle.

That's enough, though, isn't it? She clung to the assurance that Devin wasn't dead. Surely their bond would let her know if the worst happened. *This is bad enough. What now?* She didn't waste time on the possibility that Ted had taken Devin to his own house; there would be too much risk of discovery, even if Pam and Mr. Gaines had left.

She could wander aimlessly around the area, hoping to hit upon some clue. Not a very sensible or hopeful course of action. She returned to her car and headed back home. The conventional solution, calling the police, occurred to her. Even more than her awareness that Devin wouldn't approve, her lack of any concrete information to offer vetoed involving the authorities. With a telepathic cry for help as the basis of her complaint, the sheriff's office would surely dismiss her as deranged, or at most politely take a report and forget about it, especially in view of the incident with Pam. *They'd conclude that Devin MacAvoy just tends to attract crazy women.*

Back at the cabin, Heather walked Sugar under the trees, while her thoughts scurried in futile circles. Her need to help Devin gnawed at her insides, yet she had no way to act on it. *Is this what the bond does to people? No wonder Devin had reservations about it.*

She renewed her attempt to connect with his mind. He couldn't hold the barrier indefinitely, could he? If the attacker had hurt him as badly as that psychic shock indicated, he couldn't spare the strength to fight her determined assault.

Good theory, but it isn't working, thought Heather after twenty minutes of agonized straining. She felt the way she had when she'd tried, and failed, to complete the required minimum pull-ups in high school gym class. Devin must simply be too skilled to be affected by a mere ephemeral's telepathic intrusion, despite their bond and his weakened state.

Quit thinking negative! That won't help. What had Britt Loren said? He needed Heather more than she needed him. If she couldn't batter her way into his mind, another strategy might work. She cast her thoughts back to the ecstasy they had shared only a few hours before. She closed her eyes and concentrated, evoking the sensations and emotions of the bond. A scarlet mist enfolded her. Electricity sizzled over her skin, raising each separate hair. Heat coiled in the pit of her stomach.

Devin! she silently called. *I know you need me. You can't shut me out. I won't let you.*

The wall melted like a sheet of ice before a flamethrower. His pain and fear sucked her in.

She caught him in a phantom embrace. *Not like that, Devin. Let me breathe--let me think. I have to find you.*

He cried in panic, *No--stay away!*

She brushed aside his feeble attempt to exclude her again. *I'm coming, so don't waste your strength trying to fight me. Now, no more words.*

Still clutching the dog's leash, Heather collected her keys and hurried to the car. With Sugar in the back seat, she started down the road in the direction of Devin's cottage. Devin's mind drew her like a beacon. Once she got used to thinking on two levels at once, she found it easy to drive while homing on his emotions.

Grinding her teeth in frustration at the slowness of the process, she roamed the tortuous back roads in a game of "hot--cold--warmer". Little by little, she drew closer to Devin's location. Through his eyes, she glimpsed woods, blurred by the glare of direct sunlight.

When no amount of circling brought her any closer to him, she parked on the shoulder and got out. The dog clambered into the front seat and stuck her head out the half-open window, whining. "No, Sugar. You stay here where you're safe. Stay!" The dog sat down, her ears flattened. Heather focused on Devin's consciousness and started walking.

A few yards under the shadow of the trees, she came upon a car wedged in as deeply as the forest growth allowed. She recognized it as Ted's.

She hiked onward with undergrowth snagging her socks, twigs cracking under her feet. She wished she had the vampire trick of stalking in catlike silence. After a few minutes of painstaking progress, she sensed Devin's nearness. Light slanted between the trees ahead. She crept to the edge of the clearing and peered between the branches.

She almost yelped aloud at what she saw. Fortunately, she choked back the cry just in time.

Devin stood with his back against a dead tree, upright but just barely. He had a peculiar-looking garland wrapped around his neck. Ted jabbed at him with a pocket knife. Heather noticed a pistol grip protruding from Ted's belt. She estimated that a three-minute sprint, at most, separated her from Devin and his tormentor. *Plenty of time for him to draw and fire.* She had to remind herself of that fact, to keep from dashing to Devin's rescue.

Instead, she extended her thoughts to him once more. He lifted his head to stare in her direction. She doubted he could see her through the screening foliage, especially with the sun in his eyes, but he had to know she was close by. A flood of pain/fear/hunger poured from his mind into hers. A second later, she felt him rein his emotions and struggle to shape coherent words:

Damn it, Heather, I told you not to follow me. His mental voice quivered with fatigue on top of all the other stresses.

Did you really expect me to leave you in this predicament? I'm here now, so shut up and let me rescue you.

Yes, my lady. How do you intend to accomplish that?

Maybe I should start by talking to him.

Despair shrouded Devin like a dense fog. *Sweet Heather, that's hopeless. He's lost his grip--bought into Pam's obsession. He won't hesitate to hurt you.*

She felt him wince, as Ted made another cut with the pocket knife. *Enough time wasted,* she thought. *We were friends, sort of,* she sent to Devin. *I'm going to speak to him now.* She strode into the clearing.

Ted faced away from her, completely fixed on Devin; he didn't notice her approach. She felt the heat of Devin's gaze upon her, though. Her legs trembled and her stomach clenched, as if she had run the distance from her cabin to this spot.

A few yards from the dead tree, she stepped sideways into the man's peripheral vision and quietly said, "Ted? Please stop what you're doing and listen to me."

He switched the knife to his left hand and pulled the gun out of his belt. "Why are you butting in?"

"Because Devin's my friend."

"Then I feel sorry for you. You're another victim, and you don't even know it." Ted backed several paces away from Devin and leveled the pistol at Heather. "Don't interfere, and you won't get hurt."

"I'm not a victim. I know what I'm doing." The pulse hammered in her temples at the sight of the gun's muzzle trained on her chest. "Why are you torturing Devin?"

"If you don't know what he is, you must be under his spell. He practically drove Pam out of her mind. I'm trying to make sure it doesn't happen to any other women." He wiped his eyes with the back of the hand that held the knife. "After you're free of him, you'll thank me."

"I doubt it." Irritation at his perception of her as a puppet almost obscured her fear. "I don't know what you think he's done, but is it worth getting yourself thrown in jail or a mental institution? Let him go."

The man shook his head. "Not a chance, not after what I've seen. He can't stand garlic, the sun hurts him, and wounds close up like magic--he isn't human."

At the mention of garlic, Heather realized what the garland she'd barely noticed was. *It's making him sick.* "Ted, you can't be implying what it sounds like. That's crazy--horror movie stuff."

"Does he really have you snowed? Or do you know the truth, and you're defending him anyway?"

"I'm here because I--" Her voice cracked. She swallowed the threatened tears. She couldn't afford to have her thoughts or her sight clouded.

"You really *care* about this--whatever it is?"

Devin's thoughts spiked with alarm. *Heather, don't let him know that!*

Too late, he's obviously figured it out, she replied. Aloud, she said, "What do you have planned for him? Do you really want to become a murderer?"

"Not murder, execution." Ted's gun hand shook, and he steadied his grip with a visible effort.

"What about me?" she said. "You don't expect me to let you get away with this, do you? To keep me from reporting the crime, you'll have to kill me, too."

"After this monster dies, and you're not under his control anymore, you'll change your mind about that. If you don't--well, in that case, you'd be incurably tainted, and you'd be better off dead."

Exasperated, Heather told Devin, *I give up; he's obsessed. Isn't there anything I can say to get through to him?*

Probably not. I tried hard enough, with advantages you lack.

Heather edged away from Ted toward the woods, hoping he would follow her, removing him farther from Devin. *So far, I've managed to provoke him more than distract him. Nice going.* She made one more try: "Listen to yourself, Ted! Do you really believe all that? I don't blame you for being upset about Pam, but you don't have a right to take it out on innocent people."

"Innocent, hell!" He took a long stride closer to her, thrusting the gun forward. "I'll show you what this friend of yours really is. Get over here!"

Confused by the command, Heather didn't move.

The pistol fired. An ear-splitting bang and a puff of dirt sent her stumbling back. A wave of impotent rage from Devin crashed over her. Regaining her balance, she realized with dizzying relief that Ted had shot at the ground.

"I said, get over here!"

This time she obeyed.

As soon as she stepped within his reach, he sliced an incision across her left forearm.

The quick cut barely stung. She stared, astonished, at the oozing red line.

Tossing the knife to the ground, Ted grabbed her right elbow and dragged her toward Devin.

When she realized what he was doing, she stopped resisting. Instead, she matched his pace. When he shoved her at the tree, she wrapped her arms around Devin.

Don't, he silently pleaded. *Don't let Ted see how you feel.*

It's already pretty obvious. Good grief, you smell like an Italian restaurant. Though she found the aroma more appetizing than not, she sensed Devin's nausea and labored breathing. Hooking her fingers under the fishing line strung with garlic bulbs, she tried to loosen the cord in hopes of slipping it over his head.

"Cut that out!" Ted poked her in the ribs with the pistol. A grimace of disgust distorted his face. "You won't be so lovey-dovey with him when he shows his true colors. Go ahead, monster, there's dinner--what are you waiting for?"

He's right, Heather, you're too tempting. Get away from me.

His hunger ignited an answering fire deep within her. She thirsted to feed him as powerfully as he thirsted for her. *I can't, Devin. Go ahead and take what you need.*

No! He tried to thrust her away with a violent mental recoil.

Since his heart wasn't in the gesture, it had no effect on her. *Why not? It'll make you stronger.*

Not in front of him. If he sees you donate willingly, he'll have no reason not to murder you, too. Devin turned his face away from the gash on her arm, perilously close to his mouth.

Reluctantly Heather removed her arms from around him. "See?" she said to Ted. "Your theory doesn't hold up. Devin isn't about to attack me." When the young man stared at her in indecisive silence, she moved away from Devin. Better to divide Ted's attention. "Why don't you give me the keys to those handcuffs and padlock? I'll release him, and you can go home. Nobody wants to make things worse for you."

"Shut up." Ted struggled for a minute to bring his wheezing breath under control.

Devin silently remarked, *Even if that ploy worked, it wouldn't necessarily solve the problem. Suppose he has second thoughts and tries again later?*

What's your solution? Kill him? She had to admit Devin had a point, yet how could she endorse murder? But the civilized solution--having Ted arrested-- would risk exposing Devin's secret.

"Okay, forget the key," she said to Ted. "But at least let me get that garlic off him." Wondering how badly a bullet in the back would hurt, she dove for the knife Ted had dropped.

When she straightened up, holding it, Ted stepped between her and the tree. "No, you don't. Put that down."

"Oh, are you prepared to shoot me right this minute?" She started to sidle around him. He blocked her again and aimed at her midriff.

Heather, don't! This isn't worth it!

He won't kill me for this, Heather replied to Devin's mental scream. *I'll bet he's having second thoughts.*

Devin gave no verbal answer, but she sensed him broadcasting a call, a summons not directed at her.

She wondered what he was trying to do, but had no time to speculate. Ted backed up, standing in front of the tree so that she would have to shove him aside to get to Devin.

"Like you said, I'll probably have to kill you anyway," he said. "Too bad; we could've had a good thing together."

No second thoughts, after all? Giving the problem only a few seconds' reflection, she spun around and flung the knife as hard as she could in the direction of the woods.

Ted stared after it in baffled anger. To get it back, he would have to take his attention off Heather. Obviously deciding that was a bad idea, he didn't move. "Quit screwing around," he said. "If you want to stay alive a few more minutes, get back over there with your *friend*."

She returned to Devin's side and cuddled up to him. Irrationally, the contact comforted her. Recalling Devin's remarks about psychic nourishment, she visualized herself channeling energy into him.

Thanks for trying, dear. It feels good, but it won't be nearly enough--not against all this. He resumed the wordless cry, like a silent wolf-howl.

Devin, what on earth are you doing?

He didn't answer.

Ted said, "Well, monster? Are you going to take a nibble from your girlfriend, or do I put a bullet in her right now?"

Devin didn't move.

Heather told him, *You know what? I think he's unconsciously stalling. He doesn't want to kill anybody. Maybe we still have a chance to finish this without either of us getting hurt.*

Heather, my sweet, you have a touching faith in human nature. Devin slumped, resting his chin on the top of Heather's head as she nestled against his chest.

Ted barked a cough, then said, "Get your arm up where he can reach it."

She obeyed. *Why don't you do what he wants, Devin? That might keep him entertained a while longer. He'll want to observe for a few minutes, make sure you're exactly what he thinks you are.*

We can't rely on that. The sight of such repulsive behavior might goad him into violence instead. He turned his mouth away from the wound, from which a steady trickle of blood flowed to stain her T-shirt. *Please--you're driving me mad. I don't know how much longer I can resist.*

Better that than getting shot.

True, he conceded.

Her stomach knotted in sympathy with his suffering. She felt Devin's muscles tense.

Help is on the way, he told her.

Huh? What help?

Just trust me, Devin answered. *On my signal, get out of the line of fire. Move around the tree, so it's between you and Ted.*

But then he'll shoot you instead!

I don't think so. He planted a light kiss on her arm, his tongue flicking out for a single taste.

Ted emitted a hiss of surprise, as if he hadn't truly expected that behavior.

Devin straightened up. Heather felt energy coiling within him like a serpent about to strike. *Now, Heather!*

She darted behind the tree. At the same instant, Devin's form melted into mist. Peeking around the trunk, she saw a blank space where he'd stood.

Ted staggered, waving the gun in wild circles.

Her head spinning, Heather groped around the tree trunk to reassure herself that Devin was still there. She felt his solid bulk, though she still saw nothing. *How did he do that?* One of those psychic gifts, no doubt, and it must require large expenditures of energy. Even as she watched, the spot of emptiness became an indistinct patch of fog, which rippled into a ghostly outline of a man. *He's too weak to hold it for long.*

An electric current sizzled from Devin to Heather. The essence of the message conveyed, *Finally!*

A golden streak charged from the woods and plowed into Ted. He toppled onto his back. The gun fired once, into the air.

Forgetting to hide, Heather gaped at the animal that stood over the prostrate man, paws planted on his chest. *Sugar! Devin summoned her!* The leash still dangled from the dog's collar.

Devin, fully visible now, gazed intently at the dog. Sugar's jaws snapped on Ted's right wrist.

Spitting a curse as her fangs lacerated his skin, Ted dropped the pistol.

Heather darted forward and snatched it up.

"Heather," Devin called hoarsely. "The garlic."

She rushed for the spot where she'd thrown the knife. With a few quick slashes, she freed him from the garlic necklace and flung it away.

Meanwhile, Ted struggled to rise, wheezing and shoving ineffectually at the dog, who threw her whole weight against him. Her muzzle gaped an inch from his neck. He screamed.

Heather's sluggish brain caught up with what was happening. "Devin, no!" she cried. "Don't do this--don't make my dog kill him!"

The visible tension drained from Devin's knotted limbs. *Dear one, I'm afraid I'll regret your soft heart.*

Stiff-legged, Sugar backed away from her victim. Though the man didn't move, she kept her brown eyes locked on him, her canines bared. She didn't show the least recognition for the man who'd raised her from birth.

"Fix her, Devin!"

With a long-suffering sigh, Devin said, "As you wish."

The dog's ears relaxed, and her tail swished uncertainly. She sat down, glancing from Devin to Heather as if afraid she'd misbehaved.

"The keys," Devin said. "In his right pocket."

Heather dashed to Ted and knelt beside him. He lay inert on his back. Terror seized her for an instant. Groping for the pulse in his neck, she realized he had only fainted. Shoving the gun into the waistband of her shorts, she fumbled in his pockets.

She found three loose keys. Staggering over to Devin, she struggled with the locks until she'd unfastened the handcuffs, the leg shackles, and the padlock securing the chain.

Devin took one step away from the tree and stumbled into Heather's arms. Barely managing to keep their balance, they stood entwined in silence for a minute. Tears streamed down her cheeks as she hid her face against his chest.

Over her head, he said, "No time for this. Give me the keys." Easing her away from him, he tossed the keys into the underbrush. "And the gun." When she handed it to him, he emptied the clip and sent the bullets flying after the keys. That done, he strode over to Ted.

When Devin crouched next to him, Ted stirred and opened his eyes. Devin planted a knee on his chest and pinned his arms to the ground. "Guess what, Ted? I'm not going to kill you. I'll even let you have your weapon back."

"Son of a--"

Devin slapped him across the mouth. "Shut up and look at me." The whipcrack of his voice made Heather's ears ring. Ted automatically obeyed. "Listen carefully, Ted. This is what you'll remember. I went out with Pam once. She wanted to pursue a relationship, and I turned her down. Understand?"

Ted nodded. Drawing closer, Heather saw tears leaking from his eyes.

"Good. Now understand this. She was so upset about being rejected that she made up lies--fantasies. I never harmed her."

Breathing raggedly, Ted protested, "She told me--"

"She lied." The air crackled with the force of Devin's will. "Everything she told you is pure fantasy. You came to discuss it with me. We talked, and you realized I was right. Your sister is confused. She needs therapy."

"Yeah." Ted shuddered, and his head drooped to one side. "Dad's going to find her a shrink."

"Very good. You're never going to bother me or Heather again. You're too embarrassed about those crazy accusations you made. Aren't you?"

"Right," Ted whispered.

"We talked about Pam. Nothing more. I convinced you, and you went home. That's all."

Heather watched in wonder as Ted nodded emphatic agreement with this version of the day's events. Stirring under Devin's weight, he said, "You gonna let me go home now?"

"Of course. Go home and drop this matter permanently. Yes?"

"Yeah. Sure." His voice slurred as if he were drunk.

Devin got up and hauled Ted to his feet. "Now tell me exactly what happened when you came to my house a little while ago."

Swaying, Ted mumbled, "I accused you of hurting Pam. You explained how she was chasing you, and you never did anything to her. Then I went home." A frown creased his forehead. "That's right, huh? So why'm I here?"

Devin shook him. "You went for a drive to think it over. Now you'll go home and not worry about it anymore."

Ted gave a bemused nod. He wobbled in Devin's grip like a punch-drunk boxer.

"And you'll leave Heather and me alone."

"Sure."

Devin tucked the pistol in Ted's waistband and let go of him. "Now get out of here."

Turning without another word, Ted staggered into the woods. When he'd disappeared under the trees, Devin said, "That should stick. I don't think he'll threaten us again."

Stunned, Heather said, "You mentally beat him to a pulp, didn't you? How long will it take him to recover?"

"What the hell do I care? He'll live, which is what you wanted, isn't it?"

Granted, I begged him to spare Ted's life, and he did. Still, his attitude chilled her. "Did you have to push so hard?"

"Yes, to make sure he wouldn't remember anything. If he remembered, it would be extremely hazardous to his health."

"Sounds logical, but I don't like it."

Devin sighed as he hugged her. "Are you forgetting that he put himself in that position of his own free will?"

"True," she said. "But you aren't sorry about his condition."

"Damn straight, I'm not. He planned to murder me. Not to mention what could have happened to you." His embrace convulsively tightened around her.

She raised her arms to hug him around the neck. "We shouldn't be standing here. You're sick and hurt."

"And thirsty." He turned his head to lick the drying blood from the shallow cut on her arm.

Delicious vertigo swept over her. She stretched on tiptoe to press her body against his. With the fingernails of one hand, she skimmed the silken hair on his chest. He groaned aloud and nuzzled the hollow of her neck. The tips of his teeth lingered there, poised to pierce her skin.

My love-- his mental caress vibrated along her nerves *--I was so afraid for you.*

Her pulse throbbed with eagerness to slake the thirst that burned in his throat. From behind, a noise penetrated the crimson fog that enveloped her. A dog's sharp yip.

Heather blinked. *What we're doing makes Sugar nervous.* That thought shattered her sensual daze. "No, Devin, stop!"

His tongue continued its tormenting swirl on her tender skin. *Please, Heather--I'm aching for you--I can't wait.*

"Not here!" She forced herself to pull back as far as his tight embrace allowed, and placed both hands on his chest to push him away.

For a few seconds he ignored her, assaulting her senses with his raging need.

Alarmed, she dug her nails into his flesh. "Devin, listen to me! This isn't the time or place. Ted might come back, and you'd have to hypnotize him all over again. Or anybody might wander by."

He froze, stunned. The backlash of his shock at her rejection staggered her, too. A yearning to comfort him welled up in her, but she steeled herself against it. She couldn't let him control her; they had to love as equals, or not at all. "Let go of me right now." She reinforced the demand with a hard mental shove. "Let go, if you ever expect to--kiss--me again."

Chapter 13

With a shudder of effort that rocked both of them, Devin straightened up and shifted his hands to Heather's shoulders. "You aren't *afraid* of me, are you?"

"Of course not." Since their bond transmitted her every sensation to him, she knew he couldn't hurt her. "I'm only telling you to wait."

The sadness in his eyes cleared. With a rueful smile, he shook his head, wincing at the pain caused by the movement. "How did you do that? I'm supposed to be dominant. An ephemeral shouldn't be able to order me around."

"Well, live with it," she said, trying to project more confidence than she felt. "Let's get out of here."

"You're absolutely right. This isn't a safe place to hang around, and we shouldn't...indulge...in public. Even semi-public."

Heather smiled, relieved. *He listened to me--really listened.* "Then let's go home, where we can indulge all we want." She glanced at the dog, who crouched a cautious distance away, her gaze fixed on the two of them.

Heather beckoned and called, "Sugar, come!" The dog trotted over and sat down with an uncertain thump of her plumed tail. "Devin, why is she acting this way? She's nervous about you all over again."

"Of course she is. All animals have an instinctive aversion to us, until they learn better. And I made her act against her nature, attacking Ted. I hated to do it, but it seemed like the only way." He rubbed behind the dog's ears and smoothed the fur along her spine. After soothing her with a tuneless hum for a minute, he dangled his hand for her to sniff. While her ears remained flattened to her skull, at least she didn't growl or snap. She even ventured a timid flick of her tongue across his palm.

"Good enough for now," Devin said. "I'm too worn out to work on it any longer. She'll get used to me soon enough."

They hiked back to the road. Heather gratefully noticed the absence of Ted's vehicle and hoped he would make it home without getting into a wreck. In her own car, with the dog in the back seat, she started the ignition and said, "Well, your place or mine?"

The attempt at humor failed. Devin's fingers on her arm froze and seared at once. "What's closest?" he whispered.

"We'll go to mine," she said. "That way I won't have to leave you." She pulled out and accelerated, afraid that if she looked at Devin, she wouldn't be able to resist his need.

His eyes roamed over her like a tangible caress. She focused on the road, trying not to blush. The technique didn't work, judging from Devin's response.

"The way your aura glows," he said, "I think I may burst into flames any minute."

Inside her house, she bolted the doors and confined Sugar on the back porch with food and water; she wanted no interruptions. In the hall, Devin captured her in a long embrace. He didn't kiss her, only kneaded her tension-stiffened back muscles and nuzzled her hair. The mounting pressure of his leashed passion made her gasp for breath.

At last he stepped away from her. "I can't share your bed like this. I need a shower."

"Then I'll join you." Heather surprised herself with the bold suggestion.

Devin accepted it as routine, though. "Good, because I don't think I could stand to separate from you for more than a few seconds."

They did each take an individual turn in the bathroom first, though, and while he was occupied, Heather tossed their clothes in the washer-dryer. Donning a caftan, she rummaged through her father's closet for the old bathrobe she remembered noticing earlier. She hesitated only a second before appropriating it for Devin. *I was going to give all this stuff to the Salvation Army anyway. There's no Oedipal significance to a beat-up bathrobe.* She also snatched up a faded sweatshirt, in case Devin didn't want to go home shirtless later.

Within a couple of minutes they stood under the hot spray together. Devin's knife wounds had closed to thin, bloodless scars. Heather ran a fingertip along the one at his neckline. "Do they still hurt?"

"Not at all," he said, "and they'll disappear by tomorrow night. You know what I'm suffering from, little one." The words segued into a growl as he stroked the nape of her neck, exposed by her pinned-up ponytail.

Sweeping her hand down the triangle of fine hair on his lean, hard chest, she felt an impulse to giggle.

"What's that for?" he said.

"I'm naked in my parents' house with a man--who isn't even human."

"Do you think they'll come back to haunt you?"

"Not anymore. After everything we've been through, from now on it'll take a lot more than childhood hangups to worry me."

Stretching around her to lather her back in languid circles, he said, "That terrified me--watching you in danger, helpless to do a thing about it."

She tilted toward him, her erect nipples brushing his chest. "Do you get into that situation often? People trying to kill you?"

"Hardly ever." With a low chuckle, he cupped her derriere in both hands and drew her close. She stood on tiptoe, longing for more intimate contact. "I go for decade after decade living in perfect peace and quiet," he said. "We don't look for trouble, any more than your kind do. Less, in fact, because our survival depends on keeping a low profile." He enfolded her in a fierce hug. "And I'll make damn sure nothing like that ever happens to you again."

Her eyes misted with tears, she hid her face on his shoulder and nipped the slick wetness of his skin with her front teeth. His tongue probed behind her ear, sending hot and cold tremors down her spine, while one of his hands slipped down the curve of her bottom to explore between her legs. A moan escaped her as she pressed against him, writhing under the torment of his lightly darting fingertips. She bit him harder.

He removed his hand from the warm hollow between her thighs. "Easy," he breathed. "It's better if it builds slowly."

Panting with frustrated arousal, she said, "I never heard that from a man before."

"That's because you've had to settle for mere human males."

She gently punched his arm, careful to avoid the knife scratches. "I thought you were in a hurry."

He rotated her toward the spray, to rinse off the soap with which he had laved her. "Having you alone like this, where I can touch you, kiss you--" He gave a fleeting demonstration, with a mothlike flutter of his tongue on her lips. "That makes all the difference. I'm less desperate now, because your vitality in itself nourishes me."

"Like an appetizer?"

"Exactly," he said with a feral grin. "I'm nibbling on your emotions, and they're delicious."

She wiggled against him. "Well, aren't you ready for the entree yet?"

"Look here, wench, I want you so badly my damn teeth are tingling. If I can wait, so can you." His voice turned husky. "On the other hand, perhaps we should prepare for the main course in comfort." He turned off the shower and plucked a towel from the rack.

They rubbed each other dry, stepping from tub to bath mat with several interruptions, as fingers and lips strayed from the task. Heather's skin flushed pink from the massage and the humid air. She savored the titillating contrast between the marble coolness of Devin's body and the burning of his mouth on her neck and breast.

Finally he tossed the towels aside and picked her up to carry her to bed.

Arching her back, she welcomed the long strokes of his tongue over the curve of her throat. Her hips undulated involuntarily under the delicate caresses of his exploring hand. In return, she reached for him, and he curled around her to allow her to squeeze his hardening shaft.

He groaned aloud, then pierced her skin and lapped avidly at the trickle of blood.

With her thoughts melting into his, she tasted the fiery, salt-sweet flavor with him and felt the ecstasy thrumming through his entire body. At the same time, she remained conscious of the unbearable tingles of sensation at her neck and between her thighs. She soared to her peak and felt the throbbing at her core echoed in Devin's body. She clung to him as if she would shatter into a thousand fragments without that support.

Still delirious from the breathless flight, she sensed the pressure building a second time. "Devin, please--I can't--"

With his mouth pressed to her throat, he couldn't answer aloud. *Yes, you can. This is only the beginning.* He turned his head to nip his own shoulder with his incisors, then immediately returned to licking Heather. Drops of blood welled forth from his superficial wound, and he clasped the back of her head to urge her mouth toward that spot. Impelled by the desire burning in him, she complied without hesitation. Instantly his passion spiked, carrying her along.

He fitted his body over hers, and she wrapped arms and legs around him, aching to draw him in and merge with him utterly. Again and again they plunged into thought-annihilating rapture. She simultaneously tasted his life-elixir and her own. The current flowed between them in an endless circle, until at last it spiraled to rest.

Drained, quivering, she nestled in his embrace with her eyes closed until the wonder and terror of drowning in his fulfillment receded.

His lips grazed her hair. "I never knew--never imagined--" He hugged her so hard she had to fight for breath. "I've put my life in your hands."

Then it wasn't just me? she thought. *He lost himself, too.* "Will it always feel that incredible?" she said. "Or will we start taking it for granted?" If the intensity lessened when the novelty wore off, the disappointment might undermine their relationship.

"According to what I've heard from others, it never becomes routine," Devin said. "They claim just the opposite, that the bond grows stronger with time, until the dependency becomes an unbreakable chain. And the pleasure--well, they say it keeps getting better." He ran a finger over the sensitive spot from which he had feasted, making her shiver. "God, I can't imagine that!"

"Me neither." Lightheaded, she giggled. "If it got much better, I don't think I'd survive it."

"You'd better," he said hoarsely. Plumping a pillow behind him, he sat up and drew Heather to his chest. His heart had settled to its usual sedate rhythm. "When I saw you in danger, at risk of death--" He held her in silence for a few seconds, then tried again. "I knew I couldn't stand to lose you. I can't let you go, Heather. No matter what the risk, I have to hold onto you."

"What risk? That I'm going to die on you someday? To state the obvious, that's part of life." She stared up into his gray eyes. "You seem to put a lot of effort into a 'safety first' lifestyle."

"Of course we do. That's how we survive. Adventure is for ephemerals-- your kind, who know they're going to die someday, no matter what. We have a lot more to lose."

"Your kind die, too," she said. "You aren't totally immune. Nobody knows whether they're going to be alive tomorrow. So if I'm ready to accept the risk of living with you, you should be able to accept the same." *Living with? Do I really mean that?*

Devin picked up the idea just as promptly. "Sweet Heather, I do want to live with you. I want to be more than a demon lover haunting your dreams."

"If we stay together, I expect you to keep out of trouble."

"Believe me, that's exactly what I want--a quiet, safe existence." In an unsettling echo of her earlier speculations, he said, "So you're going to act as my conscience?"

"I have enough work managing my own soul, let alone somebody else's. Take care of your own conscience."

"My love, I don't have one, only a set of pragmatic ethics. I can't answer for what will happen after you--" He swallowed the word "die", but she heard it in his mind.

"Well, that's a long way off, if you manage to stay away from the fearless vampire hunters."

He grinned, trying to match her light tone. "My word of honor on that, my lady." He stretched, his sleek body catlike in its flexibility. "Hard to imagine myself in a family--a human-style family. What have you done to me, sweet Heather? I used to think I knew what havoc human females could wreak, but Judith's effect on me was only a pale shadow of your power. Legend claims that we change our donors into our likeness; instead, you've transformed me."

Slipping from between the sheets, she stood before him and laid both hands on his chest. She felt his heartbeat under her palms. Through his ears she heard the pounding of her own heart, the two rhythms automatically falling into harmony. "You've changed me, too. Neither of us will ever be the same."

His eyes avoided hers, and he seemed to drag his gaze back to her by force. "Heather, after today, I'm sure. I love you."

"And I love you, Devin. It's not just addiction." She placed a hand on his mouth. "And don't ask how I know. We have to take some things on faith."

You can find ALL our books up on our website at:

http://www.writers-exchange.com

all our fantasy novels:

http://www.writers-exchange.com/category/genres/fantasy/

All our romances:

http://www.writers-exchange.com/category/genres/romance/

All Margaret's Books:

http://www.writers-exchange.com/Margaret-Carter/

About the Author

Marked for life by reading *Dracula* at the age of twelve, Margaret L. Carter specializes in the literature of fantasy and the supernatural, particularly vampires. She received degrees in English from the College of William and Mary, the University of Hawaii, and the University of California, with her dissertation published as *Specter or Delusion? The Supernatural in Gothic Fiction*. Her other works include *Dracula: The Vampire and the Critics*, *The Vampire In Literature: A Critical Bibliography*, and *Different Blood: The Vampire As Alien*. She is also the author of a werewolf novel, *Shadow Of The Beast*, and four vampire novels, *Dark Changeling* (2000 Eppie Award winner in Horror), *Child Of Twilight*, *Sealed In Blood*, and *Crimson Dreams*, along with a fantasy novel, *Wild Sorceress*, co-written by her husband Les Carter, and a horror novel, *From The Dark Places*.

Margaret and Les, a retired Navy Captain, have four sons and several grandchildren. For fans of "Vamp Tales", please do not hesitate to visit her website: The Vampire's Crypt at:

http://www.margaretlcarter.com/

You can keep track of all Margaret's books on her author page at Writers Exchange E-Publishing:

http://www.writers-exchange.com/Margaret-Carter/

If you want to read more about books by this author, they are listed on the following pages...

Crimson Dreams

The summer when Heather was eighteen, her dream beast's nightly visits warded off loneliness and swept her away in flights of ecstasy. Now, returning to the mountains to sell her dead parents' vacation cabin, she finds her "beast" again. But he turns out to be more than a dream. She meets Devin in the flesh, apparently not a day older. His first human lover, centuries in the past, died horribly because of her devotion to him. Does he dare expose another mortal woman to that risk?

Publisher: http://www.writers-exchange.com/Crimson-Dreams/

Passion in the Blood

Cordelia and her twin sister don't realize the mother who left them soon after their birth bequeathed them a dark bloodline. They're half vampire. Although human in most respects, they possess certain psychic gifts. A friend of their late father's, Karl, also a vampire, has been watching over their family for generations in honor of his love for their distant ancestor. When her sister is kidnapped and Cordelia must beg for help from Karl, she learns the truth about his vampirism and her own heritage. In the process, she and Karl form a blood bond that leads to deeper intimacy than either one could have anticipated.

Publisher: http://www.writers-exchange.com/Passion-in-the-Blood/

Different Blood: The Vampire as Alien

Different blood flows in their veins--but our blood quenches their thirst. From Bram Stoker's 1897 creation of Count Dracula, portrayed as a foreign invader bent on the conquest of England, the literary vampire has symbolized the Other, whether his or her otherness arises from racial, ethnic, sexual, or species difference. Even before the bloodsucking Martians of H. G. Wells' *War of the Worlds*, however, popular fiction contained a few vampires who were members of alien species rather than supernatural undead.

Even more intriguing than interplanetary invaders are humanoid and quasi-humanoid beings who have evolved to live on Earth among us, often camouflaged as our own kind. The boom in vampire fiction that began in the 1970s engendered a variety of "alien" vampires, many of them portrayed as sympathetic characters. The science fiction vampire is especially suited to the presentation of vampirism as morally neutral rather than inherently evil.

Different Blood surveys the literary vampire as alien, whether extraterrestrial or a different species evolved on Earth, from the mid-1800s to the 1990s, and analyzes the many uses to which science fiction and fantasy authors have put this theme. Their works explore issues of species, race, ecological responsibility, gender, eroticism, xenophobia, parasitism, symbiosis, intimacy, and the bridging of differences. An extensive bibliography lists dozens of novels and short stories on the "vampire as alien" theme, many of which are still in print.

Publisher: http://www.writers-exchange.com/Different-Blood/

From the Dark Places and Against the Dark Devourer

From the Dark Places

When Father Michel Emeric and Dr. Ray Benson warn young widow Kate Jacobs of occult danger stalking her, she dismisses them as deranged fanatics. The eerie disappearance of her four-year-old daughter, Sara, changes her mind. Ray and Father Mike rescue Kate's child, but the fight has only begun. Dark powers from beyond our world want to destroy Kate and Sara and prevent the birth of a future child foretold to have extraordinary psychic powers and a destiny as a great warrior against evil. Kate must develop her latent wild talents and allow Sara to do the same, in a universe weirder--and more dangerous--than she's ever imagined.

Publisher: http://www.writers-exchange.com/From-the-Dark-Places/

Against the Dark Devourer (Sequel to From the Dark Places)

All her life, Deborah has known she and her older sister have extraordinary psi powers. When their mother dies suddenly, Deborah learns she's meant to use her gift against the forces of darkness in some special way. How, she doesn't have a clue, but she wants no part of this alleged fate. Yet with evil forces stalking her, can she avoid the battle ahead?

All his life, Victor has known he and his twin sister have a unique destiny. Bred to serve inhuman entities from another dimensional plane, he's instructed to either seduce a strange young woman who poses a grave threat to the cult he belongs to...or destroy her.

Unexpectedly, he finds Deborah not only attractive and intelligent but his equal in psychic power. Although his cult views religion with contempt--and she's an unabashed Christian--he's helplessly drawn to her. For her part, Deborah finds in Victor a kindred spirit. For the first time, someone other than her sister can empathize with her differences from "normal" people. Is prophetic destiny written in stone, even for two potential foes falling in love? A paranormal romance inspired by C. S. Lewis's *That Hideous Strength* and the cosmic horror of H. P. Lovecraft.

Publisher: http://www.writers-exchange.com/Against-the-Dark-Devourer/

Heart's Desires and Dark Embraces

When Margaret L. Carter first read *Dracula* at the age of twelve, her spontaneous reaction was to wonder how the undead Count saw the events in which he was portrayed as the villain. She's always been fascinated with the "monster's" viewpoint and relationships between human and nonhuman beings. Most of the stories in this collection can be described as romances, and all involve love and passion in some form. Here you'll encounter vampires, elves, ghosts, and at least one human-monster hybrid. The vampire stories in the first half of the book are part of an ongoing series in which the creatures we know as vampires belong to a naturally evolved, nonhuman species secretly living among us. Readers can get better acquainted with them in *Crimson Dreams, Sealed in Blood,* and *Passion in the Blood.*

Publisher: http://www.writers-exchange.com/Hearts-Desires-and-Dark-Embraces/

Shadow of the Beast

After the mysterious deaths of her brother and sister at the fangs of what looks like a feral dog, Jenny Cameron develops nightmares and blackouts. The quest for the truth about herself leads to her long-lost father, who deserted the family before her birth. He seeks redemption for the curse he carries, but has his bloody past condemned him beyond salvation? When Jenny discovers the secret of her dark heritage, she's no longer sure she can trust her dangerous nature enough to be with the man she loves, and she may ultimately be forced to destroy her own father. Fearing she has inherited the violence that rages in him, she struggles to find her true self under the shadow of the beast.

Publisher: http://www.writers-exchange.com/Shadow-of-the-Beast/

Wild Sorceress Series
By Margaret L. Carter and Leslie Roy Carter

In a world where hostile nations wield magic in combat, twin sorceresses separated at birth and brought up on opposing sides of the war find each other. Together, they face persecution for using wild magic, fight against traitors and assassins, explore family secrets, and discover the hidden origins of magic itself. Above all, to protect their world, they must deal with ancient, powerful dragons that most people don't even believe exist.

Prequel: Legacy of Magic

Most people in the country of Saphradea admire sorcerers and dream of having magical powers. Not Merina, a young woman who detests magic because she thinks it ruined the life of her mother, a failed sorceress candidate who abandoned her in infancy.

When Merina's fiance, Trinames, announces he's decided to go for training as a Healer sorcerer, her personal world turns upside down. Merina is heiress to a tract of rich farmland, and she wants only to manage her own property and bring up a family in peace--a dream she thought Trinames shared. Yet events conspire to force her into a realm of magic and intrigue she never wanted.

When Trinames is kidnapped and she strikes out across the wilderness to rescue him, in company with a wandering trader who turns out to be more than he appears, she runs into a crisis that awakens magical powers she shouldn't even possess.

Publisher: http://www.writers-exchange.com/Legacy-of-Magic/

Book 1: Wild Sorceress

In a world where warring nations use magic in combat, years ago young sorceress Aetria's untamed power caused a disaster on the battlefield. Temporarily banished and retrained, she's returned to the army to redeem herself as head of a company of novice mages. She uncovers a traitorous plot by her own commander, renews her bond with her "imaginary" childhood friend, and meets her long-lost twin sister. While also becoming a trusted friend of the commanding general of the army, Aetria unearths secrets of the true nature of the magic she and her comrades wield.

Publisher: http://www.writers-exchange.com/Wild-Sorceress/

Book 2: Besieged Adept

While learning to control her wild sorcery, Adept Aetria has defeated a pair of traitors trying to kill her, found a long-lost twin, and uncovered secrets of the source and nature of magic. Now she continues her research while battling the remnants of the Neo-Aggressor rebellion and integrating raw, untrained talent into the Sorcerer Corps. Meanwhile, she discovers deeper secrets of her own family background, along with a surprising new foe and a destiny she never dreamed of. Furthermore, she learns that her "imaginary" dragon friend Rajii actually exists...but so do less friendly dragons. What does their agenda mean for the future of humanity and magic in Aetria's world?

Publisher: http://www.writers-exchange.com/Besieged-Adept/

Book 3: Rogue Magess

Sorceresses Aetria and Coleni discover that both their own births and the history of their world have been manipulated in secret by an ancient, powerful race of dragons. Some, like Aetria's lifelong friend Rajii, have benevolent intentions toward humanity while others want to restore the people of the Domains to total slavery. All, however, have their own agendas with human beings and mortal magic as pawns.

Emerging from their long-lost mother's hidden home in the deserted Non-Lands, Aetria and Coleni find themselves targeted by assassins under control of the dragons. While the sisters' powers continue to grow, so do the magical gifts of Coleni's baby daughter, but will their magic provide adequate protection?

Meanwhile, still viewed with suspicion for their "wild sorcery", they can't convince most of their rivals and allies, including Aetria's old mentor and the commanding general of the army, that the dragons and the danger they pose are real.

Publisher: http://www.writers-exchange.com/Rogue-Magess/

Upcoming Books

Sealed in Blood

Science fiction conventions attract some strange people, but Sherri Hudson never expected to spend a con weekend helping a sexy man in a cape steal photos of a winged alien. When the photographer is murdered and Nigel Jamison reveals to Sherri that the "alien" is actually his sister, the situation gets intriguingly complicated. Unwillingly swept up in Nigel's quest to rescue his sister, Sherri can't help being fascinated with him. By the time she finds out he's a vampire, the fascination has become mutual--and too strong to resist.

Sealing the Dark Portal

Almost nothing Rina remembers about her life is true. Rather than the ordinary librarian she believes herself to be, she's actually a sorceress who fled from another world to ours when creatures from an alien dimension devastated her home and killed her family. Now they've pursued her to our world, summoned by a sorcerer who plans to open a portal and invite monstrous entities from the void between dimensions to overrun this planet. Rina's former bodyguard, a cat shapeshifter who was once her lover and still yearns for her, helps her true memories to awaken. She must come to terms with the truth about her past so that together they can save their new home from the fate of their old one.

Windwalker's Mate

Shannon's little boy Daniel has disturbing psychic powers. He talks to the wind--and it listens. All Shannon wants is a normal life. She wants to forget the cult of the Windwalker, a dark god from another dimension, and the

terrifying night when her child was conceived. But her first love, Nathan, son of the cult leader, contacts her for the first time since that horrific ceremony. He claims his father is stalking Shannon and Daniel. Whose child is Daniel, Nathan's or the Windwalker's? Nathan's father plans to use Daniel to open a gate between dimensions and unleash chaos on our world. To save her child and become reconciled with her first love, Shannon may have no choice but embrace the strange powers she previously rejected.